THE GALATIAN EXCHANGE
Book One: Karma and Rafe

Pepper Pace

THE GALATIAN EXCHANGE

Book One: *Karma and Rafe*

PEPPER PACE

This top faved *Kindle Vella* story is now an epic book series!
Now a Podium audiobook!

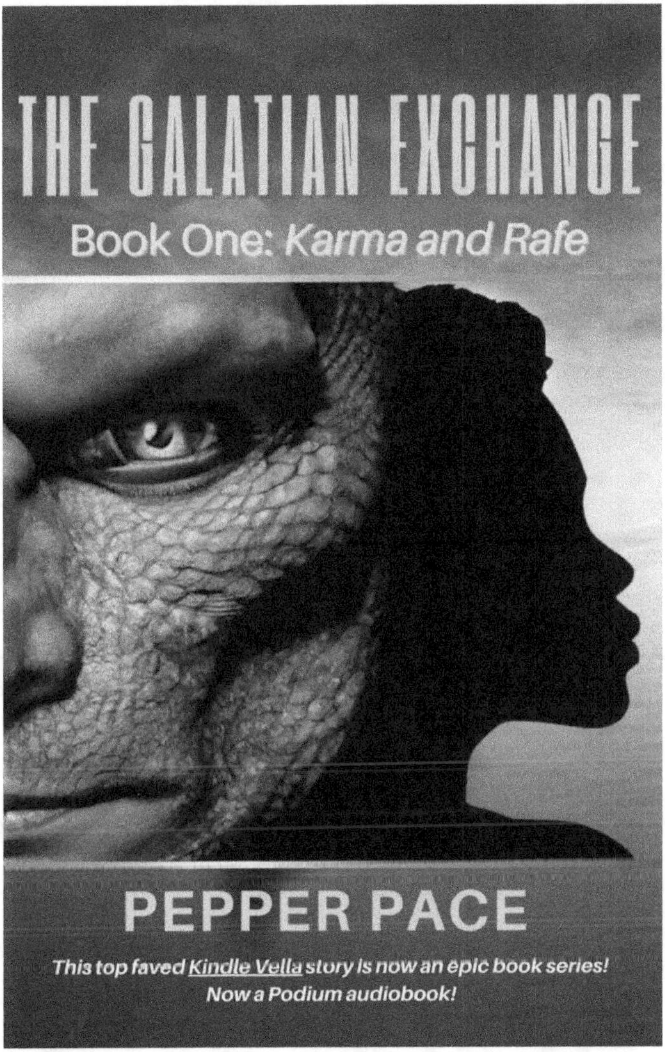

©Pepper Pace Publications
Editors: Firstediting

ISBN: 978-0-9911749-9-7

Reviews

5.0 out of 5 stars Pepper Pace Delivers!!
Reviewed in the United States on August 8, 2021

I'm hooked! Karma and Rafe are very entertaining. I like how we're gradually being introduced to these characters. Their differences, similarities and attraction! The anticipation of what's coming is killing me!! Loving it! Thanks Pepper Pace

5.0 out of 5 stars Juicy inter-species romance!
Reviewed in the United States on August 13, 2021

…I can hardly wait for the next installment!

5.0 out of 5 stars Scifi with a brown girl lead
Reviewed in the United States on March 4, 2022

I love fantasy, science fiction, and romance. I think this is a pretty good job of incorporating all three. I like that because it's a continuously building story you are allowed a chance to look at other subplots.

5.0 out of 5 stars I LOVE this story!!!
Reviewed in the United States on November 10, 2021

The Galatian Exchange hits all the right notes. I fell in love with Rafe and Karma (and Dorf) instantly. It's something about this dystopian romance that makes you think beyond the storyline. I absolutely LOVE a story that will trigger all your emotions and keep you wanting more. This is why Pepper Pace is an automatic buy. Every. Time.

About The Galatian Exchange

Corruption runs rampant even in a not-so-distant future where the biggest lottery is rigged so that the only winners are rich and white. But in a world that has been ravaged by a destructive alien attack, an opportunity for a lifetime of riches in exchange for serving as consort to one of the alien defenders is indeed a great prize.

Karma, down on her luck, will become the first Black consort, despite her belief that being an alien whore is only marginally better than serving humans. This epic tale of Afrofuturism explores a world that is chillingly plausible, where survival, identity, and resilience are put to the ultimate test.

Adult content. Mature readers only.

TABLE OF CONTENTS

A note from the Author

The Galatian Exchange first appeared on Amazon's Kindle Vella in July 2021. Since then, it has had amazing success with a consistent ranking within the top 25 of faved stories!

Unfortunately, at the time of this publication, the KV platform is only available within the United States. However, my readers are all over the world! And many have been anxiously awaiting the opportunity to read this series.

For that reason, I have decided to bring TGE to book form. But, while it has been edited from the original, there have not been any major changes made to the book form. If you have enjoyed the Kindle Vella version, the only changes are basic corrections to names, dates, and continuity.

I do want to confirm that this is _not_ a new story and is _not_ an extension, prequel or epilogue to the Kindle Vella series.

For those unfamiliar with the Kindle Vella platform, be aware that the stories are structured as short episodes within an ongoing series. Meaning; there is no end. With that said, we incorporate 'seasons', which ends a storyline while introducing new ones. So, do not worry, there are resolutions to the conflicts!

I hope this clarifies any questions. Please enjoy!

-Pepper Pace

Chapter One

Karma hurried past the woman that leaned against a post as if she needed it to support her. It was a streetlight that illuminated the pre-dawn night sky, but it also gave the woman an unfortunate spotlight.

She wore a thin, purple skirt that barely covered her skinny butt. An army fatigue jacket was her only means to fight the cold. Beneath that was a tank top that was just a wife-beater whose lower half had been torn away. Mud was splattered all over her worn boots—and hopefully it was only mud.

The woman changed her position, and Karma wondered if she was trying to strike a sexy pose or had just stopped herself from falling to the ground.

She gave her a worried glance, a variety of thoughts in her head. Was she hurt? Was she a pickpocket? Or was she just high?

She had to have been the dirtiest whore Karma had ever seen. The only whores that ended up like her were the ones that had hit rock bottom. She had mangy, brown hair that could have been dreads but was more than likely just snarls from months of neglect. She was technically a white woman, but dirty, so she was dirt-colored.

The insult was in the word *dirty*, not *whore*. There were call girls, prostitutes, and then whores. Sex work was not only the oldest profession, but once it had become legalized, they had formed the biggest union in the world: SWU, Sex Workers United.

Karma doubted that this woman was in the union, though. They had a great drug program, and this one definitely could have used their services.

When the woman opened her mouth to place a cigarette between her lips, Karma saw that her few teeth were black.

A meth smoker. But if your only recourse to survival is standing on the streets selling hand and blowjobs because even the derelicts knew not to get too close to what might have developed between your thighs, you'd blow out your last brain cells on meth too.

Karma kept walking, vowing that when the day came that she was forced to become a sex worker, she would never walk the streets for money, and she would damn sure never resort to meth. She'd find other ways to disappear.

She pulled her jacket close around her, making sure that her knit cap was low on her head so the only thing exposed was a bit of brown flesh and alert, dark eyes.

It was cold, but that wasn't the reason. She didn't want anyone to know that she wore earbuds. If anyone knew she had earbuds in, then they would know that she had a device to play music. And if that happened, she would be robbed within seconds. Getting from Cross Town, where the poor lived, to Newburgh, the affluent part of the city, was a fine dance in not getting mugged and showing up to work with a black eye. Again.

Today she was listening to *Songs in The Key of Life* by Stevie Wonder, released in 1976 by Motown Records.

Strange how even though it was close to 500 years since that album was released, things weren't much different. In 2426, most of the world was now a Village Ghetto Land.

Karma checked out the clock in the clock tower and then sped up her steps. She could not risk missing the train. They were unpredictable on this side of the city. If they said they'd arrive at 5:00 p.m., then you'd better get to the station by 4:45 p.m., and you could be kept waiting until 5:15 p.m.

However, once the trains transferred to the nicer ones on the other side of the city, then everything became timely, down to pinpoint accuracy. Yet another disparity that everyone got used to. The government ran the entire public transportation, but Guardian forbid if the train ever arrived late in one of the government-populated areas.

It only took one complaint to lose a cushy civil servant job. Everyone vied for them, and you went in knowing that you could easily be replaced. If that happened, then you just waited for Job Placement Services to find you some low-paying shit job making shit money. Well, unless you were white. White men were always placed in a government position. White women were next. Black, brown, red, or yellow people basically cleaned toilets. Of course, there would always be the option of selling sex.

The train depot always stayed crowded, and Karma pushed her way to the turnstile to scan her pass and get onto the platform. Once on the platform, she had room to move without having to be mindful of sticky fingers trying to dip into her pockets.

Those that filled the depot weren't only waiting for trains. The homeless gathered here to stay warm. The government only opened the safe houses during extreme weather. One didn't have to turn into a solid block of ice before you died from exposure, but the government sure

3

thought so. Right now, she had shelter, although it cost every bit of money she made. She could only save money once the shelters opened, and then for about three months she had a bed for the night, rent-free.

A group of guards stood together wearing wool coats and boots, doing more smoking and laughing than keeping order. The guards were always young white men who had been hired to keep the order, but they didn't see that as their purpose. When they got bored, they actually started fights with the scrubs — their word for people like her, people who had to scrape out a living.

She kept away from them, preferring to stay closer to a group of scrubs who kept a careful lookout for pickpockets and troublemakers. Those types would just bring the attention of the guards and then innocents would get their heads cracked. Yeah, she'd much rather be standing next to a scrub than a guard.

The train arrived without too much of a delay and she quickly boarded, searching for a seat. When there weren't any available, she gripped a strap and hoped no one in the crowd got touchy-feely or went searching her pockets for something to steal. She wasn't stupid enough to keep things in her pockets, and she didn't feel like elbowing someone in the nose. The last time she'd gone to work with blood on her jacket, the mistress of the house had looked at her as if she had a disease.

Heinrich's mouth was filled with a pale tit topped by a sweet strawberry nipple. His eyes were rolled to the top of his head. How could he ever let Mayva go? She

4

was perfect in every way. She had been groomed since puberty to please the Galatian animals so of course, she knew how to please him.

She rolled her hips over him and he released her sweet breast so he could stare into her glazed eyes as she rocked her pelvis, capturing him within her depths, her hips swirling in a beautiful dance that couldn't be matched by any woman on Earth or even outside of this galaxy.

Mayva was his ideal woman—impeccably beautiful. She was as white as alabaster. She had told him that the rays of the sun had never touched her. Her delicate porcelain skin was as perfect as a baby's bottom. Her long, blond locks swept a perfect, little ass. She was so petite, but her pussy could take all of his six inches with no trouble, magically gripping and holding him in place with each upward thrust of his hips.

She loved it too. Like most of the girls in the Exchange, they wanted to experience a human man before being defiled by one of the Galatian monstrosities. He had, of course, tasted many of them. But none of them was like Mayva; all of them sweet, but not worth the punishment for more than a brief romp.

But Mayva was the exception. She loved fucking. She had sought him out, explaining that she was tired of practicing with dildos and wanted a real man. She had used all of her sexual tricks on him, sending him to heights he could never have fathomed, but not only sexually—just looking at her made his heart swell with something he'd never experienced before. He was a forty-six-year-old politician; a forty-six-year-old *married* politician who thankfully only had sons. Sons could never be sold into sexual servitude the way Mayva's parents had sold her.

After a mere year of secret rendezvous, he knew he couldn't live without her. He would leave his wife and sons and run away with her where no one would ever know what he'd done. He had manipulated records and moved funds so that he now had enough wealth for Mayva and him to live happily for the rest of their lives.

Heinrich knew the punishment for sex with a consort. The Galatians considered it rape, even if the female consented. The Galatians had already claimed the consorts, and no one could enjoy them until after their servitude ended.

Stealing wasn't an issue — the Galatians didn't even know the humans had been taking a kickback for decades in order to get the preferred selectees through the lottery. But claiming a consort would lead to a fate worse than death. If it was ever discovered that he'd dared to touch their property, his dick would be removed — ripped from his body — and he would be left to bleed to death.

"I don't want to risk you, my darling," Mayva spoke while bathing Heinrich's brow with a cool, wet cloth. He lay on his back, panting after his labors. He was a bit overweight, but had been working on that over the last few months.

His beautiful Mayva deserved a man that, although nearly thirty years her senior, still held onto some vitality. There was not much he could do about his balding head and short stature, but Mayva didn't care about any of that. She loved him for who he was.

He reached up and cupped her beautiful face. "Don't worry your lovely, little head. I'll replace you in the Exchange and we will be gone before anyone is the wiser."

"Yes, Heinrich," she said gently in a voice that sounded like soothing wind chimes to his ears. "But no one has taken your offer to replace me. They are afraid that when the Galatians find out, they will be punished."

He waved his hand, dismissing her worries. "They would never hurt a consort."

"But she won't be a consort. She'll just be an untrained human," Mayva said with concern. He pulled her down to kiss him, lathering her face with the attention of his thin, wet lips.

"So? We will be long gone. Don't you worry your pretty, little head. Papa bear has taken care of everything. Once my men find your replacement, we will be long gone before anyone's the wiser."

Mayva smiled lovingly at her man. "I love you, Heinrich. I cannot wait until we're able to really be together."

He pinched her little, pink nipple and felt himself rising. He hadn't even needed the assistance of one of the potency pills he'd used with his wife. His life was going to be so wonderful with his one true love.

He pulled Mayva on top of him and rolled her onto her back. Now it was time to satisfy her. He slid down her body and spread her legs.

"Yes, Heinrich, my love!" she shouted while pressing his face deep within the V of her love. He did not see the look of disgust on her face, and could not know that as soon as she had her freedom, she planned to take his life, and his money — in that order. And once she was free, she would never be used by any man, human or Galatian.

Chapter Two

Karma was a bit hungry, but Minnie the cook would make sure she had something for her to eat before the family had their breakfast. Minnie always said that it wouldn't do to drool over the family's meals, so Karma wasn't sure if she gave her food out of kindness or out of necessity.

She had been the one to tell her to be sure to always arrive to work well-groomed. Karma was insulted at first, until she understood that she had meant that she needed to wear her regular clothes until she arrived, and needed to keep the uniform at work.

After she got off that first train, she walked a few blocks until she arrived at the subway. It was much nicer than the depots. No one but well-dressed officials and decent-looking laborers were anywhere around. Men and women actually read newspapers while waiting for their trains to arrive, containers of coffee in hand while they chatted with others dressed smartly in warm, wool coats.

Karma looked away, sick of them—jealous of them, if she had to be truthful. It hadn't mattered if she had done well in school or if her parents had taught her to have a sense of self-respect. She hadn't been able to get a civil service job the way all the counselors had promised. No one with brown, yellow, or black skin ever got the civil servant jobs and there wasn't a damn thing anyone could do about it.

Corruption ran deep, but there was no use complaining about the racial injustice, police brutality, and bad conditions of the areas relegated for the poor and sickly.

She had seen one of the Galatians being interviewed on television years ago when she'd been a kid. They had promised to take care of the humans and to protect them against further harm from intergalactic threats. And even though much of the world was in the process of being rebuilt after the ruin the Tybernees attack had left it in, the Galatians obviously didn't understand that the humans that had been left in charge were just as much of a threat to mankind.

She sat on a bench and picked up the newspaper that had been abandoned on the seat next to her. The headlines were all about the upcoming Galatian Exchange, where the girls that had spent years being schooled on becoming a consort to a Galatian would finally be matched with their alien. The girls lucky enough to have been selected in the lottery were interviewed, proud to service the Galatians that protect us. Karma smirked mirthlessly. Funny how they thought they were so different than the whores that walked the streets down here on Earth.

After leaving the subway, Karma walked to the bus stop, which let her off fifteen minutes later a few blocks from where she worked as a maid. She didn't really agree that she was a maid, although that was what she was told by the employment agency that had placed her. She was actually a slave. The only difference was that she got paid for the privilege of being mistreated.

She was happy that she had arrived at the house with a few extra minutes of time.

She hurried to the small room that had been relegated to the servants and directly to its simple adjoining bathroom and toilet. The bedroom contained a twin-sized cot in case a servant was required to stay overnight to attend to some function that wouldn't end until after the trains and busses stopped running. If more servants were required to stay, then two people squeezed into the bed and the others made pallets on the floor.

Karma actually didn't mind the times she'd had to sleep overnight. It was better than a corner in the train depot, where she had often slept when times had been hard, and even better than the small motel room she currently shared with two other girls — both thieves who would rob her blind if she didn't keep everything she owned on her person.

After using the toilet and washing her face to confirm that she hadn't picked up some grime, Karma re-did her ponytail at the back of her neck. The rubber band that held her springy, dark hair was barely a match for the Afro that threatened to spread across her head.

She got one of her uniforms out of the closet and slipped it on. They were supplied by the employers, but were nothing special, just a simple, gray dress, white hose, black flats, and a white apron. They didn't require her to keep her hair beneath a bonnet or scarf as long as she kept it braided or pulled back into a ponytail.

She finished up just as Callista entered the room to change into her uniform. They nodded in greeting. No one had time for true friendships. Friends were just people that tried to ingratiate themselves into your life so they could stab you in the back. Even at twenty-three, Karma had learned that life lesson.

She checked her appearance in the floor-length mirror and saw a girl staring back at her with empty, lifeless eyes. She recognized the smooth, brown skin, the nose with nostrils that flared out above lips that were full and darker than the rest of her. But she had stopped recognizing her eyes long ago. They had not always been empty, dark orbs that reviewed a world she no longer wanted to be a part of.

Karma looked away and then quickly hurried out of the room. She helped Minnie in the kitchen. The older Black woman had made scrambled eggs and bacon for the family, and the kitchen smelled so good that her stomach began to cramp. But Minnie shoved her a slice of bread filled with some of the eggs and dripping with bacon grease and then she sent her into the basement for ice.

Karma hid the small sandwich in the folds of her apron and hurried downstairs, where she quickly inhaled the offering. It would take the edge off, but she was still hungry.

Later, after Mister Tolbert left for the office, the kids had gone off to school and the mistress went about her business, Minnie served the staff breakfast. In addition to the leftovers from the family's breakfast, she fried potato skins with onions—the potatoes themselves would be served for lunch. Mrs. Tolbert kept a tight watch over the food, but didn't care much about the leftovers.

Karma had worked for them for eighteen months. She had been assigned to care for the children, but Mrs. Tolbert often took advantage of her skills with numbers to help keep the household books. The little boys were mischievous little scamps, but she didn't mind, since all children should have an opportunity to be mischievous without the threat of being sent to reform school.

Mrs. Tolbert was another matter. Tall, graceful, and aristocratic, she was also as cold as she had probably once been beautiful. Her platinum-dyed hair always stayed perfectly coiffed. However, her face was another matter. Too much plastic surgery had left her with a plastic appearance and as a result, she wore too much makeup and made it her life's goal to seek out new and better plastic surgeons — easy to do, since she was wealthy enough not to have to work for a living.

Mr. Tolbert had been born into money and had therefore inherited a nice government position as the director of the Galatian Exchange; something that wouldn't require too much energy, as he basically managed the Galatian Lottery.

It was a good job with aloof employers who basically left you alone to go about your duties, and for a maid, that was the best kind.

Karma helped Minnie wash the breakfast dishes and then she went to the market. It was better to shop in the morning because you could be assured that whatever you wanted was available.

The stores in the rich areas were obviously much better stocked, but the prices were higher. Mrs. Tolbert didn't care, as long as she got her imported coffee, a chicken for roasting on Sunday, and a pot roast each Friday.

Karma showed her identification and then purchased the items on Minnie's list. She paid using the Tolberts' credit account, which Mrs. Tolbert scrutinized every single day, down to the penny.

Once she returned to the Tolbert house, she began her cleaning routine. Each of the three bathrooms had to be cleaned each day. Every other day she had to wash, iron, and fold the laundry, as well as change the sheets on laundry day. She scrubbed the kitchen each night before heading home, and if time permitted, she had to help Minnie with food prep for the following day.

She liked helping Minnie the most. Even though the older woman rarely spoke, she passed out scraps of food, even if it was just the peels from apples — but she would sprinkle those peels with a bit of sugar and cinnamon so it was a delicious treat. When she peeled potatoes and carrots, she would sauté the peels in butter and sprinkle them with salt and pepper. Not much went to waste in Minnie's kitchen.

That night when preparing to leave, Karma saw Mr. Tolbert sitting in his car smoking a cigarette.

Mrs. Tolbert forbade cigarette smoking in her house, but he usually sat on the enclosed porch, where he enjoyed a glass of whisky and read the newspaper. She nodded her head briefly at him when he followed her with his eyes.

"Karma!"

She was surprised he knew her name. Karma's back stiffened. Now she would have to get another job. Sleeping with the boss was a sure-fire way to get thrown into jail. The wife always found out, and then she'd set the maid up by pretending she'd been robbed. It happened all the time. Besides, she would never sleep with Heinrich Tolbert. He was a sleaze. He worked with the Galatian Exchange peddling young girls off to aliens in the name of alien-human good will.

"Yes, Mr. Tolbert?" She watched as he rolled down his window.

"I'll drive you home."

"Uhm…" Her mind thought rapidly. "No thank you. I have some shopping to do."

"Then I'll take you to the grocery store."

"Well…" Her mind wasn't working fast enough. She did not want to get into the car with that man.

"Karma." He frowned at her. "Get in. I have a proposition for you. Don't worry." He gave her a once-over, and she could tell he didn't seem physically interested in her. "I won't touch you."

She hesitated. It would be very hard to get another job. If she didn't pay her share of the rent she would be out on the streets, and winter was coming. She moved to get into the back seat but Mr. Tolbert reached over and pushed open the passenger door. She slipped inside, keeping her hands folded on her lap as she stared straight ahead.

He put out his cigarette and pulled out of the driveway.

"Relax, Karma. I'm not interested in you—not like that."

She gave him a curious look and he glanced at her. She wasn't bad-looking. If he got her fixed up a little, maybe no one would figure out that she was a scrub…

He hadn't been successful in his attempts to secure a replacement for Mayva. He'd spoken to a few men he knew, ones who had daughters that hadn't made it into past lotteries. He had proposed his offer—one that any

14

man that cared about the future of his daughter should have snapped up. They were all interested in having their daughters join the lottery, but once they understood that it went past that and he meant for them to go straight to the Exchange, they each balked.

Each exclaimed that without the proper training, there was no way a human could properly serve a Galatian. Heinrich had tried to entice them with the wealth and rewards that their daughters — and therefore, their families — would receive after the service period ended.

But none would sacrifice the supposed well-being of their daughters. Heinrich had even offered to pay one man to allow his daughter to fill the empty seat that would be left by Mayva. He had to be careful here, not to tip off anyone of his plan. But the idiot wouldn't accept the sweet deal. His daughter was a dog. There was no way she'd ever get a better proposition. But the man had turned him down flat in fear for his daughter's safety if it should ever be discovered that the Galatians had been duped.

Heinrich couldn't take any more chances with his colleagues becoming suspicious. He had not considered that none would jump at the opportunity. His entire plan was hinged upon slipping in someone that could pass as Mayva and then stealing away with the love of his life.

Why would no one take this opportunity to do something they had planned to do anyway; whore off their daughter? None would be the wiser — although if it did become discovered at some point in the future, he and Mayva would be long gone.

Heinrich had been forced to search the common people, call girls that were used to whoring themselves. But the pretty ones laughed at him and said they didn't have to be slaves to hideous aliens when they made good money servicing hideous humans. He'd had to downgrade to streetwalkers, but no fool would think that the unclean filth that walked the streets had been groomed over periods of years to be a Galatian consort. The Exchange would be held in two days, and he was desperate.

Karma wasn't the standard consort introduced into the Exchange but he was desperate, and this was his last chance.

Chapter Three

"Are you hungry?" he asked with a smile. She didn't believe that smile.

"No, sir." She was starving, but would never admit it.

"Well, I'm hungry. You can join me for a late-night snack while I tell you about my proposition."

She inhaled a strained breath. "Mr. Tolbert, no disrespect, but all I want to do is the job that you hired me to do."

He drove quietly for a few moments. "Do you like donuts? There's a place up here that sells the best pastries, and their coffee is imported from the Costa Rican province. The tariffs are out of this world for imports, but you really can't say that you've had a cup of coffee until you've had a Costa Rican blend. What do you say? Humor me?"

Her stomach ached, and the talk of food only made her hungrier.

"Okay," she replied. At least she could listen and get something to eat out of the deal.

He chatted about stupid things, weather, politics — everything under the sun except what he wanted from her. They finally pulled into the parking lot of a nice diner, one where the staff wore uniforms instead of street clothes like in her part of town.

Once inside, the smells made her stomach growl loudly and Mr. Tolbert chuckled. "Well, it's a good thing we stopped. You're hungrier than you thought."

She resisted glaring at him. They went to the counter, and Karma's eyes grew large at the array of beautiful confections. Heinrich ordered two apricot Danishes and a fancy whipped drink. She had no idea what an apricot was, but knew strawberries. They were rare. She ordered something called a strawberry cheese crown along with a large cup of coffee.

She poured lots of cream and sugar into her coffee and took a drink. She'd never had a drink that tasted better. Once they were at a table tucked away in the corner, she watched her boss suspiciously.

He smiled that sneaky smile again and gestured for her to eat. He took a bite of one of his Danishes and she picked up her cheese cup and nibbled the pastry. It was so good! She took a bite, capturing a strawberry that was surrounded by sweet, red gel.

"Good?" he asked. She had nearly forgotten about him.

"Yes, sir."

"Karma, I understand that things aren't easy in this economy. Not much of the Earth is habitable anymore. If the weather doesn't destroy the plants, then it's blight and disease that does. Even though the Tybernees are long gone, they made sure that bringing Earth back to its glory won't be easy."

Blah blah blah was all she heard as she continued to nibble her pastry and drink her hot coffee.

"Which is why I want to offer you an opportunity. The Galatian Exchange is going to be held the day after tomorrow."

She let out a relieved breath. He just needed her to join the cleaning crew for the event. Well, all he needed to do was just ask. What fool would turn down that opportunity? She'd get paid extra, and there was always extra food and drink that the workers divvied up afterwards. She could eat for a month at what she'd get from the Exchange—although generally, it got sold.

Helping with any of the many Galatian events was considered an enormous boon for humans. The gossip was plentiful, and sometimes the staff ended up in the newspapers—obviously in the background, but it was a status symbol to be seen wearing the crisp, white shirts and black pants while carrying the trays ladened with strange Galatian treats.

"Karma, how would you like an opportunity to join the Exchange?"

She smiled. "I'd be honored! Thank you, Mr. Tolbert!" She thought about the crisp, white shirt she'd get to wear. She'd always wanted a white shirt, but it cost too much to maintain purely white things.

"Karma, I think you misunderstand. I don't mean that I want you to work at the Exchange. I want you to *participate* in it."

She just stared at him in confusion.

He tried again. "I want you to become a Galatian consort. One of the women is unable to fulfill her duties and in truth, it was my responsibility to see to the health of the girls. Now that she's incapable of serving, I find myself in the terrible predicament of being one consort short—"

She stared at him as if he was insane. "What?"

"Karma, you do understand the benefits of being a Galatian consort, don't you?"

"Yeah, but, Mr. Tolbert, people train for years—"

He waved her words away. "Nonsense. You serve our family, and have done so for years—"

She rolled her eyes. "Yes, but sex isn't involved—"

He looked around quickly and lowered his voice. "Sex is sex. They're trained in the art of pleasuring a man. But if you want to know the truth, you just need a working vagina. There. Period. The main thing is looking after them while they are stationed here on Earth—"

"Yes, sir. I know," she replied. "For seven years. And you can't break the contract."

"And at the end, you will be set for life. You will never need for anything."

She didn't reply.

Heinrich continued quickly. "Seven years where you will never be cold, never be hungry, will have a roof over your head. Seven years where—"

"I'd have to have sex with an alien," she said.

"They are aliens, but they look a lot like us."

She shrugged. "If you think seven-foot-tall green men with scales look like us, then yes, they do look a little like us," she replied dryly.

"Women say that sex with a Galatian man is quite pleasurable—"

"Mr. Tolbert, I don't want to talk about sex with a Galatian. Even if I agreed to do this, I would stand out. Mr. Tolbert, all of the consorts are white women."

She didn't pull back on her words and refused to look down although his cheeks turned pink.

"Well…uh…it seems Galatians like that sort, so supply and demand…"

"I don't fit the mold. I'm tall, I'm Black, and my hair does not flow down to the back of my knees." It was another common trait. The consorts grew their hair as long as they could and when they walked across the stage, it was considered the height of beauty for them to swish their loose hair until it moved like golden waves.

"Long hair isn't a requirement." He looked uncomfortable. "There is nothing in the agreement that says you *have* to be white. In the end, they would be lucky to have you. You know how to serve." He smiled at her. "The ones that went through training have never had to actually serve anyone a day in their lives."

That was true. They were all the pampered daughters of the wealthy.

He continued when she didn't say anything. "You can work as a maid for the next seven years and end up just where you were the day before. Or you can replace my missing consort and become a wealthy woman by the time you're thirty."

She studied his eyes. There was no saying no to his request and returning to work at his house. He'd given her this opportunity but in actuality, it was just an ultimatum.

She thought about the girl she'd seen this morning, strung out and selling herself for enough money to smoke more dope. If she turned down Mr. Tolbert's offer, she would be out of a job tonight. And tomorrow she'd put her name in at the employment agency with the other hundreds of women waiting to be selected to fill shit jobs making shit money. In two months she would be right out there selling herself too.

Sex was the one commodity she possessed that could support her. But if she would be forced to sell it, then she wanted the best return.

"What if..." she said hesitantly.

"Go on?" He leaned forward, sensing that he had her.

21

"What if they don't want me because I don't look like the others?"

He leaned back and smiled. He had her. "Why wouldn't a Galatian want you? You're pretty, you're smart, you're capable—and they're obligated to take you. The contract can't be broken."

"I won't allow any man to beat me." She narrowed her eyes. "I don't care about contracts. I draw the line at that."

He relaxed. "Don't you know anything about Galatians? They don't hurt humans. They think they created us and *have* to protect us."

She knew all about that. Over two hundred years ago when the Tybernees arrived, stealing the Earth's males in order to enslave and force humans to fight in their wars, the Galatians had suddenly swept in.

Appearing like human Titans, they fought off the Tybernees and then explained the true origins of man. The Galatians explained that mankind was nothing more than a Galatian experiment. When the Earth was new, Galatians had travelled to the planet and injected their DNA into organisms that eventually turned into man. Man was left to their own devices while the Galatians watched from afar, protecting the Earth's galaxy from the other intergalactic creatures that had long since figured out the puzzle of space travel.

Many humans refused to accept that they were considered a lower species. But not Karma who could care less what words others used to describe her. Others always tried to define someone else. She was who she was.

"The Galatians say they won't hurt humans, but behind closed doors—"

"No," Heinrich said without hesitation. "They have this entire honor system. They would never hurt us. The most they do is uproot and relocate us if we piss them off too much."

And whenever that happened, that city died, Karma thought. The Galatians helped to rebuild what was broken, city by city. They fixed the soil so plants grew without the effects of the radiation that had been dropped by the government to destroy the Tybernees. The Galatians had the technology to harness the sun's power instead of polluting the environment with the poisons that man had used in prior generations. But if the rebels pissed them off too much, they simply pulled up stakes and moved to a different city.

The Galatian Exchange helped to keep them rooted to Earth in order for man to continue receiving the valuable aid.

Karma had finished her pastry and was sipping her coffee as she thought about Mr. Tolbert's offer. Right now, she wasn't hungry. The coffee had made her alert, but wouldn't it be nice not to have to take two trains and a bus to work six days a week to work for someone else? Wouldn't it be nice not to worry if one of your roommates had sold your clothes, or trying to make sure any money you made was hidden so that if they set you up to be robbed, no one would take everything you owned?

"Mr. Tolbert, I do have a condition."

Heinrich's grin grew broader as relief washed over him. Thank goodness she'd accepted this offer. The alternative would have been a lot of threats and calling the police to report that she'd stolen from his house. She didn't know it, but his wife's pearl necklace was in her coat pocket even at this very moment.

"What's your condition?"

"I don't want to attend the Exchange looking like I'm a scrub. I want a gown like everyone else."

He eyed her. The gowns took weeks to be made, and she was much taller than the others. There was no way she could fit into Mayva's gown. He hadn't considered her attire, but they'd go shopping. He'd spring for something. Hell, he'd spring for something nice. She had just saved his hide!

"Of course. You'll need a wardrobe," he replied. And she'd need a makeover. She'd be the first non-white involved in the Exchange and it would surely create a stir. He couldn't care less about the controversy and the resulting public backlash. He just needed for her to be presentable long enough for him to get away with his girl and the money.

Pity the girl wouldn't ever reap the benefit of the Exchange, as she wasn't likely to survive her first time fucking a Galatian.

Chapter Four

Rafe marched alongside the cell that held the two prisoners. It hovered a foot off the floor. Its bars were titanium, and required three different keys to unlock. There was an emergency override that required simultaneous input from three command centers—located on three different planets.

No one had ever broken free of a Galatian cell. Rafe's team had been hunting the two Malnamanian intergalactic pirates for two full years. Even though the Galatian Exchange was to be conducted later today, seeing that the prisoners were properly transported was top of his mind.

Selling humanoids was becoming a hot commodity. The Galatian Guards had the temperament for the task, or so thought the Interplanetary Collective. Even the strongest aliens known to the universe did not possess the sheer strength of the Galatians. They were basically pure muscle.

"Rafe, the last transport back to Earth is about to leave. If you intend to make the Exchange, you'd better go. I'll take over."

Rafe gave his captain a brief shake of his head. "I'll take a pod down to Earth. I need to see this through."

One of the prisoners snickered. "Big, bad Rafe Sigur giving up his position as head of the Galatian Guards to babysit a bunch of humans?"

Rafe ignored him, not reacting to the words that still inflamed him. He'd requested to be allowed another tour in the Guards. It had been denied. They wanted him to find a mate and settle down to have an offspring, which couldn't happen until after he'd spent his term on Earth. After which, he would receive his land and home back on Galatia, where his union would hopefully be fruitful and he could be blessed with a child.

He did want those things, but he'd watched his brother struggle with his queen. They'd lost a baby during the final months of pregnancy after years of trying. His brother's queen had become despondent. He didn't want to see a queen suffer like so many. He knew it was his duty to try to replenish the Galatian race, but he believed there should be alternative ways to keep their race thriving.

He thought the experiments in which they took their DNA and created other life-forms should be continued. Galatians had created several humanoid races using themselves as the map. But races like Malnamanians were too ruthless, and Earthlings were too self-destructive. There were others, but they were still developing, too new to determine how they would turn out.

Once the cell was secured into the ship's hold for transportation to Gong, the prison planet, Rafe gave the two prisoners one last opportunity to lighten their sentences.

"You know that humanoid trafficking is punishable by life in prison. We know you are working with the Tybernees. You give us their home base and we will lighten that sentence."

"To what?" one of the prisoners asked. "Half a lifetime on a prison planet where everyone's in the pockets of the Tybernees? Get out of here with that shit."

"Hey!" Rafe's tail swished beneath his skirts. "You give us what we need and you won't ever have to worry about the Gong. We can send you to a Galactic prison on your home planet. Visits from your family...your mama and papa still among the living?"

The prisoner stood on his spindly legs. He was lucky that he had no true bone structure because Rafe had tried to fold his body into submission during their battle.

"My mama and papa are of no consequence to me," the alien spoke. "I won't make a deal with you. No one in this universe would."

Rafe turned to leave without another word. His tail, however, slipped from beneath his skirts to observe the alien. The Malnamanians truly had no family loyalty. They would sell their own mothers for a brigget or two.

Karma was surprised that Mr. Tolbert had bought her an entire wardrobe. She didn't know that she'd raise suspicion if she didn't arrive at the Exchange with a trunk filled with finery.

It didn't cost him anything. The money wouldn't be coming from him but from the government credit account, which legally allowed him to freely make purchases until the weekly accounts were taken. He wouldn't dare stick his hands into his personal accounts until the day he fled his screeching shrew of a wife. She kept as tight a hold on the finances as she did on his prick.

Instead of returning to her motel, Karma was set up in a hotel room that, by his standards was a fleabag, but by Karma's was luxurious. The mattress had pristine, white sheets, but even better than that, she didn't have to share it with two other women. There was a television set and a radio, so she turned them both on. She took a hot shower and washed her hair with shampoo instead of the bar of soap.

Mr. Tolbert told her there was no time to sleep. He sent over two women to help get her prepared for the ceremony, even though it was two days away. She wanted nothing more than to slip between the sheets and sleep—after all, she'd been awake since before 5:00 a.m. the day before. But the women had taken one look at her and announced that it would take the full two days to make her presentable.

As insulting as it was, she had to admit that each torturous treatment gave her improved results.

She was waxed, plucked, massaged, manicured, and pedicured. She'd received skin treatments, hair treatments, teeth whitening, and underarm bleaching. There had been no time for laser treatments to permanently remove the hair from between her legs and underarms, but she'd received a colonic and was inoculated—not to protect her from diseases, but to make sure she didn't pass any onto her Galatian owner—she refused to use the word master.

When she felt too sick the next morning to rise, she'd been given an IV and instantly felt energized.

The Exchange would be held tomorrow, and the two white women still didn't know what to do with her hair. They were only used to curling and brushing out fine, pale strands of hair that could be moved into ringlets at the slightest urging.

Once her hair had been trimmed, she was left with a perfectly round Afro that could no longer be stretched into its normal puffball ponytail.

"Do you know anyone that can put in extensions?" one lady exclaimed to the other.

"It's too kinky!" came the response.

"Well, what about braids? I've seen some amazing braids—"

"For the Galatian Exchange? Never!"

Karma peered at her hair in the mirror. She liked the sight of the little ringlets that stood out over her head. Besides, even if they pressed it, curled it, braided it, or put in a weave—one day, the Galatian would know that this is the way her hair was meant to look.

She peered at them through the reflection of the mirror. "I need some Black hair care products; moisturizer, gel, and argon oil."

They just stared at her, evidently trying to translate those items from their dictionary of white hair care products.

"Send someone to the Dollar Store in the Black or Mexican part of town," she replied while placing a fifth slice of bacon into her mouth. "I'd go, but I think you said I needed that second massage."

Rafe landed his pod and strolled to the commander's sector. Everyone he passed either gave him a second look or stared after him in surprise.

"Hey!" someone called after him. "Aren't you supposed to be at a binding ceremony...uh, now?"

Rafe's brow drew down in annoyance. "Shut the hell up," he growled without a backward look.

The men hurried along.

When he reached the commander's sector, his assistant gave him a look of surprise. "Sir, I think you're late for—"

"I need to speak to the commander," Rafe interrupted.

"Of course. Right away, sir!"

After a brief announcement, he was buzzed into a large office.

Commander Einar turned to look at the clock. He was dressed in the formal attire for the Galatian; a pleated skirt that nearly swept the floor and a matching vest made of a copper-like metal that could only be mined in Galatia. The metallic hue perfectly complemented the commander's sleek, green scales. They had been oiled so they shined.

"What are you doing here, Rafe? You're late for your own ceremony! I was just preparing to leave for the second half—"

Talk of that damned ceremony made Rafe's scales prickle. They were on the verge of tracking down a key rebel cell and all anyone could talk about was that damned ceremony. It was as if everyone else was on the verge of binding themselves instead of him.

The commander would surely understand how important it was for him to continue with his position with the Galatian Guards after the capture of the two Malnamanians.

They couldn't afford for their toughest Defender to be saddled here on Earth babysitting the humans.

"You heard about the capture of the two Malnamanians."

Commander Einar gestured to the computer at his desk. "The information is in the report. Rafe, you're not even dressed for your own ceremony."

"Commander, you can't honestly expect me to leave my duties—"

"Lieutenant, we talked about this."

"But—" Rafe interjected, his arguments at the ready for why he should be allowed to be replaced by another Guard. Most looked forward to their opportunity to leave the dangers of battle and retire to be catered to by a docile human companion.

But he wasn't like most. He didn't think humans should be treated as completely helpless. Yes, they lacked much of the sensibilities needed to survive intergalactic predators—they were nearly wiped out multiple times by viruses—yet he could give them credit for prevailing for as long as they had.

The commander swiftly pulled out a short sword. It's point was at Rafe's throat within a split second—not that it would have done much damage, even though his neck was one of his most vulnerable areas.

"Look, Rafe. If you are even thinking of deserting your duties . . ."

"Deserting? No, sir," he said quickly.

"Your duties are to follow your orders," the commander stated. "So let me make it clear; if you aren't at that binding ceremony to accept your human, I don't care how many criminals you capture, I will send you to Gong. And not as a Guard!"

Rafe swallowed and then nodded. He quietly turned and left the office.

"Shit!" he cursed in Galatian. He checked the time and then sprinted down the corridor to his transport pod.

"Stand up straight." One of the women prodded Karma in the side. "Remember that you'll be on display for the *universe* to see."

Karma swallowed. "I'll stand up straight when I'm on display. Are you sure you ordered everything I asked for?"

"It's on the way. Now it's time for you to get dressed, and we need to be quick about it. It's going to take forty minutes to get you to the city center."

She didn't know the names of the women. One was tall, thin, and snippy, while the other was shorter, younger, and less snippy.

They'd spent the last hour on her makeup. She hadn't bothered to look in the mirror. They would never get her to look like one of the white women they wished she looked like, so why should it matter? Besides, did they plan to do her makeup when she woke up tomorrow in the company of her alien owner? This wasn't for her or for him—this was for the world, and Karma literally didn't give a damn about what anybody else in the world thought.

There was a knock on the door and Karma dashed forward. Both women stopped her by hooking each of her arms.

"Oh, no," one tsked. "Remember that no one can see you."

The woman hurried to answer the door while the other pushed her to the bathroom.

"I don't like that everything is so last-minute," the lady holding the package snapped once the door was closed and locked behind her. Everyone was tired, but Karma instantly came alert at the sight of the brown-paper-wrapped package. She snatched it and flopped down on the bed to unwrap it.

Inside was a leather case, which she quickly unzipped. A broad smile took over her face at its contents. She removed the old-fashioned CDs. *Thriller* by Michael Jackson, *Saturday Night Fever* by the Bee Gees, *This is Life* by Johnny Broho, and finally the best album every created, *Metaphorical Music* by Nujabes.

My life is complete, she thought with a smile. *I can withstand anything with my music.*

The two assistants exchanged disbelieving looks. "You were given the opportunity to ask for anything to add to your dowry and you chose old-fashioned CDs? They don't even make CD players anymore!"

Karma carefully returned the CDs to the leather case and slipped it into her new trunk, which contained less personal riches — ones that Mr. Tolbert said she wouldn't be able to do without. She'd also placed her wool coat and hat in it, although there was a much finer one ready for her. But they were her items, and she wouldn't toss them away so easily.

"Don't you worry, I have a CD player," she said. She had saved for half a year, opting to sleep in the train station to save enough to buy it from a pawnshop in Newburgh, where she was less likely to be cheated.

She would have shown it to them, but then they would know the hiding places that she'd slashed in the lining of her coat.

A smart person carried their possessions with them or they might never be seen again.

"Can we resume?" the snippiest of the ladies asked.

Karma stood and allowed them to dress her in a slinky, white gown that hugged her body.

"Well, she's thin enough," one said while appraising her critically.

"Poor people usually are," Karma muttered.

"But she's filling it out nicely," the other commented. "I dare say, she might even look better in her dress than the others will look in theirs." Karma was surprised by the compliment—even if it was slightly backhanded. All she'd heard for the last few days was how much work it would take to get her even partially presentable.

"The white was a good choice," Snippy stated.

"Yes, it contrasts amazingly with her skin tone," Less Snippy replied.

"It might be her saving grace."

"Not with that horrendous hair."

"I rather like it."

"Look," Karma interrupted. "Can you two stop criticizing me like I'm not here?!"

Snippy smiled for the first time since Karma had met her. "I think it's time to look in the mirror, young lady."

Young lady? For the last two days, she'd just been "girl"—if they called her anything at all.

Karma looked at the other woman, who nodded in encouragement. She moved to the mirror, walking in the way they'd instructed, allowing her body to sway as she glided across the room.

Karma froze as she scanned the image before her. She opened her mouth just to confirm that the set of rouged lips actually belonged to her.

The makeup was exquisite. *She* was exquisite. Not only had she never imagined that she could look so pretty, Karma had never, ever, seen any person so richly dressed.

Diamond earrings hung from her ears while jewels dripped from not only her neck, but also her white gown. Even her high-heeled slippers looked as if they were cut from glass, like a modern-day Cinderella. Jewels sparkled in her short hair, catching the glint of light from several directions.

"Do you like it?" Less Snippy asked softly.

Karma couldn't find her words so she simply nodded. Snippy hurried for a white fur cloak, which she slipped over Karma's shoulders. The hood was pulled over her head until it concealed her face.

"You will make a grand entrance—mostly because you're already late," Snippy sighed, and added in a gentler voice, "but also because you're a vision."

Karma tried to swallow back her fear. "Thank you—for everything."

Chapter Five

Mr. Tolbert had sprung for a limo. He had said that appearance was everything.

She hadn't seen him since the night he'd given her this opportunity, and the two women that had assisted her were not going to join her, stating their job was over. She felt completely abandoned.

She left the building for the first time in two days and saw a uniformed man waited by the limo to open the door for her.

"Madam," he said politely. Karma had been cautioned to keep her head down until she was safely inside the City Center, at which point she would be assigned an official escort.

She was thankful that she wouldn't have to decipher any of this alone. Information about what happened behind the scenes during the Galatian Exchange had been shrouded in mystery, including the consort school where the lottery winners were trained on how to please their new alien masters.

There were many rumors about the consort training, but Mr. Tolbert seemed to think that her years in servitude was the only training she would need. She wasn't so sure about that.

Karma fidgeted in the back seat, too afraid to even admire the rich décor. Of course, she'd been inside many limousines—as the cleaner. She longed to pull out her music, which was about the only thing that might put an end to her nervousness.

"Excuse me," she said while leaning forward towards the front seat.

"Madam?" the driver replied.

"Can you play some music, please?"

"Certainly, madam. Would you like to listen to the classical channel? Or perhaps jazz?"

"Jazz is fine," she replied.

She finally relaxed as low music began to fill the vehicle. But then her mind began to replay all that she knew about the Galatians, and the fact that she knew pitifully little made her nervous again. She'd never seen one in person, only on television. They were always on television. It seemed as if humans could not get enough of them.

But television was not something she could afford, so her knowledge of Galatians was based on what she read in discarded newspapers and magazines.

They looked much like humans—if humans had reptilian snake scales instead of skin. Their scales differentiated them from each other, as did the scale patterns—the way a cobra was different from a copperhead. Maybe that's how they differentiated themselves racially. Which scale pattern did they consider the low alien on the totem pole?

One thing she knew for sure was that Galatians were bigger than humans. Their average height was seven feet tall—and some were even taller. Their muscle structure was more enhanced—either because they worked out obsessively or because they just had a superior muscle and bone structure.

The Galatians considered themselves superior to humans in all ways, and not just because they were man's creators. But Karma figured that if you could fly through outer space, whup the asses of your intergalactic enemies all while solving Earth's problems, then your superiority was a no-brainer.

There had been all kinds of medical research done on them, trying to determine how closely related the two species were. But it was moot to her. Everyone knew that ancient Galatians had infused their DNA with prehistoric life-forms to create man—even if that knowledge still caused people to fall into fits of mass suicide.

Many called them ugly, but she didn't actually feel that their differences made them ugly. It was like calling a wild horse ugly just because they ran on four legs instead of two. She knew about the ugly in people, and having snake scales instead of skin didn't disgust her, nor the tail, nor did their tongues, which were human-like, but as long as a reptile's. Even the slits that replaced their noses didn't bother her.

The only thing that gave her worry was the thing that people talked about in whispers or in dirty magazines; a topic that was made into X-rated movies where humans with fake penises wore snake suits and played the role of a Galatian ravaging beautiful women.

It was said that they were extraordinarily well-endowed. Photos had been leaked from research facilities that looked doctored to her. One thing for sure was whether Galatian or human, a prick was still a prick.

Karma gaped at the congestion of people that crowded the streets surrounding the City Center. Some

38

were protestors that held signs stating their dislike of species-mixing. The rest were just people interested in seeing their favorite celebrities, and possibly a glimpse of a real Galatian.

As they drove past, she tried to glimpse the red carpet, which teemed with paparazzi. Richly dressed celebrities posed or waved at fans. She didn't see any Galatians, though. They typically didn't pose for the paparazzi.

The limo drove around to the rear of the large facility. After passing through several levels of security, the driver stopped at an entrance that was far less fancy than the one in front. The rear entrance was flanked by armed guards wearing military uniforms. Humans protecting Galatians? That seemed unlikely. They were present to protect the consorts.

Military personnel were no longer used to fight wars—the Galatians took care of all that. Soldiers served as bodyguards or were used for covert missions.

The driver quickly hurried to open her door and then handed her an envelope.

"You'll need this, ma'am."

She made sure to keep her head down while she accepted the envelope. It was thick, and had her name written across the front in fancy script.

He led her to the door and once again showed the same card that had allowed him entrance through the security gate. The guard opened the door for her.

She hesitated when the driver didn't come inside with her and then the door was firmly closed before he could even turn away. A greeter was instantly at her side holding a clipboard.

"I hope you're Karma Chambers," the woman said quickly. "Because we have had a huge snafu! I'm not sure how it happened, but we had your name wrong in nearly every system!"

Karma pulled back her hood.

The greeter gasped and took a step back. "What is this?"

Karma handed her the envelope. "I think you'll need this."

"Is...this a joke?" she asked, and looked at the guard over Karma's shoulder, gesturing for him to come forward.

One of the guards moved to join the greeter, his steps faltering when he caught sight of Karma.

"Is there a problem?" Karma asked. Her voice didn't reflect her fear — mostly because she was becoming more angry than afraid. But her knees still quaked and her palms began to sweat.

The guard quietly slipped the envelope from the shocked woman's hands. He removed the contents and examined them thoroughly before passing a small identification card to the greeter.

The woman snatched it from him and stared at it for a long time.

"This can't be —" she sputtered.

"It has her photo and her name," the guard said stiffly. "She's the property of the Galatians, and you won't hold her up any further."

The woman's back quickly straightened. Her lips snapped closed and then she thrust the envelope and contents back to Karma without replacing them in the envelope.

Karma accepted them, surprised that she felt relieved at being considered the property of aliens.

The woman turned and began walking away.

"Follow me," she commanded.

Karma wanted to test something. She momentarily ignored the woman and turned to the guard.

"May I know your name?"

The guard seemed to come to attention, his body growing rigid and formal. "I'm Sergeant Adam McPherson, ma'am."

"Thank you, Sergeant. I'd like to let my owner know who has been kind, as well as those that...haven't been." Karma looked over her shoulder at the greeter, who had stopped a few feet away. Her face grew pale. "What's your name?" Karma demanded.

The woman hurried to her, suddenly all smiles. She looked to be in her mid-thirties, and probably enjoyed her cushy job working the Galatian Exchange. No one with such a prestigious position wanted to lose it because they failed to kiss the right ass.

"My name is Pamela Shriver, dear, and please accept my apologies if I seemed short! It's just that we've had a number of problems today, from late arrivals to missing information—but none of it has to do with you, dear!" The woman practically fawned over her.

"Let me take your cloak! Would you like a beverage? I can get you a light snack—"

"A beverage would be nice. Coffee. No, a mocha Frappuccino," she said, recalling the drink that Mr. Tolbert had ordered.

Pamela Shriver accepted her cloak and tried not to gape at her gown. She snapped her fingers and a young woman hurried to her side, gaping at Karma as well.

"Bring Ms. Chambers a mocha Frappuccino! And make it quick!"

The assistant hurried away, carrying the cloak.

Karma took a deep breath. If these people were being so rude, she could only imagine the reaction of the Galatian when he saw her instead of one of the white girls they were accustomed to.

In the long run, it didn't matter. At the end of her seven years of service, she would be wealthier beyond her dreams.

"Let's sign your contract, and then we can get you to the ceremony! Maybe your Galatian will even be there..."

"What?"

The woman hurried them through a set of doors and into a corridor with cement floors and walls.

"Oh, no worries, dear. You are one of two last arrivals, so the others have already selected their consorts. You missed the binding ceremony, but it's okay!"

Her voice had gone high and her smile broader, as if she was trying to convince herself that everything was okay.

Karma didn't really understand what the selection ceremony was, but she was happy that she missed it. It sounded too much like BDSM. Besides, she didn't want to ask questions. That would be a sure-fire indication that she shouldn't be here. Mr. Tolbert should have told her about all of these steps.

They entered an elevator, and the woman continued to chatter.

"I did not know that the lottery had been won by..."

Karma ignored her. When the elevator doors opened, she finally saw the luxury that she had been expecting. The walls were covered in lush, red wallpaper, and the dark wood furniture gleamed like glass. They entered into the expansive room, which were teemed with scurrying workers.

Every one of them stopped and stared at her.

"I'm sure you all have better things to do than to stare!" Pamela clapped her hands and everyone went back to their duties while still giving Karma discreet looks.

They entered an office, and Pamela gestured to a chair opposite a neat desk.

"Okay," Pamela said as she took her seat and opened a folder. "Karma Chambers. It says it right here..." She passed her a sheaf of papers bound by a clip.

"This is your standard contract, the terms of which I'm sure you learned over the course of your education at the consort school. Just sign here."

Karma quickly signed. The door opened and a young woman hurried forward with a tall mug of something frothy and hot.

Karma's mouth practically watered for it—but then she imagined herself dripping the liquid onto her pristine gown and she knew she had to turn it away.

She thanked the woman because she looked completely out of breath, but regretfully Karma left it untouched on the desk.

"Initial here." Pamela pointed to another area. "And here. Perfect." She took the paper back and then stamped it, signed it, and then gave a shaky smile. "All signed, notarized, and you are now legally the property

43

of the Galatians for a period of seven years. Congratulations!"

Karma wasn't quite relieved. Her owner still hadn't signed. In fact, he wasn't even here. Had he somehow found out that she had replaced the true lottery winner?

"Is everything still legal if he hasn't signed?"

"Absolutely. No worries," Pamela said. She leaned forward and spoke in a low voice. "I hear that you got a very good one. He's a lieutenant. He's called Rafe Sigur. Had he been here on time, he would have had first choice and you wouldn't have gotten him.

"But at least you'll be able to join the end of the ceremony and see the others with their owners. I'm sure your master will be along shortly."

Karma's heart pounded in her chest. Despite what Pamela said, she wouldn't feel safe until Rafe Sigur signed his name on that contract.

Rafe tugged at his vest as he hurried down the corridor. Shit! He'd gotten turned around. This place was too big! Maybe he shouldn't have ignored the guard that had offered to escort him, but he'd been here often enough at others' binding ceremonies. They were held once every five years, at which time seven Galatians that retired from service would claim their prize.

He tried not to growl—not sure if he was more upset about being late or the lucky prize winner. It was his own fault in being overly confidant that the commander wouldn't be able to do without him. But if he had to be completely honest with himself, he'd hand-picked and trained many of the soldiers, and knew they were fully capable of carrying out the mission without him.

It was he that couldn't let go. Bringing the Tybernees to justice had been his life mission, and now he was expected to learn how to become domesticated.

He turned a corner and recognized the corridor. He quickened his steps just shy of running. His leather skirt swished around his ankle boots, making an annoying swoosh swoosh sound while his ceremonial sword knocked against his side.

He thought about his human and how she must be feeling at his tardiness. They prepared most of their lives for this event and he'd ruined it for her. Guilt caused his tail to hit the ground but he drew it back beneath his skirt. It was protocol. Humans were used to them by now, but giving them a tail to gape at was an unnecessary annoyance.

Humans were completely rude, but it wasn't all their fault. Galatians hadn't stuck around to instruct them better; a folly that they now were hell-bent on correcting—at his expense.

He stopped short at the door and smoothed his hands down his vest and skirt. He'd quickly oiled himself and hoped he looked smooth. He opened the door and stepped into the room.

The room was filled with people milling about, and he scanned it quickly with a practiced eye.

"Rafe!" Carlisle and Esteban hurried to him.

"You missed it!" Esteban said.

"I missed the entire thing?" Rafe's belly sank.

"No." Carlisle grabbed his arm and pulled him through the crowd. "You missed your human's entrance."

"Where is she?" He craned his neck.

"Rafe…" Esteban was shaking his head and smiling much too brightly, the orange tint of his scales too close to laughter. "Do you see the paparazzi?"

Rafe didn't. "No. Usually they surround us at these events like *carmight* on a *letnaleede*."

"You don't see them because they're all over your human."

"What?!"

Several of his comrades spotted him and before he knew it, he was being ushered by half a dozen Galatians. All were talking over each other in their mother tongue.

Was his human okay? What was going on!

"Lieutenant Sigur!" a human yelled, and the next thing he knew, he was surrounded by cameras. People were yelling questions at him while soldiers held them back from physically accosting him.

His friends used their tails to circle him, keeping the humans at bay.

"How do you feel?!"

"Did you know?"

"Will you keep her?"

"Where is she?!" he demanded.

It seemed as if the crowd parted as a hush fell over the humans and Galatians alike. And that's when he saw a woman dressed in a long, white gown that hugged her form like a second skin.

His eyes took in everything at once; her short-curled hair, her big, frightened eyes, and her deep-brown skin.

Chapter Six

Karma was terrified when Pamela escorted her into the room where the ceremony was being held. It was even more amazing than the previous room, which had been where the Selection Ceremony had been held in privacy, away from the eyes of the public.

This is where everyone's first sight of the lucky winners would take place. Fancy tables were set up with exotic-looking food—most of which she couldn't even identify. Chandeliers sparkled in the dim light and expensive, red brocade covered the upholstery.

Servers in pristine uniforms walked among the richly dressed guests. Karma gawked when she spotted several Galatians speaking to each other in groups. It was impossible to compare them with what she saw on television or in the papers. They were so much more than she could have ever imagined. Their sheer size dwarfed even the tallest human.

They were lizard and human mixed together, and her knees began to knock at the idea of living with one of them for seven entire years. She had made a mistake, a terrible mistake. One angry glance would be enough to send her cowering in a corner. She couldn't do this—fool them, cheat them, risk their wrath.

She nearly turned around, but Pamela exclaimed that the others were at the head table speaking to reporters. Pamela took her arm and practically pulled her through the crowd. Karma didn't even care when she saw her favorite singer and several popular movie stars.

She stared at the six Galatians and their chosen consorts. *Chosen* was the pivotal word. She hadn't been chosen. She could tell the ones that had been paired together. The women doted on their Galatian, serving them choice pieces of food and keeping their glasses filled. They smiled for the cameras and giggled at the reporters.

Karma didn't think she'd ever giggled a day in her life. She cocked her head as they got closer. Wait…why did all the consorts look so much alike? They were all blond with white highlights, and their makeup accentuated the paleness of their skin.

She'd never seen so much pale skin in her life. One of the Galatians took his human's hand and examined it as if he'd never seen a human hand before. He blinked at her and Karma thought she could see his apprehension despite the fact that he had no expression. Could a big, strong Galatian be intimidated by a frail human woman?

"Hello, ladies and gentlemen. Here is our missing consort. Let me introduce you to Karma Chambers."

There was not another word spoken. The other six consorts gaped. The Galatians came to their feet and bowed politely. But then the reporters converged on her.

"Did you say that this woman is a consort?"

"You're the first Negro consort!"

Karma wasn't the only Black person in the room. Several of the celebrities present were people of color — but they had some type of talent that pulled them from the slums. They could entertain others. But even they couldn't bid for the lottery.

As questions were shot at her, Karma wished more than ever that Mr. Tolbert was there. But he wouldn't be here. Mr. Tolbert would never show his face around here again, and that was something Karma had known from the beginning. He'd dangled this opportunity in front of her like a carrot, but only because he stood to get something bigger out of it.

She just hoped she survived this.

"Who are you?" a reporter asked.

There was no backing away now. She had to follow through because Mr. Tolbert wasn't going to help her. She'd have to do what she'd always done; she'd just have to help herself.

Karma forced a smile. "I will gladly answer all of your questions—if my owner permits it."

They now wanted to know who her owner was, and now the others in the room had begun to crowd around her.

The Galatian owners might have appeared docile with their humans but they swiftly moved in front of her, blocking her almost completely from the paparazzi their normally green scales tinged a deep purple like a chameleon.

The humans wasted no time backing away.

"Where's Mayva?" a consort hissed at her.

"I'm sure I don't know what you're talking about," Karma replied. A different woman turned to the first one.

"You know damn well where she is. She got away with it, and we're going to give her a chance to do it!"

"She's a fool!" the first one replied, but she had quieted some.

"Get her out of here!" one of the Galatians directed to the soldiers. Karma looked up at him. He was a titan! His strange eyes studied her and when he blinked, the thin membrane of his eyelids allowed his green-and-yellow slitted eyes to remain partially visible.

Pamela gripped Karma's arm and whisked her away, along with a small military escort and a large number of paparazzi which followed closely behind.

Mr. Tolbert, what did you do?

They were heading to a rear exit when she heard several voices say that Rafe Sigur was here.

Karma wasn't sure if she was relieved or even more afraid. She ignored the calls and questions from the paparazzi as she tried to compose herself. But then a hush fell over the din of noise and her shield of bodies parted, exposing her to a Galatian that stared at her, silently taking in every inch of her from the tips of her toes to the top of her head.

Half a dozen Galatians flanked him and he seemed bigger than them all, not taller –although he was surely over seven feet tall, and not even broader—as some were very bulky. It may have been in the way he held himself, or perhaps the way the others flanked him as if he was showcased.

She took in the exposed areas of his body. His strange, metallic vest showcased well-muscled arms and shoulders. He was both sleek and athletic, and while the others were impressive, he was a definite standout.

He was definitely more man-like instead of lizard. His hairless head was sleek and perfectly formed and his almond-shaped eyes were different, but fit him.

She wished she could see the rest of his body. Galatians didn't wear pants, so she didn't know how big his legs were. She'd once seen pictures of men in a place called Scotland that wore kilts, and his leather skirt reminded her of that. He was…regal.

She took her attention from him long enough to look at the tails of his comrades. They had formed a circle around him, keeping the news people at bay. She found the sight of those tails most curious of all.

Her owner, Rafe, turned to address a man that had stuck a camera in his face. His voice came out sounding deep, but not completely human. She couldn't put her finger on it, but it reminded her of someone morphing the growl of a lion into words.

His eyes narrowed, and she realized that Galatian's faces didn't really move. This must be the way they frowned. He was not pleased, and his tail came from beneath his skirt to brush the man away.

It was one powerful tail because the man stumbled backwards, off balance. Rafe returned his attention back to her while his tail hovered behind him as if it was taking stock of his surroundings.

She realized how strange that thought was but that is what it seemed to be doing.

He suddenly approached her, moving so quickly that she didn't expect it and had to stop herself from retreating. He held out his hand and waited for her to accept it.

She placed her hand in his.

Rafe was surprised at how delicate the human's hands were. He'd never touched the hand of a human female. How did they ever survive all the perils of the world with bones that could be crushed with so little effort?

"My apologies for my tardiness. I should have been here to shield you from…" He looked around.

"We can leave from the back," Pamela said, and ushered them to a nearby rear exit. Rafe guided his human, unconsciously making sure that nothing but him touched her. When someone with a camera came up behind them, he used his tail to brush them aside, causing the man to reel back into several other people.

His comrades made a formidable barrier, falling wordlessly into a protective formation that made it impossible for anyone to follow them.

Rafe allowed only the human attendant through the exit with him and his human. He knew his comrades had created an impenetrable barricade that no one could breach.

"Lieutenant Sigur, we should go to my office to complete the contract. Ms. Chambers has already signed. I'm sorry you weren't able to make your own selection but…" Pamela's mouth formed a pout.

Oh my goodness! Karma thought. Was she trying to flirt?

"My own selection?" Rafe asked.

"Yes. As the senior officer, you would have been given first choice in the selection of your consort."

Karma heard a low growl come from him.

"Are there some better than the others?" His voice had become low, and Pamela gave him a surprised look.

"Oh no! Not at all. Just look at her! She's certainly…striking."

Karma tuned out Pamela's annoying voice and focused on Rafe without turning to look at him.

"You would do well to remember that this individual is mine, whether I selected her or not."

"Of c-course! I m-meant no disrespect!" Pamela stuttered. "Ms. Chambers and I have gotten along so well—"

"Sigur," Rafe said. "As a reminder, a consort is no concubine. She takes my last name. Please keep that in mind when referring to my consort."

Karma looked up at him. His voice was stern yet his face was placid. If he was mad about not getting his choice of consorts, he certainly didn't show it. And by the way—why didn't she know that she would get her owner's last name? This was beginning to feel less like ownership and more like an arranged marriage.

"Yes, sir. Of course, sir." Pamela hurried ahead and didn't say anything else until they had reached the office.

Once inside, Rafe didn't bother to sit. He took the contract and quickly scanned it, although he'd seen it months earlier and had gone through it in detail. He looked at the signature of his human. Karma.

He had not known her name. It sounded right for her. She was Karma. Karma Sigur. A protective surge settled around him. They said this would happen, but he hadn't believed it.

He never noticed human females beyond simple curiosity. He loved Galatian women. Nothing was as beautiful to him. But Karma would be the only female that would ever share his last name. When he married a Galatian, he would proudly bear her name to show his honor and respect.

He paused in his reading to glance at her and found her large, brown eyes watching him.

Humans had eyes that made it so easy to want to protect them. It was said that puppies and babies had the exact same effect on humans.

He picked up the pen and quickly signed his name.

Rafe saw Karma's shoulders relax and he wondered what worried her. And more importantly, why hadn't the others claimed her for themselves? They were good brothers to allow him the honor of acquiring the most unique consort that had ever been contracted.

"I would suggest that we join the others, but the cameras are too disruptive," Rafe said to Karma once he'd signed his portion of the contract and left Pamela Shriver's office.

"I don't know if I'd be comfortable with cameras watching my every move," she replied.

"I'm sorry I wasn't here to escort you. It won't happen again." He offered her his arm and she took it in surprise. This was going much smoother than she could have ever hoped. He didn't seem at all disappointed that he hadn't gotten one of the other consorts.

"I missed the beginning of the ceremony also," she said. "I think we were paired because we just happened to be the last to arrive."

"That explains it."

Her smile faded. Well, if he didn't like the choice he'd been left with, then he shouldn't have been so late.

"We can go to our home. I haven't seen it yet."

Karma swallowed and nodded. "I'd like that. I can make us a meal if you haven't eaten."

He nodded. "I am hungry. But you're not supposed to cook on your ceremony day."

She wasn't? She smiled. "Things aren't going exactly by the book today."

"You'll have plenty of time to service me," he replied.

Karma swallowed.

Did that mean she wouldn't have to sleep with him tonight? Rafe had been kinder than she could have ever hoped for, but he still technically owned her.

Chapter Seven

Rafe had a driver — another person in military attire. The vehicle they used this time felt like a tank to Karma. It had to in order to accommodate Rafe's legs.

"Have you selected a location to live?" Rafe asked. He watched her steadily, and Karma tried to hide her confusion. Weren't they on their way to their new home? Did he mean seven years from now once she'd earned her freedom?

"I'm unsure," she replied, pretending to understand. "I've never lived anywhere but here, so I don't know much about other places."

He nodded once. "I like places on this world where you can experience different seasons. I do not think living where there is always sun, or always snow, would be desirable. But of course, it is your decision as my consort to select our permanent home."

Karma digested that information. They were on their way to a home, but it was evidently a temporary one. Damnit, the things she didn't know would be her undoing. There had to be a booklet or manual that she could get her hands on that gave her facts.

"How long will we live here?" she asked.

"That depends on how long it takes you to choose our new residence." Rafe looked out the window. He wished he had a say in these matters. Where his human chose would determine the type of work he would do here on Earth. He absolutely did not want to spend the next seven years working in an office — even though he would have a crew of employees to command. They would be humans, and he didn't know as much as he wished about the species. Obviously, biologically he knew everything there was to know about them, but their personalities and what drove them was a mystery to him.

He looked at his little human. Maybe she would be willing to help him understand how to work with those of her kind.

But if he knew anything about consorts, he knew they did nothing but what was required of them. And as they already had the contract, they had all they needed.

Rafe noted that Karma watched him curiously before finally turning to look out her own window. Her stares didn't bother him, as they needed to familiarize themselves with each other. But consorts were supposed to act as if they already knew everything there was to know about Galatians. Consorts had been instructed that Galatians hated being stared at, so they never stared. Consorts knew they loved having their scales rubbed, so they always touched.

But Karma stared at him, and she didn't continuously touch him or talk in the way humans called chitchat. Also, she looked much different than other consorts. They had always been told that the selected lottery winners were the most beautiful of the beautiful, and therefore, it wouldn't matter which one they selected. But Karma was brown, with dark eyes and hair, much different than what the humans in charge of the Exchange described as the standard for human beauty. Already, having a human was much different than what he had expected.

Rafe wondered about the things consorts had been taught that the Galatian owners were never meant to know; how to stay in their favor, how to neutralize their hair triggers, how to keep them satisfied.

But there were many things humans could never understand about Galatians. There were many things they were never meant to know. Humans thought themselves very good at manipulation, but they were not better at it than those that had given them the trait.

The driver eventually approached a large building. She stared up at it through the window of the car, craning her neck to see the top of the skyscraper. One thing was for certain; only the richest people in the city lived there.

After entering a set of gates guarded by armed security, the vehicle drove around back where a massive door rolled open, allowing their vehicle access to an internal garage.

When her door opened, Rafe stood with his hand poised to help her step out of the car. The vehicle was taller than she was accustomed to, and although there was a built-in step, it was still a long way from the step to the ground—especially while wearing crystal heels.

She placed her hand in his and remembered the feel of it from the first time he'd taken her hand, back when he escorted her away from the paparazzi. Rafe's palms didn't have scales but smooth ridges that reminded her of the underbelly of a lizard. Each of his fingers was tipped with dark, short talons, and when her hand was enclosed in his, it was like being swallowed by a goliath.

It should have been unsettling, but it wasn't. His light grip, despite his strength, represented protection.

Not necessarily physical protection, although she didn't doubt he'd offer that, but most importantly to her, protection against other humans that treated her unkindly.

Rafe released her hand, and Karma suddenly felt exposed. She drew her cape around her shoulders, not bothering with the hood. They approached a set of doors that presumably led into the building. It was manned by a doorman dressed formally.

"Good evening, sir, madam." If the doorman seemed surprised by her, he didn't show it. More than likely, he'd already heard all the gossip on the news. Karma wondered how long it would be before the authorities of the Exchange showed up to question her. Apparently, it wasn't going to happen tonight.

She'd signed the contract and her face was plastered all over the news, so there was no way they would make her "disappear." There was absolutely nothing that anyone could do about it—besides pissing off the giant that walked beside her. She gave Rafe another discreet look.

Rafe walked ahead to the front desk and gave his name while Karma followed behind, trying to take everything in.

The lobby was richly decorated. It had a towering ceiling, with painted panels like portraits that hung in a museum. The polished marble floors gleamed, but Karma couldn't help but wonder at the amount of work it must have taken the cleaning crew to maintain it.

The human at the counter handed Rafe two cards, and Rafe passed one of them to her. It was a black vinyl card and surprisingly, her new name was written in gold print across the back: Karma Sigur. Her belly flipped and flopped. For the next seven years she was Karma Sigur.

"This will allow you access to all areas of the compound," the man said while staring up at Rafe. "I'll call the concierge to give you a guided tour—"

"Not today," Rafe interrupted. "My human and I are tired."

"Of course. I'll have someone escort you to your apartment—"

"That won't be necessary. Just tell me how to locate it."

The man pointed to the elevator and gave brief directions. Karma had figured out something about Rafe. He was either impatient or simply liked doing things for himself. The latter would be a win for her.

Rafe placed a light hand on her back and gestured to the elevator. "The desk clerk said that your belongings are in our quarters."

"Already? That was fast."

"As it should be," he said while pressing the button to go up. She smiled to herself. It was interesting that the Galatians had better expectations than even the poorest humans of the world.

When the elevator doors opened, Rafe hurriedly stepped inside and she followed noting that it was huge, even bigger than the bedroom of her apartment. "There will be food available for us in our quarters. Is there anything else that you require to meet your human needs?"

When Karma met his eyes, she tried not to stare at the slitted pupils or his translucent lids that were so different from human eyes.

Was he asking if she needed a toilet? She hadn't consumed enough today to need the toilet. The only thing she needed was food and a place to rest without this slinky dress and these high heels. One day's rest before she'd have to begin her duties was more than she could have wished for.

When the elevator opened to their floor, Karma realized that they were in the penthouse. A short entranceway led to one door.

Rafe wasn't quite sure what to expect. Whenever he'd been stationed on Earth, he'd always stayed in a den with his men. He knew about the palaces that he'd eventually live in—both here on Earth and then later on Galatia, once bound to his soul mate. But no one talked much about the transition house that was used until his home was built.

Rafe used the key card to open the door, going inside before Karma. They nearly collided. He gave her a warning look. This was the second time she'd tried to walk ahead of him. She needed to be mindful of safety issues. He went before her in every location they travelled together, to secure the area.

Once Rafe was inside the apartment, Karma scowled at his back. *Rude.*

The lights were already on, and she saw before her an expansive space. Dark slate floors and marble and stone walls made up the interior. One of the stone walls had a water feature that actually had a built-in grotto.

Karma had never seen anything like it. She was blown completely away, especially when she realized there was some type of cavern beyond the waterfall.

Dim, inset lights were embedded in the floor, ceiling, and walls, which illuminated the room, but there were also lights within the rocks of the grotto and the cavern that lay beyond.

"Wow..." she said. It was the most amazing thing she thought she'd ever seen.

"It's perfect," Rafe added. This would be his personal quarters, and he longed to shed his clothing and swim, and then relax along the rocks to relax. He looked up and saw that there was a skylight, and wondered if it could be opened to allow him to experience the elements.

Maybe not. Humans didn't seem to enjoy living among the rain and snow or the other things that might find themselves inside his den.

"That is an actual cave..." Karma said in awe while trying to peer into the dimly lit space beyond the waterfall.

"It's my den," Rafe replied. "Let's go inside."

Karma quickly looked down at how she was dressed. Was she supposed to go for a swim? But then saw Rafe move to the wall where he pressed a square metal pad. A door opened in the wall and Rafe went inside, with Karma following.

It was a cave! The room had to have ceilings that were twenty feet tall; tall enough for stalagmite-type structures to hang from the ceilings. Water streamed and dripped from above, where a skylight revealed the night sky.

She tentatively walked around the area. The floor was made of rock, with living moss and water grass in areas. Smooth stone ledges surrounded a large pool. Karma reached down to test the temperature where water bubbled and steamed like a natural spring.

Rafe grabbed her wrist to stop her. "Not there. That will likely be boiling hot for you." She was alarmed at how quickly he had moved to close the space between them. He moved as fast as a lizard might dart across the ground, only on two legs instead of four!

"Come." He turned to leave the room. "Let us explore your quarters."

Her quarters? So, this was his den...they wouldn't sleep together? Oh, thank the Guardian!

Karma followed him back into the main room, noticing for the first time that there was a large, plush, gray sectional sofa, but also large, decorative stones — some with and some without cushions.

Opposite the waterfall was a huge projection screen where a screensaver showed a moving image of a strange land. She saw smooth mountains with openings like caverns. Flora of varying colors could be seen covering much of the surface. Below the mountainous caverns could be seen a large pool of water, something akin to an ocean.

The atmosphere seemed to glow purple, but she wasn't sure if it had to do with how it had been filmed.

"That's my home," he said while standing next to her.

"I've seen pictures," she replied, "but they never looked real to me. It's so beautiful."

"It is," he agreed.

Karma noticed the music players — three different types! She hurried to them and reverently ran a fingertip along the silver metal.

"I'm sorry it's not very grand," Rafe stated. When she turned to tell him how wonderful everything was, Karma saw that his scales had subtly changed their tint.

She couldn't help but to stare. He'd done that before, back when they had been in the presence of that Shriver woman. She had never heard about anything like this happening. What did it mean?

Rafe was uncomfortable because he was more than pleased with his quarters, but knew that humans preferred their living accommodations more elaborate, with gold and jewels. This room was very simple; but maybe her personal quarters would be better suited for her.

Karma clamped her mouth shut before exclaiming how beautiful it was. Maybe this place was trash compared to how the lottery winners normally lived. She had no intention of putting her foot in her mouth!

Rafe turned and rounded a corner and then reached a short corridor with a single door. After opening it, he walked inside and Karma sighed, wondering why Galatian's didn't know that men opened the doors for women to enter.

Karma's bedroom was fancy, the way the city center had been fancy, with gold and brocade material. A plush, gold carpet covered the floor and the wood and marble-topped furniture sparkled, with not even a speck of dust.

She spotted her trunk in the corner but resisted the urge to run over to check on her music collection. Instead, she spotted a white vanity to one side topped with makeup and perfumes. She'd seen similar pieces of furniture in the homes of the people she had worked for. She always hated this particular piece of furniture. Every single day, they had to be cleaned and then repolished as they became hopelessly stained by makeup or hair care products.

The room was large enough to have a sofa and chairs in front of a fireplace. French doors opened to a glass sunroom. And this was all for her?

Karma's breath was literally caught in her throat. She was going to suffocate and then black out in front of her alien owner. Instead, she looked at the one thing that sobered her.

The four-poster bed.

It was bigger than any bed she'd ever seen. Sheathed in gold, it was so massive that a stool was needed just to climb into it.

It meant that Rafe would also use this bed. She swallowed nervously.

"Is this to your liking, Karma?" he asked, jolting her out of her thoughts. He watched her, curious at her mannerisms. He wasn't sure if she liked her quarters.

She just nodded. "It's very beautiful."

"Let us look at the kitchen. We can have food, and then I will introduce you to Dorf."

Dorf? She wouldn't ask, because he said the name as if she should know about Dorf. Maybe he was the butler, or hopefully, someone that would help her keep this place in order.

They entered the kitchen next and while it was nicer than any kitchen Karma had ever worked in, she was more interested in the buffet of food that was spread out on the counter.

Karma didn't think about changing out of her fancy dress. She didn't think about offering to make Rafe a plate of food. When her belly began to growl in need, she hungrily scanned the array of food. Everything looked delectable, including the strange food that she couldn't identify.

Karma went for what she knew, piling a plate high with ham, fried chicken, corn, salad, and dinner rolls. She stood there in front of the buffet with a mouthful of food before she realized that Rafe was watching her.

Karma froze. She was acting like an animal instead of a cultured lottery winner! She should have served him before she took one bite of food.

She put down her plate. "Rafe?" she asked tentatively. "Is there anything I can get you? What would you like to eat?" She could practically feel his anger radiating from him.

Rafe's scales began to take on a faint, purple tint. Karma ate as if she was starved! Had someone neglected to properly care for his human in his absence? He'd seen prisoners locked up before arriving to the Galatian Guards for transportation to Gong. They ate like her, with eyes that didn't see anything but the food that was being shoveled into their hungry mouths.

"Karma," he growled. "You're starved. Who is responsible for this?"

She heard a tapping sound and saw that the tip of his tail repeatedly hit the floor like a human might tap his fingers in annoyance against a tabletop.

As if in response to his anger, Karma grabbed a plate and began putting food on it hoping to appease him. It was food she didn't know, so figured it was food he would like.

Her brain searched for some type of explanation as to why she had just acted like a glutton.

"What do you mean, who is responsible? I was just so busy that I didn't eat." She handed him his plate. "You should eat, something."

After a pause, he accepted the offering. "Bring your food and sit with me at the table."

Her cheeks grew warm. "Yes." *Like a civilized person,* she imagined him saying.

Chapter Eight

Once seated, Karma ate slowly, although her stomach was far from satisfied. She noticed that Rafe ate with his fingers, scooping up something that resembled beans in a savory red sauce with three fingers. He did it expertly, not spilling one bit of sauce. Afterwards, he sucked his fingers clean and went for more.

Whatever he was eating looked good. She tried not to stare at the way his tongue slid around his digits in an oddly enticing manner. She cleared her throat.

"How is the food?"

"It's acceptable. Not like home, but it's not easy to make our dishes here on Earth."

"Oh?" she asked curiously.

"Well, the fermentation process is difficult without the rich Galatian soil. And even though we share a similar carbonate–silicate geochemical cycle, even a small difference in volcanic activity can make a huge difference. Regardless of what we grow in our soil, it will be different if grown here versus there." He paused to register her understanding.

"I look forward to the meals you will prepare using ingredients shipped directly from Galatia," he continued.

She smiled. First thing on her to-do list was to get a Galatian cookbook.

Rafe's lips turned up slight at the corners — the first that she'd seen his expressionless face move. Was he smiling? It was a bit unsettling.

It wasn't that she focused much on him being a different species. Humans had had years to get used to that. It was just that she wasn't used to simply being around anyone else. Her life was solitary. She only had time to focus on what was necessary to keep herself safe and fed. For the first time since losing her parents, Karma could see a future where she could finally focus on just enjoying being alive.

"How is your meal?" Rafe asked after swallowing what looked like several sauceless meatballs.

"It's very good."

"When you've finished, we will pay a visit to Dorf. He has his own sleeping quarters."

"I'm finished," she said, although her hunger had not quite been satisfied. She was now more curious than hungry — although she intended to eat more — but maybe after Rafe turned in for the evening.

He licked his fingers clean and then got up. Karma liked the way he ate. Some humans from different cultures ate with their fingers and basically, she needed to think of Rafe in that way — as a man from a different culture.

She followed him out of the kitchen and back into the main room. He crouched down by the wall near the entertainment center and rapped on a small panel that was no more than two by three feet.

What was he doing?

She noticed another square button near the panel, but it was much smaller than the one that led to Rafe's den.

After a moment, the panel slid up and a little animal walked out.

At first, she thought it was a large, fluffy, white cat, until she realized it wasn't covered in fur, but in snow-white feathers. Was it a bird or an animal? It was like a mixture of both, with small wings and four legs.

The creature walked using slow, sinewy movements. When it was out of its room, it stretched in the way a feline would and gave Rafe a bored look before yawning.

It had a round, catlike face, and Karma decided right then and there that it was the cutest thing she had ever seen in her life. She had never heard of this type of alien, but there were more non-human creatures in all the universes than humans would ever truly realize — maybe even more than Galatians knew about.

"This is my Japoxillian. Dorf, this is my consort, Karma."

"Oh my goodness," she said in delight while moving to crouch also. "He is so cute!" She reached out to rub his pristine feathers and Dorf bared his teeth and bit her hand.

Karma yelped and jumped back, jerking her hand from the creature's mouth. His teeth were like little daggers, sharper than even a cat's teeth!

Rafe just looked at her curiously before standing.

"Dorf is here for your use as well. Please call on him anytime you find yourself in need of his services."

Karma rubbed the scratches that had been left on her hand. She gave Rafe a shocked look. He hadn't said a thing about that thing biting her! She had no idea what it was supposed to help her do, but it could stay in its little room for all she cared.

"Have you settled in, Dorf?" Rafe asked.

She half expected the creature to speak, but it watched her with an unnerving, accusatory stare before finally moving closer to Rafe's tail. It swatted the tip of it with little, catlike paws before clamping down on it with his sharp teeth, as if in retaliation for Karma not allowing it to bite her.

Karma expected Rafe to howl. Instead, he crossed his arms before him while looking at the small, ferocious beast.

This little shit was going to have to go!

"We'll talk about it later," Rafe said. He wasn't looking at her, but at the Dorf. "Give it time, Dorf!" he snapped, and the creature released his tail and walked away before curling up and licking its feathers with its adorable, little, pink tongue—a total contradiction to its vicious demeanor.

She looked from Dorf to Rafe in complete and total confusion.

"I'm sure it will take time to become accustomed to our ways," Rafe said. "I've been with Dorf for nearly ten years, and he can be a bit—"

Dorf made a barking sound.

Rafe made it seem as if she was the one that needed to adjust to living with a monster that willfully bit others.

Rafe shrugged. "Karma, I need to go to my den for a while and take care of my needs. You should get familiarized with our home and relax. Tomorrow will be a busy day."

"Busy?" Because if it was going to be busier than today, she wasn't sure if she'd make it.

"Of course. Tomorrow is the final ceremony with the brothers and their consorts." Rafe's tail swished and

71

he sighed. "There are so many formalities. I just wish..." He gave her an apologetic look. "I'm sorry, Karma. I know you train for this for many years and these are potentially the most important two days of your life. But for a Galatian, it is a lot of foreign rituals that I am not familiar with."

Karma gave him a relieved look. "Rafe, this might surprise you, but consorts don't always want all of these rituals either. I'd prefer to just get on with our lives together and be done with news reporters and ceremonies." They were legally bound, and the thought of parading herself around for the curiosity of others made her feel sick. It was hard enough trying to navigate her role in Rafe's life without the added burden of trying to impress the humans who were responsible for the laws that had kept her out of the lottery in the first place.

Rafe was already nodding enthusiastically. "That would be completely acceptable to me. This is very foreign to me."

Karma smiled. Rafe was so easy to get along with. "Good. We're in agreement."

His tail swished even faster, as if he too felt relieved. "We don't need a full-on ceremony to consummate our relationship. Until tomorrow, Karma," he said while turning to retire to his den. "Then, you will legally be mine through Galatian law."

Karma's head tilted. "Wait. What? I'm already yours. We signed a contract—"

Rafe opened the panel while laughing. "Human laws don't bind Galatians. That contract was to bind you to me. What binds me to you will be our mating."

She virtually froze. "Are you saying there is still a chance I might not get my rightful rewards?" she stuttered.

"Of course not." He walked back to her. "That has never happened before. No Galatian has ever rejected his consort." He took her hands. "I have no intention of rejecting you. You please me. But after tomorrow, I wouldn't be able to reject you even if I wanted to."

Karma bit her lip. Shit. She was still not in the clear. For all she knew, any second now authorities from the lottery could kick down the door and drag her out of here for fraud!

Rafe released her hands. "Now forgive me, Karma, but I need to swim and unwind." He turned back to his den.

No. She needed to complete this now.

"Rafe? May I swim with you?"

Rafe looked at Karma with surprise. He'd never heard of a human that wanted to get into Galatian waters—they preferred their own pools filled with chlorine to keep it free of the bacteria that his body craved.

"You'll keep to the center of the pool where it won't be too hot or too cold?"

"Yes," she nodded.

Rafe found that he liked the idea. He liked this human that was so different than anything he expected.

"I would enjoy your company." He took her hand and led her into his new quarters. Once inside, Rafe went to the wall where there was a large silver button.

Once he pressed it, another hidden panel opened to reveal a walk-in closet containing articles of clothing hanging carefully from a metal rod. There were also shelves containing other items that he would need for this world.

Rafe sighed and stripped out of his clothing. Leaning on his tail, he removed his boots and placed them next to his other footwear. When he turned, it was to see Karma gaping at him with her big, brown eyes.

She was still completely dressed and wearing those ridiculous glass shoes. He hoped she didn't intend to swim in those articles. He was quite curious to see her nude body.

The lottery winners had studied Galatian form in great detail—or so he had been told. She, however, acted as if she'd never seen a nude Galatian.

His kind had taken great strides to keep certain types of photos out of human circulation. Although nudity was completely acceptable by Galatians, humans used such photos in extremely inappropriate ways.

And while he had seen a multitude of nude humans, he had never been in a room with a nude human female, as they were described as being too modest for such things. Rafe typically respected the values of other cultures—usually. In this case, it was she that had asked to swim with him.

Rafe turned and climbed into the pool, giving her time to adjust. It was only normal for Karma to experience a bit of trepidation—which is why it surprised him that she had chosen to forgo tomorrow's ceremony, where she would be given the elixir that would allow her to go into a twilight state—making the loss of her virginity much less stressful.

He'd hoped she wouldn't want it. Galatian females did not need to be drugged in order to mate. It would please him a great deal if she chose to be conscious during their first mating. After all, she had been surgically prepared to physically accept him. He'd been told there would still be some pain, but his human would adapt.

He was intrigued. He had been told that sex with a human was exquisite. But that was the last thing he wanted to focus on this evening. She would have her one day of freedom.

After tomorrow, he would claim her in all the ways that he desired, just as had been promised to the Galatian males stationed on Earth since the inception of the Exchange.

This is not going to work. This is not going to work. This is not...

Karma heard people make crude jokes about someone being *hung like a horse*. But as a city girl, she could not have imagined what that could have meant.

Rafe strolled out of his closet completely naked. Any woman would have found the sight of his toned muscles exciting, regardless of whether his body was covered in sleek scales and not skin. But she could only focus on the appendage that hit mid-thigh—and his mid-thigh was much bigger than the average human's mid-thigh.

His penis wasn't even impossibly thick. But at about fifteen inches, flaccid, it was ridiculously long—and would only get bigger.

Her mind began to retrace the steps that it would take for her to leave the building. She'd have to be cool about it, of course, so she wouldn't raise suspicion.

"The water should be acceptable here in the center with me," Rafe said. He was leaned back against smooth stones, with his hands spread and his head partially reclined back.

He appeared completely at peace, while her heart was beating a mile a minute.

How am I going to get away from this?

Wait...

Karma calmed her beating heart. Human women had been having sex with Galatians for generations. If they were killed in the process, then the rich wouldn't be offering up their female offspring. In fact, she had seen stories about retired winners and they always looked happy—mostly because they were filmed in their huge estates.

Karma studied Rafe, knowing that she had not manufactured his kindness. She felt deep down that he would never intentionally harm her. Maybe they didn't fuck the way humans fucked. They must have some special way of doing it so it wouldn't completely destroy her nether regions. That was the only way any of this was possible...

Karma thought about the meth user she'd seen earlier in the week—the one that had made the choice of losing herself in drugs rather than face the harsh reality of what she needed to do. She had to complete the contract. She had to consummate this relationship.

Karma slipped the straps of her dress from her shoulders, allowing the thin, satiny fabric to pool at her feet. She stepped out of her shoes, not even recognizing the relief to her feet and calves once out of the heels. Finally, she slid her G-string down her thighs and stepped out of it until she was left completely and totally nude.

She saw Rafe's eyes slowly scan her body until they finally moved back to her face and rested there for an uncomfortably long time.

Chapter Nine

Karma's brown skin mesmerized Rafe. The white fabric of her gown had been a magnificent contrast but now, without any clothing, he was able to appreciate the many hues that actually made her brown.

Humans were quite unique, having skin tones that ranged from nearly the palest white to almost the darkest black. Karma's skin was that of burnished wood polished to maximum sheen.

His eyes moved to linger at her small breasts. The nipples were exposed, like many of Earth's mammals, and not protected by scales. He found the nipples curious. Maybe they elongated with pregnancy, as with Galatian mothers.

The skin around her nipples was darker than the rest of her skin, causing him to want to explore the texture of the puckered flesh.

His eyes next moved downward, stopping at the sparse, dark hair between her thighs.

From the moment he'd set eyes on her, the short, brown curls on top of her head had taken much of his attention. He could not imagine what it would be like to have hair, but wished to rub the strands between his fingers so he could understand why it didn't cause her to scratch her head until every curl lay on the ground.

The hair at the V of her thighs was barely visible, and he wished it was wild and curled the way the hair on her head was. By comparison, she was otherwise hairless—with none on her legs or arms, although she did have very slight eyebrows.

He finally stared at her big, dark eyes. Why were her eyes so big? And why did it touch him in such a protective way? He sensed her nervousness, and he wanted to assure her that he would never allow any harm to come to her. She was his, at least for the next seven years.

"Karma. The water should be acceptable here with me." He waited patiently for her to walk to the pool. She moved with slow, graceful movements, which he tracked and put to memory. If she wore a mask and a full bodysuit, from this moment on, he would be able to recognize her just by the way she moved.

Once she was near the roughened stone, Rafe stood and offered his hand to help her. She took it while she stepped over the ledge and onto the stoop bordering the inside of the pool. He didn't release her hand until she was safely seated on the ledge at the pool's center. He was big enough that he didn't need it and could float comfortably along the pool's surface.

"How is the temperature?"

"It's nice," she replied.

He dunked his head and swam a short distance beneath the water. His tail stayed above the water, taking in her comfort level. Now that much of her nudity was concealed by the green-tinged water, she appeared to relax. After about a minute or two of underwater swimming, Rafe stood, allowing the water to stream down his scales, invigorating him.

"Do you swim?" he asked. He saw her staring at his prick, and he suppressed a chuckle when her eyes quickly shot up to his face.

"I've never swam. Never had time." She gestured to the side where the hot spring was located. "That heat doesn't hurt you?"

"No. Not unless I'm in ecdysis — or what you call shedding or molting." She appeared to digest that before inhaling a long breath.

"Rafe? Can I touch your ski — scales?"

Instead of answering, he swam to her where he patiently floated.

She reached out and tentatively ran her fingers down his chest.

His breath caught in his throat at the unexpected way her touch caused him pleasure. Galatians needed to have their scales rubbed, but could make do unless it was right before they lost them. It was one of the few times that they came in contact with the females of their kind, who helped to relieve the incessant need.

But Karma's light touch was almost a tease. He closed his eyes and held his breath as she continued to explore him with a touch that was slowly becoming maddening.

"When do you go into ec-ecdysis?"

"It differs, depending on what is happening," he replied with eyes still closed in enjoyment. "It can be as few as once a year, or as many as four."

"What triggers it?"

He sighed in pleasure. "Didn't you learn this in consort school? You probably know more about me than I'll ever know about you."

"Then maybe it's you who should be touching me."

He opened his eyes and saw her slight smile. His heart leaped and his prick flinched. Her voice had taken a seductive turn.

He reached up to take a few strands of her curls between his fingers, satisfying his curiosity. He knew he could have touched her anywhere, but it was her hair that he longed to explore. It was both thick and soft. There were actually jewels embedded in it that shimmered in the dim light. He liked it a great deal.

His hand eventually traced down to her face, and Karma closed her eyes and leaned in to his touch. Her skin was so soft and so delicate. How did humans go about life without injuring themselves at every turn? With every bump?

His fingers then lightly skimmed down her torso, mimicking the way she had touched him. He heard her soft sigh and the blood began to surge to his prick.

This is not the time, he chastised himself. *She has one more day before I claim her completely.*

He saw that her nipples had hardened and grown thicker right before his eyes. Not able to resist, he circled the bead of flesh with the tip of a sharp nail, careful not to scratch.

Karma's eyes popped open and he stopped but she spoke, her voice urging him on.

"If you touch me there, it makes me feel really good."

He was surprised by how gruff her voice had grown. His mouth parted and it took two beats of his heart before he found his words. "If you touch me anywhere, it will make *me* feel good." His words didn't sound familiar to his own ears, but it had been a very long time since another's touch had caused his nature to rise.

In response, Karma's hands suddenly moved up to his face, where she cupped his cheek in her hands. She stared up at him and Rafe couldn't move. She had him captured by her stare.

"Karma." He placed his hands over hers and gently removed them. "We should rest—" If she didn't stop soon…

"No. We shouldn't rest." He felt the fingers of her hands wrap firmly around his prick.

For Karma, it was a very powerful feeling to know that a man desired her. In that moment, it didn't matter if that man was human or alien. She hadn't felt desired in a very long time—if ever.

Her two previous lovers had been brief flings—the first in order to know what sex was like, the second because she hoped to feel something more than the drudgery of her existence.

In both cases, she hadn't felt much of anything beyond disappointment.

She didn't, however, have human expectations of Rafe. And yet he treated her with more humanity than any human other than her parents ever had.

She could close her eyes and pretend—pretend that he was a man with skin and hair—but she really didn't need to do that. When he touched her, her body reacted. She wouldn't lie to herself by pretending it was because of how long it had been since someone had desired her. Her body reacted because she liked the way he made her feel.

When her hand reached for his hardening prick, she actually liked the way he rapidly grew due to her touch.

It was the first time in her life that she felt empowered.

"Rafe. I don't want to wait until tomorrow. I want to consummate our relationship tonight. Now."

Karma was becoming accustomed to Rafe's being reflected in the subtle color change of his scales. They now had a soft, blue undertone. This wasn't anger, or annoyance. This was the color of Rafe's desire.

The next second, Karma was being lifted until she was facing Rafe eye to eye.

"Karma. Are you sure about this? Because it is your right to have this last day as your own person before we are truly united—"

"Rafe. Do I have to ask you again?"

"No," he growled. He pulled her close and she reflexively wrapped her arms and legs around him, clinging to his tall, lean frame. Rafe moved quickly, surprising her with his graceful speed while she clung to him. But one of his hands held her securely to him, and not for one second did she fear that he would drop her.

Rafe leaped from the pool and with two long steps was out of his den. He moved swiftly through the front room and was in her quarters within seconds. She was gently placed on her bed before she knew it.

Karma wouldn't look at how big his erection had grown. She focused on his face while her heart drummed madly in her chest.

"You tremble," he said while gazing at her as she lay before him. He crouched over her until his face was inches from hers. She saw him inhale as if he was trying to breathe her in.

"I-I'm afraid," she admitted. "Just...make me feel good first, okay?"

He smiled and then nodded. "Of course."

Rafe lowered his body and eyed her thickened nipples. He would no longer deny himself. He wanted to taste her more than he had wanted anything in a very long time.

His tongue circled the darkened flesh around her nipple and her body arched. Yes. She liked when he touched her there with his tongue. He knew other places that human women liked to be touched with a tongue. But first he wanted to explore these two beautiful peaks.

Rafe gently drew one of her nipples into his mouth. Her tender flesh felt odd in his mouth. His teeth could destroy her if he wasn't careful. He used his tongue to flick her tip while his mouth held her breast within his grasp. He stroked her other breast lightly, enjoying how it hardened against his fingertips.

A soft moan spilled from her lips and Rafe's prick grew harder. Reluctantly, he released his mouth from her breast and moved lower, his tongue tracing a path down her body. He circled her belly button curiously and felt her body tense and relax. Another place she enjoyed being tasted.

Rafe hooked his arms beneath her knees and gently spread her legs. He stared at the delicate folds and the way her dark curls glistened with signs of her arousal. Her scent had become imprinted in his memory. If she ever became aroused while in his presence, he would now know, able to differentiate between her and any other consort...any other human...any other creature in the universe.

His tongue flicked the tiny sensory bud at her core and her legs began to tremble uncontrollably. He held her in place so his teeth wouldn't hurt her. And then he burrowed his face into her V, lapping at the juices that now coated his tongue and face.

The sounds that came from her had intensified as her body trembled and her hips gyrated against his touch. When her opening began to pulsate rapidly, Rafe came up on his knees and turned her onto her belly.

Karma was surprised at how quickly she responded to Rafe's touch, but his tongue had more dexterity than the average human tongue—not that any man had ever troubled themselves to do this for her.

Maybe if they had, then the act of sex would have caused her to actually *feel*.

She was ready for him to work more of his alien magic, but then he turned her over onto her belly. Not sure what he planned, Karma looked over her shoulder as he lifted her rear, lining it up with his groin.

"W-what are you doing?"

"Is this not the position that you require?" He watched her with intensity.

"Uh..."

"What would you like?" His voice was a low groan of need.

She paused. "Whatever you do so it won't hurt me."

"This is the only way that allows me complete access." He placed the tip of himself at her opening, but then paused. "Do you want me to stop, Karma? This is your night— "

Stop? No! There was no going back now!

"I'm ready, Rafe." And then she was met with the exquisite pleasure of him entering her, taking away the last of her fear as he slid gently into her.

He was bigger than her other lovers but it wasn't uncomfortable—at first. At first, Karma enjoyed the way he methodically and yet gently pushed forward.

But soon, it was too much.

She fisted her sheets and squeezed her eyes closed. Was he going to stop? Karma knew of one sure-fire way to make a man stop, and that was to make him orgasm.

Taking control, Karma straightened and turned. Planting her hand on his torso, she firmly pushed him back. Repositioning herself so that she was lying on her back, Karma wrapped her legs around his body. Rafe hissed slightly while following her lead as she took him in hand and guided him to where she wanted him. He was much too big for more than three or four inches of him inside of her, but she gripped his shaft, working it in her fist, squeezing him hard when he tried to enter her too far or too fast.

Karma rolled her hips, her muscles working the most sensitive portion of his prick. Her fist pumped him and, in the end, just like any male would, he cried out loudly in pleasure moments before he filled her depths with his seed.

She had never felt so much semen at once. It was an impossible amount. Something like that would have normally made her worry about pregnancy—but everyone knew it wasn't possible to cross-breed with the Galatians. They could barely procreate with their own, hence the reason they'd crossed galaxies creating life-forms in their image.

86

Karma's mind was relieved. It had gone her way, with Rafe lying beside her on the bed, breathing heavily. But it wasn't without a toll. Karma's body ached, and felt battered in places one would never want to be bruised. He'd gone so deep that he literally could not have gone further.

And had she not finally taken control, Karma wondered if he would have tried to create an opening for himself.

She wanted to pop a painkiller, get into a hot bath and squeeze her eyes closed until the aches in her body receded. But Rafe watched her, his eyes never moving from her face, as if he was taking stock.

She knew how to put a stop to that.

Karma moved close to him, her body molding to his hard, yet yielding form. She buried her face into the space beneath his chin and felt his hand come around her to hold her close.

A moment later, she felt his head lower to her hair. He inhaled deeply, again breathing her in.

She ached. She was afraid. She didn't know what was in store for her as an alien's consort. She was so accustomed to always being alone in her pain that it felt strange to find comfort with another person.

He's not a person...

But an alien could be a better person than a human.

Chapter Ten

Was it possible that the surgery did not take? Rafe had returned to his den to relax in his pool while Karma met to her needs in her own bath.

She seemed more resilient than other females of her species. Thankfully so. Had she not rejected the ceremony, she would have slept through their first mating and he very well could have mortally wounded her. He just didn't understand how this could have happened. The additional opening within her body was supposed to be there for him.

What if he had just pushed forward, not knowing that her delicate flesh was not going to yield for him? Rafe closed his eyes. It was unthinkable. He would have been the first Galatian to kill his consort. Of course, that wasn't what most bothered him. He could plainly see that his human was unique. The loss of someone like her would torture him—especially with the knowledge that he was the cause.

He had not liked seeing the pain on her face. She had clung to him afterward—

He was going to find out who was responsible for this and strip them of their position, if he didn't first strip them of their skin!

Dorf strolled into the room and then carefully leaped onto the edge of the pool. The little Japo watched him, but Rafe was not in the mood for Dorf.

"Keep an eye on Karma. You know how easily humans are stricken with a coma." He'd seen it happen with just a slight knock on the head.

Dorf stood and then lifted his leg and pissed in the pool before neatly leaping from the ledge and strolling out of the room. Rafe closed his eyes and rubbed his brow with his webbed fingers.

Karma didn't find painkillers, but the hot bath helped some. The tub was nearly as big as a pool, with a waterfall feature she used as if it was a shower in order to wash the faux jewels from her hair.

It had already been filled, and she found temperature controls and various aromatherapy settings.

She had cleaned a number of rich people's houses, but had never seen anything as luxurious as this apartment. Why should they ever move? She couldn't imagine anything better.

Karma closed her tired eyes and sank down into the soothing water until it reached her chin.

It was over. The battle had been won. Oh, but she was sore...and yet it hadn't been completely unpleasant. Rafe had been surprisingly gentle, despite his strength and size.

An alien...

She'd whored herself to a non-human.

Karma stamped down a wave of revulsion. But she recognized the feeling of disgust because she'd felt it when she'd walked down the streets to the leers and catcalls of men who barely saw her concealed face but felt it was their right to objectify her because of her female body.

She had known revulsion when cleaning the homes of grown-ass people who pissed or vomited openly just because they knew someone else would clean it.

She'd watched guards beat and stomp sleeping homeless men, women, and children out of sheer boredom.

She'd slept on cold cement floors with nothing but the clothes on her back and threadbare blankets to cover her while praying that the guards would keep walking past her.

And she'd met a Galatian that treated her with kindness. It wasn't disgust and revulsion that she should be feeling for him.

It was gratitude.

Karma vowed at that moment that no matter what was to come, she would never think that her human was better than Rafe Sigur's alien.

Karma finished washing and then stepped from her tub. She dried herself with a thick, fluffy towel that dragged the marble floor, and thought of the two women that had prepared her for this day as she rubbed lotion and oils onto her skin, paying particular attention to her feet. They had complained that her feet were atrocious. They probably hadn't ever had to wear boots from a thrift store without socks. Now her feet were as smooth as whipped butter.

She oiled and brushed her hair and then padded naked into her bedroom to retrieve her sleep bonnet from her trunk.

Dorf was sitting by the door and Karma jumped. How in the hell did it get into her room? The door was closed.

She walked warily to the trunk, keeping an eye on it in case it tried to attack her. Dorf didn't, only following her with a steady, steely-eyed gaze.

She quickly slipped on one of her new gowns. She'd unpack tomorrow, when hopefully, she'd feel better.

She pulled the soiled comforter from the bed and left it on the floor. She'd tackle that tomorrow as well. She knew how to soak out these types of stains from a variety of expensive fabrics. Luckily it was a thick comforter, because there had been a great deal of fluid left behind.

Karma climbed between her satin sheets but before dozing off, she got up and retrieved her portable music player and slipped on her earbuds. Karma fell asleep to the sounds from the 1977 soundtrack from *Saturday Night Fever*, by various artists including super group the Bee Gees.

When Karma awoke the next morning, she found that the earbuds were no longer in her ears and that Dorf was curled at the foot of her bed, snoring softly.

She sat up and then groaned in pain, moving more gingerly as a deep-seated ache flared to life, reminding her of last night's events.

Dorf opened his eyes and then stretched his front paws.

She blinked. He was wearing her earbuds! What kind of animal was this?

"How did you like the music?" she asked tersely, not expecting an answer, but fully prepared to receive one.

Instead of answering, he walked to her and made to bite her hand. Karma jerked away and quickly got out of bed, ignoring the aches and pains in her body. Why was he so bitey?

"No!" she said while shaking her finger at him. "Bad! No biting!"

Dorf snatched the earbuds from his ears, jumped out of bed and ran to the door. Standing on hind legs, he easily reached up to turn the doorknob and left the room with two angry barks.

"Jeez..." she said while rubbing her hands. He was pissed.

Well, if he didn't like being yelled at, he shouldn't go around biting people!

Karma checked the time. It wasn't even 5:00 a.m. She was still on her previous maid's schedule. But there was a lot of work to do.

Karma didn't have anything but "nice" clothing to do her daily cleaning in. But she figured that her owner would not want to see her dressed like the help. So, after going to the bathroom, she dressed in a blue pantsuit with matching blue jacket.

Her small Afro had dried into tiny, tight curls and after moisturizing them, she finger-picked them into shape.

Next, she grabbed the comforter, wondering where the laundry might be. She headed for the kitchen, knowing there would be a ton of food that would need to be disposed of.

Too bad she hadn't thought about how to get it to the hungry at the train depot. It was a sin to throw away so much food. But, in truth, she didn't even know where she was. Somewhere in Newburgh; but she'd never heard of anyone working in an apartment building like this.

But when Karma stepped into the kitchen, she saw that there was a cleaning crew present, busily cleaning and cooking.

Everyone stopped in surprise when they saw her. There were two women and one male dressed in black-and-white maid's uniforms.

"Apologies, ma'am! Would you like us to leave until later?"

"No. I just didn't...no. Please finish what you were doing."

The male approached and gently took the comforter from her hands. "We will take care of that, ma'am."

Karma turned to leave and then stopped. "Uh...is there some type of manual or guide?"

"Ma'am?" One of the maids gave her a confused look.

"Never mind," she said, and quickly left them to their work.

Well, what the hell am I here for?

She thought back to last night. *Just sex?*

Rafe had fallen asleep worried about Karma and had awakened the same way. Dorf hadn't reported anything at odds with her but he wouldn't be relieved until he saw her for himself.

He left his pool and dressed in his everyday attire; a long skirt made of material that mimicked leather pleats and a double-buckled harness for his sheathed sword and transmitter.

He slipped on boots and left his den, deciding he would get a start on tomorrow's work assignment while his human rested.

But he was surprised to see her curled on the sofa with a portable music player on her lap and what looked like CDs on the table in front of her.

She came to her feet when she saw him and then slipped on shoes with more of those ridiculous heels.

Rafe glanced at the window and saw that the sun had yet to rise.

"Rafe." She gave him a tentative smile. "You're awake. Good morning."

"Yes. I hope that it will be a good morning. And to you, as well. How do you feel?"

"Oh. I'm...fine. A little sore," she added softly.

"If you need more of your cream, I will arrange for it to be delivered."

"More of my cream?" she asked.

"I'm sorry, I don't know what you call it. The cream that you use to relieve your pains. We've used it in battle, but it's not really engineered for our needs, it is suited to you."

The humans' medicines and creams were comparatively mild, but could be useful for minor scratches and scrapes. But in the event of a real injury, Galatians used their own salves that were so strong they would be damaging to humans.

"I would like if more salve could be ordered," she said.

Rafe nodded once. He reached down and picked up a CD.

"These are old," he commented. "We have much music, if music is what you like."

"I love music," she replied. "It was the only thing..."

Rafe waited, but she didn't continue. "You can listen using the speakers," he said.

"I didn't want to wake you." She gestured to the waterfall. "Even though that waterfall is pretty loud, this room opens right into your den."

He didn't mention the speaker controls. Humans hated even the slightest suggestion that they didn't know something.

"I don't mind music, and neither does Dorf." Especially Dorf had a love for music. But he'd tell her more about that once she warmed up to him. It wasn't easy for humans to be around Japoxillians. "Have you eaten, Karma?"

"No. I wanted to wait for you."

He nodded and led them to the kitchen. He selected the food that he wanted, wishing the servers did a better job of preparing Galatian food. The grimlock was hot and the tzochin was cold.

But soon, his consort would take over preparing all of his meals and caring for their home. Consorts spent years learning how to prepare Galatian meals and tomorrow she would prepare one of their biggest ceremonial dinners. It was said that a good human cook even rivaled the best of the Galatians' in meal preparation, and that this was the most important thing about gaining a consort.

But last night's events surely put doubt to that. Karma had done unexpected things to bring him pleasure.

He watched her enjoy her meal. She didn't eat nearly as quickly as she had last night, but he could tell she was enthusiastic.

Good. He would prefer her bigger, heartier. Although, from this moment on, her weaknesses or strengths would no longer affect her ability to survive. She would live the remainder of her life in wealth and security.

"I'm sure you will want to visit your sisters today before their ceremonies."

Her brown eyes rose and locked with his. "Won't they be busy?"

"I thought you liked being together to...prepare yourselves."

Karma sipped hot tea. "I'm already prepared." She smiled softly, and Rafe felt a jolt to his prick.

"Yes. I suppose you should spend the day resting. I have to leave to prepare for my new position. Dorf will be here if you should need anything. And I will return in time for my brothers' ceremony."

"Yes, Rafe," Karma replied.

After Rafe left, Karma grabbed her key card and left the apartment. She needed to know where she was, exactly. And she needed to find some type of instructional book on how to be a Galatian consort.

The first would be easy. The second would require her contacting her 'sisters'.

Karma went down to the lobby, where the concierge waited behind the front desk.

"Mrs. Sigur. How may I be of assistance?"

That name gave her a jolt. She was Mrs. Sigur. Karma Sigur. It felt weird to say that in her head—even stranger to realize the potential of that title.

She looked at the man's bronze name tag. "Geoff, I need the exact address of this building."

"Absolutely." He handed her a card with neatly printed writing. The Washington at Newburgh Circle. Beneath that was the address and a fax and phone number.

Karma tapped a polished nail on the desktop.

"I need for you to arrange for all of my leftovers to be neatly boxed and left on a table in back of this building."

"Ma'am?" The concierge tilted his head.

"I'm going to have a few…acquaintances come by to pick them up."

Geoff's face began to turn red. "I'm very sorry, Mrs. Sigur, but no one is allowed on the premises except those authorized by the Galatian Interplanetary Collective." He discreetly gestured to a large picture window.

Karma saw that scores of news reporters were camped outside the gates of the building.

"What the…?"

"It's all on the news if you want to…" He picked up a controller and a big screen materialized before them. A moment later it came to life and showed a newscaster with the backdrop of a photo of her at yesterday's event.

Karma's mouth fell open.

She was so regal that she didn't even recognize herself!

She listened to what the newscaster was saying. "At this time, representatives of the lottery have not responded to questions. It is thought that the first non-Caucasian consort is of Arabian descent, and might possibly be the daughter of one of the billionaire princes of the former United Arab Emirates.

"The woman is rumored to have skin that is darkened further by the sun. But no one knows how her inclusion in the lottery had gone unnoticed until yesterday's Galatian Exchange.

"She is mated to Lieutenant Rafe Sigur, a highly decorated warrior within the Galatian Guard." An image of Rafe leading her out of the crowded banquet hall was then shown. He was a giant compared to her, yet she saw how he protectively kept the crowd from swarming them.

"Lieutenant Sigur recently led his crew of warriors to the largest intergalactic human traffic ring known to the Collective. Because of their endeavors, hundreds of humans will be returning to Earth in the coming weeks—free of the tyranny of the Malnamanian and other space pirates who still engage in the illegal trafficking of humans."

Karma turned away and headed for the elevator, gesturing for the concierge to turn off the broadcast.

"Mrs. Sigur? What about the leftovers?"

"Just...pack them up and give it to them." She gestured to the people gathered around the building.

The lottery officials had to know that she was no Arabian princess that had been accepted into their precious lottery. So, when was the other boot going to drop?

Karma stopped suddenly and turned back to the concierge.

"Geoff. How can I get in touch with my...sister-consorts?"

The man hurried from behind the desk. "You can simply call them from your home's telephone. Just press zero for the concierge desk and ask for them by name."

"I don't know their names…"

"I can give you that information," he said without even the slightest blink of his eyes although he had to know that she should know the names of the sisters that she'd gone to consort school with for most of her life.

He hurried back to his desk and retrieved a folder. He slipped a sheet of paper from it and quickly offered it to her.

She skimmed it. It had the names and pictures of each consort and their Galatian owner — with the exception of her. Opposite Rafe's photo was one of a lovely, blond-haired, blue-eyed woman. The name Mayva had been stricken out and Karma was written beneath it.

"Thank you." She eyed each of her sisters while getting back into the elevator.

Chapter Eleven

Back in her apartment, Karma searched for the telephone, finding one in a wall niche in the front room.

She dialed zero for the concierge desk.

"How may I help you, Mrs. Sigur?"

"Let me speak to..." She looked at the photo of the woman that had told the other consorts that Mayva had gotten away with it and they were going to give her a chance.

This woman might not necessarily be on her side, but she seemed to know that Mayva had planned to escape the Exchange, and she wasn't interested in ratting her out. Her name was Madeline.

"Madeline, please. Madeline...Eng—"

"Engström."

"Yes."

"One moment." After a pause, the phone began to ring.

"Engström residence." The voice was smooth, self-assured, and cultured.

"Uh...Madeline?"

"Yes. Who is this?"

"I'm...Rafe's consort."

There was a pause. "Hold on a second." After a minute, Madeline returned and hissed into the phone, "What in the hell is going on!"

"We should probably speak in person."

"Yes. Drago is busy preparing for this evening's ceremony. I'll call the other girls. I assume Rafe is out?"

"He won't return until this evening."

"Good. We'll be there directly." The phone disconnected.

Karma heard sounds in the kitchen and when she went to investigate, saw two maids collecting the leftovers from breakfast and placing them in neat boxes.

How had they gotten into the apartment? When they saw her, they bowed politely in her direction and then a hidden door opened and a third man exited a small elevator at the rear of the large kitchen. He seemed surprised to see her and practically gawked. She quickly left them to their duties.

She returned to the front room. Where was Dorf? She didn't quite trust him. He was probably in his little hidey-hole, and good riddance.

After twenty minutes of pacing, she heard her doorbell ring and hurried to answer it.

Six women crowded through the door. Their attention was split between looking her up and down and gawking at the large room.

"This place is much bigger than my apartment," someone said in awe.

"Check out that waterfall!" another said.

"Thank you for coming." Karma finally spoke.

"Who are you?" a woman asked in a snooty voice. In her defense, this was basically the only voice that Karma was accustomed to having directed at her from the rich people of the world.

Like the other consorts, she wore a face full of makeup and her long hair ran in waves down to the small of her back. They were all dressed in silken robes that were so long, they brushed the floor. The only difference was the variety in the intricate designs.

"You know who I'm not. So, let's start there," Karma said.

"You have a lot of nerve!" another woman hissed. "You illegally infiltrated the lottery—"

"Shut up." Madeline glared at the women. "We're not here to bicker."

Karma glanced in the direction of the kitchen. "Let's go to my room. There are others here." She led them to her room and then firmly shut the door.

"This room is so...big." One of the girls swirled around, taking everything in.

"Of course it is! She got Rafe Sigur. She got the penthouse."

"She's not going to get away with it." The first snooty woman spoke. She walked up to Karma until she was standing less than a foot from her. She gave her a distasteful look. "After you die, it will leave Rafe free. I'm going to petition for your position."

"Don't be stupid, Jayne!" Madeline said. "We'll be going through the ceremony at the same time. You'll already be mated and it will be too late."

Jayne smirked. "Oh, it will work. I won't mate with him until I'm good and ready."

"Why should *you* get him?" the woman who had admired the room asked. She folded her arms in defiance. "I want him too. And I'm just as good as you."

"Let's be frank." Another woman spoke as she plopped down on Karma's neatly made bed. "Neither of you ever had a chance with Rafe. He was always going to be Mayva's. If she hadn't figured out a way to escape the Exchange, she would have snagged him as first choice, and with her gone, only I would have had second choice."

Karma's eyes moved to the 'second choice'. "What do you mean by first and second choice?"

"*They* don't choose us. We choose them, and Mayva already chose him weeks ago. It's our status that determines who gets to choose first." The woman's eyes lingered on Karma. "Perhaps your status would have outranked us all—if you truly are the daughter of an Arabian prince."

They were speaking of wealth and power.

"Well, something or someone arranged for you and Rafe Sigur to be the last two arrivals." It was Madeline who spoke. "It secured his availability, since it was assumed that the real Mayva would eventually arrive."

"Well, Mayva is gone, and this one is as good as dead!" Jayne spat angrily with fisted hands on her hips. "And I *will* step in to claim the preferred position as consort to Lieutenant Rafe Sigur. And if any of you stand in my way, I'll make these next seven years the worst seven years of your pitiful lives!"

A few of the other women rolled their eyes while others remained quiet, either because they were too shy or too afraid to speak up.

"And what makes you think I'm going to die?" Karma replied, as if unconcerned. But she was thinking of the human military soldiers the lottery officials might send after her. "The Galatians won't allow anyone to even get near their consorts—"

"But you're not truly his consort until after the first mating," Jayne interrupted smugly. "And you probably got your surgery in some third world province so it probably won't even take. Then you'll die by prick before you die by military sword."

"Surgery?"

Madeline pulled Jayne back a few steps while Jayne snatched her arm away. Madeline gave Karma an apologetic look. "I don't know who did your surgery, but you need at least six months to heal before you can *do it*. Did your handlers tell you that? Because I would be more worried about that than being caught."

Karma gave her a confused look and someone giggled.

"It didn't take dear, if you can't remember it."

"Shut up," Madeline said. "She could have had the surgery when she was younger than us."

"I hurt for three weeks," someone said. "It's nothing I'd ever forget, regardless."

Jayne looked at Karma. "Surely you knew about their pricks? How did you think it was supposed to fit inside of you?"

"The same way a baby comes out," Karma said in dawning realization.

"You're stupid," Jayne said conversationally. Someone giggled and covered her mouth while her cheeks turned pink. Jayne continued. "It doesn't work in the reverse. A prick cannot enter a cervix the way a baby squeezes out of one. It's too tight, and it's not even in the right position."

Guardian have mercy…

These girls had been surgically modified to allow their cervixes to be used for sexual entry.

"They really didn't tell you what they were doing to you?" Madeline asked with sympathy.

Karma simply shook her head. It had not even occurred to these girls that she might not have had this sexual accommodation surgery. And yet Heinrich had not even considered her safety and well-being concerning this secret surgery, because all that mattered to him was escaping with his mistress!

Second Choice spoke lazily from where she was now stretched out on Karma's bed. "What the surgeons did to you and to the rest of us was reposition and then permanently open our cervix so that our mates could find a way to fit themselves into us. And that pesky old uterus that would have caused us the inconvenience of menstruation. Gone."

She looked at the blank faces of each woman, attempting to hide her horror. The Galatians claimed to value life, but they condoned the barbaric practice of surgically sterilizing their consorts just so that they could have intercourse!

"It's the price of winning. Unimaginable riches in exchange for seven years of servitude to a Galatian and yes...the loss of ever bearing children," Madeline confirmed.

"What exactly happens during this mating ceremony?" Karma asked.

"We will share a ceremonial drink, and then our master's queen will prepare them while we prepare each other. Once we're in a twilight state, our masters will fulfill our destinies as their consorts. From that point onward, he will never allow another female to touch him...down *there*...until we have completed our term and return him to his queen."

"Queen? The Galatian females?" Karma asked.

"Yes," someone replied. "They call their females queens."

"How do the queens prepare the masters?"

The consorts looked at each other with smirks and red cheeks. "With their tongues," Jayne snapped in annoyance. "A queen will help them spill their seed so they're not too aroused and kill us during the first mating. It's when we know for sure that our master will fit...you know, inside."

She had never heard even a hint of this information before, beyond the fact that Galatian females rarely came to Earth because their men were highly protective of them.

Two of the women giggled. They were women in their twenties, but they acted like schoolgirls. No fault of their own, Karma relented. They were ignorant, despite their schooling. She didn't know who they were by name, and didn't think she would ever care to learn. Besides, they looked too much alike to care. Talking to one was just like talking to the others—maybe with the exception of Madeline—and of course, Jayne.

"How do the consorts prepare themselves?" she asked.

"We put on our robes," the woman on the bed responded while lifting her arms in a dreamlike manner. "They're so beautiful, don't you think? Then we use a cream that makes us numb. That way, it won't hurt."

Karma gave the woman a doubtful look. "Does this cream of yours allow you to feel pleasure?"

"I'd rather experience a lack of pain than a miniscule amount of pleasure," someone else replied.

"Not me," Second Choice said.

"Let me just get this straight," Karma stated. "Once they mate with their consort, they can't be touched sexually by anyone else, not even a Galatian queen?"

"Why are you asking these questions?" Jayne asked. "It won't matter. Your surgery doesn't even sound like it took. And if it didn't, you can't satisfy your master."

Maybe she would attend the ceremony, just to see Jayne's reaction when Rafe wouldn't allow anyone but her to touch him.

"Look, Karma," Madeline said. "Mayva and I were friends. She was one of the first girls I met when I got to consort school, and we were lucky enough to be selected for the same Exchange year. I know her parents are worried sick and raising hell about her whereabouts. If you can tell me anything about what happened to my friend, I'd appreciate it."

Karma sighed. "I'll tell you anything you want. But you're going to have to help me first—"

Madeline was already shaking her head. "There's not anything I can do to help you. You tricked your way into becoming a consort--"

"I'm not asking you for that kind of help. If I survive this then I want a manual. Something that will help me understand all the things I'm supposed to do."

Jayne laughed. "That's a big wish list you have. But we don't write it down. There is no manual for someone to get their hands on and leak it to the media." She gestured to the window. "It's because of you that those animals are out there waiting for the smallest scrap of information about us!"

"That's what your Japoxillian is for," Madeline continued. "Look, we have to finish preparing. In truth, the least of your worries is how to continue this charade.

Mayva's parents won't want a scandal, and neither does the lottery. They've probably already concocted some lie. If I were you, I would be worrying about finding a way to escape before it's too late."

Karma still had many questions, but the women were leaving. Jayne was the last of them to go out the door. "See you tonight," she smirked.

"Yes, you will." Karma gave her a smooth look.

The apartment was quiet. Rafe was gone, the cleaning crew had collected the leftovers, and she had no idea where Dorf was.

She was filled with nervous energy. This battle still hadn't quite been won. The other consorts posed a threat to her. But after tonight, they would realize that she was indeed the number one choice and the most powerful among them.

In truth, she wished she had been selected by one of the lesser-ranked Galatians. Maybe they wouldn't care as much.

Karma moved to turn on the television but knew that seeing herself under so much speculation would just increase her anxiety.

She went to the music player and scanned the music collection. It was probably the only thing in the world that had any potential to soothe her.

The various disc covers intrigued her. It was an impressive collection. She only recognized a few of the artists; the others were apparently from different areas of the world. She went through each and every one of them until she stopped at a disc cover that had a photograph of a Dorf creature.

Karma examined the photo carefully. They were exquisite creatures, so she understood why someone would want to capture it in a photo. This Dorf was very regal. Its wings were spread slightly to make it look even bigger, and each feather was in perfect position. The title of the disc had strange writing that she couldn't understand, but intrigued, she slipped it into the player.

The music began as simple piano but it was much more melodious than any piano she'd ever heard. After a few beats came a genderless voice. She could not tell if it was young or old, male or female.

Karma stood for a moment as the tinkling of the piano and the melodious voice melded.

It was the most beautiful thing she'd ever heard.

Moments later, the sound of a full orchestra was introduced. The strings and gentle horns did not distract from the voice that sang out with so much emotion. She had no idea what the lyrics were, or even what the song was about, but like an opera, the melody told a story, and it felt like one that she was very familiar with; the story of loss.

It ended much too soon for her so Karma replayed it, this time turning up the volume so she could hear every nuance. She sat on the couch and thought of things she had long ago buried.

She had been nine years old when the Malnamanian monsters had rounded up the men from her housing unit. Paid by the Tybernees to "snatch and grab" as many human men as they could, the Malnamanians had no thoughts of the families that had been destroyed that day.

Most didn't have much, but when a family unit strived to make it work, they were sometimes able to manage a passable existence, and that is the way it was for Karma's parents.

They were poor, but her parents worked the rooftop community garden, which gave them food when the rations barely gave them enough to keep their bellies from groaning each night. Her father also worked as a custodian and handyman while her mother was a maid. Even as a child, Karma worked. She ran errands for the whores; mostly getting them food or hygiene products or other odds and ends.

No one that she knew had ever seen a Malnamanian in person—and certainly not the deadlier Tybernees that had been run off decades before by the Galatians. But still, the Malnamanians did their dirty work with their boneless, blob-like bodies that could be manipulated into different shapes. They were the perfect instrument for infiltrating small spaces.

And yet hearing about an attack on the radio in some distant city didn't hit home for a nine-year-old child whose only thoughts were if she had collected enough petty change to buy a sweet.

Those invasions happened in other parts of the world, not here, where it was civilized. It was even hard for a child to believe that aliens were real. It was a story whispered by the other kids, who talked about the horrible things that would happen to a man if he was taken by the aliens.

The worst being that they never, ever, came back.

But then the screams of terror filled their housing unit and when she looked out the window, she saw them slithering up the wall with a speed that defied reality. They quickly broke through the windows of the homes, and even those that had bars offered no barriers for the creatures who just slid between them.

Her father's eyes were frantic when he told her mother to hide under the bed so he could surrender without them searching the unit and locating the two of them. But her mother knew she would never see him again and wouldn't let him go.

The Malnamanians shattered through their barricaded door as if it was made of matchsticks. One of them grabbed Karma's father while she listened from her hiding place beneath the bed.

The many screams of the terror-stricken people in her housing unit filled Karma's entire existence, but the sound of her mother's screams cut through everything else as she begged for her husband.

And then her screams were cut short.

Her dad had been wrong about them not searching the small apartment after they had taken him. They tore everything upside down and topsy turvy searching for more males and when they found her, prepubescent and small, they lifted her into the air and ripped off her clothes. When they didn't find testicles and a penis dangling between her legs, they unceremoniously tossed her naked body to the floor.

Bigger and much stronger than humans, they cared very little that they had broken her collarbone and given her a concussion.

And still she had fared better than her mother, who had been sliced with a Malnamanian's deadly talon until her head was nearly completely separated from her body.

That was the first time Karma truly understood the meaning of complete and total loss.

When the song ended for the second time, she wiped her wet eyes and thought about the things that not even wealth could replace.

When she stood, she saw Dorf watching her from the middle of the room. For some reason she didn't quite understand, she didn't want him to see her tears. She turned quickly and replaced the disc in its jacket and put it away.

Chapter Twelve

"Who is she?" The commander watched Rafe with an intensity that caught him off guard. The commander was no one's pushover. He was known for stripping those that angered him of their scales.

Rafe knew that even he was subject to that treatment, despite being in the commander's favor — although *favor* was not the most accurate description of their relationship.

Rafe had just learned that there were rumblings of suspicious activity surrounding the lottery, and even yesterday's Exchange. And it was very close to home, as it involved his consort.

He was still reeling with news that the true lottery winner was nowhere to be found when he had been summoned to the outpost by his commander.

His commander had asked who the human was that he'd been mated to and the truth was that he didn't know. He didn't even know how he was supposed to feel; whether to be angry or just disappointed.

"When was it ever our jobs to know the history of our chosen?" Rafe's voice hinted at his mood.

Commander Einar ignored the tone in Rafe's voice and rifled through a folder. "Karma Chambers," he said while passing Rafe a folder. "This is the little that we know of her." Rafe accepted the documents. "She has no known ties to any rebellious factions."

Rafe met his commander's eyes at that statement. Did they think Karma was a spy? That was ridiculous. The rebels hated all aliens and would never allow themselves to have sex with a Galatian. Besides, this was all too messy for that.

Rafe looked over the pages, finding pitifully little information. She had worked as a maid up until about a week ago, when she had been reported as missing by her employer.

She was orphaned at the age of nine when her father was kidnapped by Malnamanian slave traders; her mother had been killed in the process. There was little information about a stay in an orphanage but that was only months after the death of her parents. There was no record of how she survived after their deaths. Her records picked up again after she applied for work with the Ministry of Employment. Her work history only consisted of short jobs in the service industry with positions as either a maid or custodial worker.

Rafe handed the folder back to his commander. "You know more about her than I do." He was curious, though. "What about the other one...the one that was to be my intended?"

"Mayva Heath."

"Heath?" Rafe's interest was piqued. "The oil family?"

"Exactly," Commander Einar stated. "They are one of the more prominent families in the North American province. And they don't know where their daughter is. Mayva Heath's file has been completely eradicated from the Galatian Exchange, which means it is unlikely that she was kidnapped by rebels or enemies of the Heaths."

"This is an inside job..." Rafe stated.

Commander Einar stood and began to pace. Rafe found it difficult to determine his mood as his scales had changed to a muddy brown, a tactic used to conceal one's thoughts.

"We've uncovered years of corruption within the Exchange. We were able to trace it back to a high-ranking lottery official. His name is Heinrich Tolbert. We've uncovered years of embezzlement within the discretionary funds, which culminated in half a billion dollars being stolen one day before the Exchange. His wife reported him missing the day of the Exchange and stated she hadn't seen him in days."

"How is it possible that our checks and balances didn't prevent this from happening?" Rafe asked.

"It seems that Tolbert was in charge of those checks and balances. Initially, he only embezzled from the discretionary funds. The numbers from each worldwide province go through his office right here in North America."

"Easy for him to access funds from around the world," Rafe realized.

"And if he took only a few thousand from the many funds and then subsequently approved them all, they would have been small enough to stay under the radar."

"That explains the discretionary funds, but not the half-billion from the Exchange's accounts. We're in charge of those and we audit them on a monthly basis; *we,* not them." The Galatians funded the Exchange so that it paid for their needs while on Earth. The discretionary funds were a gift to the humans to assist them with their needs as it pertained to the Galatian Exchange. Humans thought of it as an allowance.

Galatians did not accept actual monetary payments from their protectees, but garnered their wealth from an exchange of goods; mostly intergalactic items that Earth provinces found necessary to help them to rebuild even better infrastructures after the destruction of the Tybernees wars.

The commander continued. "The humans could never get away with embezzling our funds because of our audits, which we tell others are done monthly, but they are actually done weekly. Tolbert, of course, knew about this. He arranged to disappear one day after the embezzlement."

Rafe shook his head, anger finally manifesting in the purple tint of his scales. "With Mayva Heath...my intended?"

"Three humans disappeared right around the time of the Exchange." Commander Einar returned to his desk for the file. "Karma Chambers, Heinrich Tolbert, and Mayva Heath. The only one that has resurfaced is Karma Chambers." He handed the file back to Rafe. "Now it's your job to figure out where the others are and to take Karma Chambers into custody until we get to the bottom of this."

Rafe had accepted the file but gave his commander a sharp look. "She is my consort."

"Or a murderer of your true intended."

Rafe blinked. "Commander..."

"Rafe. What's the issue? She's not truly yours until after tonight's mating ceremony."

Rafe closed his eyes and rubbed a hand over his face. He finally looked at his commander.

"We mated last night."

"You did *what?*" The commander's response wasn't anger, but awe.

Rafe refused to repeat the words.

Karma's idea...Karma had not wanted to wait...Karma had seduced him...

"Without the queens?" the commander continued.

Once again, he looked at his commander. "I didn't need the queens..."

"You risked your consort without a queen?!" Now the commander roared in anger.

"She was awake, Commander."

Commander Einar gave him a look of surprise. "For her first time? I didn't know that was possible." Commander Einar looked off into the distance. "When I took my consort for the first time, she...even in her twilight state, she was still in a great deal of pain." He shook his head as if to shake away the memory.

Rafe watched him in curiosity. "She was not aroused?"

"No," Commander Einar snorted. "She was never aroused in the entire seven years she was mine. I am very happy to be finally bound to my queen."

Rafe knew that each union was different, but yesterday, Karma had become aroused. He could smell it on her.

"Rafe, have you selected an Earth career?"

Rafe turned his attention back to his commander. "Yes. I've chosen a military career." If he could no longer work as a Guard of the Interplanetary Collective while stuck here on Earth, then he at least wanted to hone the earthlings under his command to be better warriors.

The commander nodded for a long time. "That would have been a fine career for a warrior such as yourself."

"Would have...?"

"You're now assigned to head the Galatian Exchange and to identify any other areas of corruption."

"But that's a North American assignment. My consort selects—"

"Your consort is a fraud who is very lucky that she tricked you into fucking her before the ceremony! You'll do as I say, Lieutenant, or I will take her, regardless of whether the mating has been completed!"

Those words stopped his arguments. He knew the commander would never do such a thing, but even the threat of it cut down deep—even deeper than not being able to continue doing what he did best; combat work.

Rafe nodded once. He had already intended to find out who was behind the inconsistencies with his consort. And now he knew that she was the one behind them.

Karma was curious about Rafe's den. She didn't think it was off limits, but he might not like her snooping around. Dorf watched her, not going back to wherever he had spent the majority of his morning. But she didn't care if he watched. It wasn't as if he could snitch on her.

She pressed the electronic lever to open the door and then slowly entered the room.

It was dim, despite the skylight, yet the water was so green it seemed to offer a type of illumination. It smelled of something dank and warm, though not quite unpleasant. This was the way that green places would smell.

The green places were the settings of books she had read as a child; books about meadows and castles with princes and princesses. Living her entire life in the urban city, Karma could only imagine what these green places were truly like.

Rafe had asked where she would like to live, and she thought she'd like to live in a place where she could have this smell every single day. She would have to find a green place.

Karma walked to the pool of water, remembering Rafe had said portions were hot enough to burn her. She went there where the water bubbled and held her hand over the steam. It actually was hot, and she'd seen him swim over the area without looking as if it bothered him in the least.

She looked at a smooth rock ledge. Was this where he slept? Karma reached out and ran her hands over the smooth rock. Did he curl up to sleep, or stretch out? She wondered if she could get comfortable on a smooth rock ledge.

She'd gotten comfortable on the cement floor of the train depot, so anything was possible.

She looked at the roughened, cavern-like walls and then ran her fingers along them. It wasn't painted foam; it was actually rock! Had it been transported from Galatia? How could anyone afford to build a full-on cave in a penthouse apartment when there were so many hungry and homeless people right here in the city?

She sighed and went over to where his closet was located, remembering how he had stripped out of his clothing and turned to her as if his nudity wouldn't be a complete shock.

She thought back to what had happened between them after their swim and the way she had snuggled against him and how he had in turn embraced her, making her cheeks feel warm.

Karma smiled without realizing she was doing it.

She opened the door to the closet and stood there for a few moments just taking everything in. A low light had come on automatically, and she could see his long skirts hung neatly on rods. Shelves held his boots, along with bins that held large glass jars with salves and creams. On one wall hung a stiff-bristled brush with a long handle, a paddle, and a metal rod.

She could not imagine what they could be used for. There was another metal lever and she pressed it. A hidden panel opened and she saw weapons. There were rows of knives, swords, and guns, along with boxes of ammo.

Her hand reached out to take a knife, but she quickly drew it back. Who would she use a knife on; a trained military Guard? A Galatian who leisurely swam in boiling water?

She closed the door to his weapons closet and moved back to where his clothing hung.

Karma withdrew one of his long skirts, surprised at how heavy it was. This particular skirt was made of strips of thick leather overlapped so it more than likely wouldn't reveal his nudity.

She ran her fingers over the belt straps that would keep it secured around Rafe's waist. He was big and muscular, but his waist was comparatively small. She wondered if she could wear it, and was tempted to try but it was so long that even with her heels it would scrape the floor, and it was not the type of leather that would yield.

She turned to leave the closet and saw Dorf had followed her and was reclining on the ledge, watching her.

Just exploring my new home. She decided she wasn't going to explain herself to a cat/bird.

She left the room and checked the time. She should get ready for the celebration, although she had no idea what time it was supposed to start.

In her bedroom, Karma dug through her trunk and was surprised to see a brightly colored robe that was exactly like the ones worn by the other consorts. She quickly unrolled it and hung it on a satin-lined wooden hanger, hoping there weren't any creases in it.

It was absolutely beautiful. She ran her fingers over the silken material, feeling the cool fabric practically flow over her fingers. There wasn't a wrinkle to be seen.

She sat at her vanity, distressed it was so white and would pick up every speck of dust and wayward fingerprint. Karma was determined she would clean the vanity herself, and not require the cleaning staff to have to bother with something as trivial as a table made for no other purpose than to apply makeup.

But Karma didn't overdo it. She didn't know why people wanted to look fake, but she didn't. She found an eye shadow that matched colors in the robe and along with lip gloss, Karma was pleased with her look.

She dug through the trunk for jewelry, but it all seemed so fancy when she wore nothing beneath her robes. Wasn't that the point of the robe in the first place? Easy access for her Galatian mate.

No jewelry.

She put away the rest of her new items but when she held her old woolen coat, Karma realized there was no place for it in her new life. She had a beautiful wool cape now.

This part of her life was gone forever.

She balled it under her arm and headed for the kitchen to throw it into the trash when she heard the front door open.

Rafe was home. Her heartbeat sped up when she saw him walk into the room.

She opened her mouth to greet him but the words froze on her lips when she saw he was crossing the room towards her at a fast pace. His eyes were once again narrowed. The first time that she had seen him like this, his annoyance had been directed at the woman from the Exchange. But not this time.

She knew very little about Galatian expressions, but she was becoming accustomed to the change in tint to their scales, and Rafe's purple was not a pleasant sight.

Karma took a step back, but Rafe grabbed her wrist.

"Where is my true consort?" he growled.

Karma's mouth fell open. She stared up at the angry Galatian in terror. How did she think she could survive this once he figured out what she'd done? They were hugely territorial of their females—she'd already experienced it when he thought she was his.

He gave her a shake, pinching her wrist painfully. "Answer me!"

Karma cried out in pain. "I don't know!" He released her and she rubbed her wrist, holding it to her chest.

Dorf was suddenly there and the animal barked and sank his teeth into Rafe's tail. Rafe didn't appear to be hurt, but he turned to glance at the little animal and it gave Karma time to raise her arm to shield her head and

122

face. She dropped to the floor into a protective ball. The brunt of his beating would land on her back and if he didn't kick her, it might not hurt as bad.

Chapter Thirteen

Rafe blinked at Karma. She was cowering on the floor before him, the acrid stench of her fear quickly filling the room. He'd not smelled her fear to this degree before and it was enough to defuse his anger completely.

"I wasn't..."

Dorf released Rafe's tail and hopped until he was standing next to Karma. He spread his wings and then hopped on Karma's back, forming a shield between her and Rafe.

When Rafe saw his long-time friend protecting his mate from him, he felt shame to a degree he'd never before felt in his life.

He would not have hurt her.

But he had. Rafe turned and headed for his den, shutting the door behind him.

Karma waited tensely for the first pained blows to rain down on her. Instead, she heard Rafe's low and hesitant voice. He said he wasn't. He wasn't what? She'd heard the sudden ruffle of wings and Dorf landed on her back. He wasn't awfully lightweight, but she realized he had spread his wings above her and was shielding her.

When moments later she heard Rafe retreat to his den, she knew she had to get out of here. For all she knew, he was going to get his weapons. She didn't care if she was dressed in thin robes with no clothes on beneath them, or that she didn't even have shoes.

She jumped to her feet, sending the Dorf creature flying and squawking into the air. With her instinct for survival sending her into overdrive, Karma ran across the room for the front door.

She had just reached for the door handle when she heard the soft, sorrowful lyrics to the song, only this time, there wasn't any music.

Confused, Karma took a moment to glance over her shoulder as she hit the lever to open the door. But what she saw stopped her in her tracks.

Dorf was singing.

It was his voice that had been on the song that had made her cry; had made her remember. His head was thrown back as he looked to the ceiling, although his eyes did not seem to be focused on anything. His wings were thrown back as he sang the saddest song she had ever heard.

It was him on the music cover?

But...

The door was open, waiting for her to run for her life. And then she remembered something she never wanted to forget while in a panicked state; running was sometimes an invitation to be chased.

Nothing was pursuing her, and the Dorf-creature was singing that song and Rafe had hurt her wrist but he had retreated to his den...

Stop.

Going against every learned instinct, Karma did just that. She stopped.

She watched Dorf sing his gentle lyrics, appearing as if he was in a world of his own and when it ended, he looked at her.

It dawned on her she had gotten it all wrong. Rafe had said he would help her, and for her to call on him for assistance. He had spoken to him as if he was a friend. Dorf wasn't a pet! He was just another type of alien.

She scratched her head, feeling overwhelmed, and Dorf walked to her. Had he been trying to communicate with her all this time?

When he was standing before her, he looked up at her and waited. Still unsure, she offered him her hand. He opened his mouth and sank his teeth into the pad of flesh on her hand along her pinky finger.

It was supposed to hurt. She'd seen his teeth. But instead, a tingling sensation ran up her spine, causing her to momentarily shiver.

"Are you hurt, child?"

Karma's eyes practically bulged when the crystal-clear voice rang out in her head. It was the voice of a male; a very human voice.

She stared at the Dorf in disbelief. The voice was in her head, not in her ears.

"Did he injure you?" the voice came again.

"W-what?" she asked in a shaky voice.

"Rafe. He can be a brute, but I never dreamed he would attack his consort."

"How are you doing this?" she whispered. "I've never heard of such a thing. You're speaking in my head..."

Dorf didn't immediately reply. "You're not who you say you are. I knew something was wrong. I thought you just hated my kind."

Karma shook her head quickly. "No! I don't. I just didn't understand."

Dorf mentally sighed. "This is a mess. But it's still no license for him to strike you— "

"He didn't!" she said quickly. "He didn't hit me," she whispered. "He grabbed my arm and I was afraid."

Dorf tilted his head as he watched her. "Afraid of your own master? Ah…but you are not who you pretend to be. That is a worry. I'll need to speak to Rafe about this. You don't appear to be completely impossible, as I initially thought."

Karma's mouth snapped open. "I didn't understand! I thought—"

"You don't have to speak aloud. It's just us two. You can speak mentally. I'm connected to you cerebrally. This is how Japoxillian communicate with others of differing species. I've helped Rafe learn to speak many different tongues. Humans are not so easy to help, as your tongues and vocal cords have limited capacity. Unfortunately, your brains do as well. But unlike Galatians, I do not believe this to be an indication of limited intelligence. Now, in order to speak to me while we are linked, you just have to think your thoughts in verbal form. Please remember that I can pick up your thoughts, but not necessarily what you intend to relay."

Karma tried to digest the information. But Dorf had given her a lot.

"Don't leave while I'm speaking to Rafe," Dorf continued.

"But he knows I'm not..." she said those words aloud, and the rest she spoke mentally. "...who I pretended to be."

Dorf sounded amused. "You really don't understand. There is no way to run from Rafe. He will never let you go—at least not for seven years. Never run from him. He will pursue you, even if it means crossing galaxies. You are his now."

Those words chilled Karma. Rafe hated her, and now he was stuck with her.

Dorf released her hand and she felt another strong chill run through her body. He gave her a meaningful look before turning for Rafe's den.

When Dorf entered the den, he saw Rafe was in his pool. He swam beneath the water when he saw the Japoxillian. Dorf leaped to the water's edge and waited patiently. When Rafe emerged, Dorf stared at him until, with a sigh, Rafe swam to the ledge and Dorf spoke to him in a language that they both understood.

"I thought you had lost your mind and struck your consort."

Rafe flinched. "I could never...purposely hurt her. Did I injure her wrist?" Shame filled Rafe. It was never his intent to injure her. He'd just forgotten himself, his strength, until he realized he'd squeezed her too tight.

"She says she was not injured, just afraid."

Rafe sighed again. "Of course, she would be."

"I told you she was all wrong—"

"I know you did, my friend. I didn't listen because I liked that she was all wrong."

Neither spoke for a moment. "This is a mess. But there is no time to tell me what's happened. I've watched this human and I've linked with her. She didn't refuse to link with me out of a need to keep her secrets. She truly thought I was your pet."

"You? A pet?"

"Yes, but it can't be helped. The lower life-forms here on Earth happen to look much like I do."

Rafe closed his eyes. "She truly was never intended to be a consort. How did she come to replace the person that was truly intended for me? And what happened to the one I should have been mated to?"

"There will be time for those answers, Rafe."

Rafe shook his head. "I can't trust myself with her. I wanted to...Commander Einar is forcing me to get to the bottom of this. I nearly treated her like a prisoner I needed to interrogate."

"It was wise of your commander to put her in your hands and not allow someone else to investigate her."

Rafe's eyes flashed in anger. "No one but me can do that. I would never allow it, even if he had not been wise." She was his mate—right or wrong, it did not matter. He could do nothing different when it came to protecting her.

"Then you already know you will not hurt her," Dorf said matter-of-factly.

He pushed away the image of her terror-filled eyes and then the way she had dropped to a defensive position, as if she had known exactly how to prevent as much injury as possible. He had no doubt Karma had never known the sanctity of the consort school, because she had lived in places where she had learned to be afraid of being beaten.

Dorf had been the one to shield and protect her, and then later, to soothe her with his special song.

"I heard you singing your Death Oath." Rafe gave his friend a meaningful look. "You did that for her. You vowed never to sing it again."

"Speak to the human," Dorf replied. "She may not be who she pretended to be, but she also isn't what you think. There is no malice in her actions. I just sense a need to survive."

"Survive what?" Rafe frowned.

"That, I do not know. But there is no time to get to the bottom of this now. You will need to prepare for the ceremony."

"We have already mated."

"Of course, I know that. But it's still an important ceremony, and this one will have the queens in attendance. You do not want to keep them waiting."

"It's not the queens that concern me. She's afraid of me, Dorf."

"And she thinks you hate her."

"Hate? I don't want to be in her company. But it has nothing to do with hate."

"Rafe."

"But I will go to the ceremony and afterwards, she will give me the answers I want!"

"Yes."

"And you will be present to read her lies."

"Of course."

Rafe got out of the pool and then went to his closet and retrieved his oil. He did the best he could without a consort to rub it on his back. He frowned. He was angry, but much of it had to do with how thoroughly he had been tricked by her. He had been so pleased she wasn't

130

anything like he had expected that he hadn't seen what any low-ranked Guardian should have seen.

Dorf had been in her presence for mere minutes before he had felt her wrongness.

Damn his attraction for non-conformity.

Rafe donned his wrap, wondering how he was going to make it through the ceremony without touching her. It was true he didn't want her in his presence. He did not want to look at her, smell her, or be aware of her. But he could not forget how it had felt to be inside of her tight opening, and then her responsive sounds of pleasure.

Commander Einar had said his consort had never become aroused while with him. But Karma had. He had tasted of the juices that streamed from her womanhood. He'd felt her taut nipples harden against his tongue. He'd heard her breath catch and the beat of her heart speed up when he entered her.

Rafe paused to close his eyes. It would be difficult, but he would not mate with her again.

He did not want to see her. He did not want to smell her. He did not want to taste her. He did not want her in his presence because he did not want to know just how difficult it would be to control himself.

Chapter Fourteen

Karma had returned to her room, where she hung her old woolen coat in the back of the closet.

Dorf had said not to run, and she wouldn't—for now. But she wasn't convinced he would not force her to leave—no matter how many contracts or rituals had been performed.

Karma went to her bathroom, cleaned herself up, and then went back to the living room to wait for Rafe to come out of his den. He and Dorf had been in there for a while. Maybe he didn't want to do the ceremony with her.

She rubbed her hand, surprised that despite the small bite marks on the side of her palm, she didn't have any discomfort.

There was so much she didn't understand. How had Mr. Tolbert thought she could ever possibly get away with this?

The answer to that question was, he didn't care if she did or didn't. He'd only set her up to do something no one else in their right mind would agree to. He'd had to find someone so down on their luck, his only resort had been a person who could have never been included in the Exchange in the first place.

There was no way this could have ever succeeded.

He will pursue you across galaxies.

If that was true for her, then it was probably also true for the consort that had gotten away…

When Rafe came out of his den, he saw Karma standing by the window, staring out into the fading day as if deep in thought.

He took in her sleek form in her ceremonial robe. The delicate fabric cascaded to the floor to pool around her bare feet. He preferred her feet bare, and didn't altogether mind the clothing. The Galatian queens could have never worn clothing so delicate. Their rough scales would have shredded such fine material.

He could see from her profile, slender yet strong legs with sizeable thighs and backside. Her profile also showcased perfect, round breasts peaked by the imprints of her nipples, which he knew would grow tight beneath his touch.

Karma turned with fingers intertwined. He was struck by how her brown skin glowed with a nervous, pink undertone, which then amplified the tones found in the patterns of her robe.

Rafe noted Karma's skin did the same as his scales; they showcased several different hues based on his disposition. He liked that she didn't hide beautifully expressive skin beneath unnaturally colored makeup — especially her dark eyes. They were lined with something dark, which did amplify them, so he did not object. It made it difficult for him not to stare into their depths.

His eyes shifted to the fluffy hair on top of her head, which glistened with some type of added sheen. He remembered the texture from last night; soft, yet wild. It was Karma herself, soft and yielding if he touched her with kindness—but wild with self-preservation if he didn't.

There was no consort in history quite like her. They had always been trained to accept without question—without complaint. Just the way human males wanted them, but not necessarily what Galatians wanted.

The thought made him uneasy. He cursed to himself. He did not enjoy thinking this hard about something as inconsequential as the inner workings of consort training. But he feared with his new work assignment, it's exactly what Commander Einar expected.

"Rafe," Karma said in a hesitant whisper, surprising him out of his reverie. "I just want you to know that...I'm aware there's a lot of things we need to talk about. I knew from the beginning this day would come." She paused. "And I'd have to explain myself. I-I just want you to know I intend to do that openly and honestly."

Rafe looked away. Time would tell if she intended to be open and honest. "There will be time for that later. We need to leave for the ceremony."

He turned for the door. His tail pushed past the pleats of his skirt to observe Karma, confirming she followed.

After quickly slipping on the terrible glass slippers, she did.

They entered the elevator and went down past even the lobby level. Karma was surprised they didn't leave the building. She looked at Rafe's broad back and narrow hips in his regal skirt. His vest seemed molded to his back, tapering down to narrow hips. His long tail split the pleats and seemed to stand at attention between them like a separate individual.

Humans could say whatever they wanted, but Galatians posed a regal figure.

The elevator doors opened and she tore her eyes from Rafe's back to the corridor stretched before them. Rafe naturally moved quickly, due to his tall frame and much longer legs. But because she was accustomed to walking along the city streets—generally in the dark— she moved quickly too, and managed to keep up with him despite the heels she wore.

When he reached a set of double doors at the opposite end of the corridor, Rafe paused and turned his head in her direction—although he didn't look at her.

"In case you aren't aware, you must bow to the queens. Follow the lead of your sisters."

Before she could reply, Rafe opened the door and stepped into the room. All eyes moved to him. The males were standing beside their mates, who knelt on thick cushions that formed a large semi-circle.

The room was unlike any of the other fine rooms Karma had seen over the last two days. The pale-cream floors and walls reminded her of the expensive tiles she only saw in the richest homes. The room was huge, as it had to be in order to accommodate the seven couples— along with the seven queens that stood in the center of the semicircle.

Karma had never seen a Galatian female, even in photos. But if she thought the seven-foot-tall men looked formidable, the females were even taller. While not as broad as their male counterparts, their muscles were more defined due to their leaner forms.

Their coloring was also different. The males had primarily green tones with smooth, multicolored scales that ran down their backs in differing patterns. But the females had more of a mud-like color, with single-colored scales.

Even with her limited education, Karma knew this was the way with nature. The males of the species were generally more flamboyant in order to be more appealing to the females. But was that supposed to cross species? Her cheeks grew warm as she thought about how confusing attraction was.

She realized Rafe had gone down on one knee and had bowed his head before the queens. She quickly mimicked the movement, although not as gracefully. Despite being a servant for all of her adult life, Karma had never been forced to bow down on her knees before anyone.

Rafe made strange clicking sounds in his throat and one of the queens did the same. He suddenly spoke.

"Forgive our tardiness, my queens."

"We only just arrived. Stand. Take your places," the queen replied.

They came to their feet. Karma could have figured out where to go but Rafe took her wrist—gently, this time—and led her to an empty cushion, which now enclosed the circle.

Karma did as the other consorts and went down to her knees on the cushion.

Everyone stared at her. The males had even turned bodily to gaze at her. Their human mates obviously didn't like that she had taken the attention from them.

They had clearly worked hard to look beautiful. Their makeup was bright and colorful and their hair flowed in perfect curls over their shoulders. But even the queens looked at her with interest, at least until Rafe moved to stand behind her instead of taking his place beside her within the circle.

The Galatian female that had spoken to Rafe cocked her head at him.

"Take your place, Rafe Sigur, so we may commence. We waited for your consort before the others drank their Twilight elixir and applied the mating compound."

"Then commence—" Rafe began. But he was interrupted when one of the consorts came to her feet.

"Forgive me, queens and Galatian brethren." It was Jayne. "But I cannot allow this travesty to continue."

"Consort," one of the Galatian males spoke in concern. "What is this?"

"Sit down, Jayne!" Madeline hissed.

"No." A queen spoke. "Speak, consort. What travesty do you speak of?"

Nervous beads of sweat began to gather on Karma's forehead. She should have run when she had the chance. Her eyes darted to the door, but the Galatians moved with a speed unmatched by humans. She could never outrun fourteen of them.

Jayne turned to Karma and pointed an accusatory finger at her. "This *person* is a fraud! She was never in the consort school with us! She infiltrated the Exchange and took the place of our dear friend who was supposed to be sitting here now!"

Karma could see the queens turn to look at Rafe now.

"Explain this, Rafe Sigur."

137

Karma was unsure why there was only one female spokesperson, but she was the one who directed the questions to Rafe. Karma held her breath.

But instead of answering, Rafe made those clicking sounds in his throat. This was their language. His brethren looked on in interest while Jayne just stared from one Galatian to another with increasing impatience.

"There's no indication who this person might be! She could be a rebel terrorist for all we—"

"Jayne." Her master spoke firmly. "You will stay quiet." She shut her mouth quickly while Rafe continued speaking to the queen.

When Rafe finished, the room had grown quiet. The queens looked at each other and began speaking to each other. Karma was so scared she was literally shaking. She suddenly felt Rafe's hand on her shoulder.

He wasn't trying to hold her down or prevent her from moving. It was gentle, as if he wanted her to keep calm.

Karma concentrated on the feel of Rafe's hand on her. She was still scared, but she didn't shiver as much.

The queen spokeswoman turned to Jayne.

"The matter is being handled, human."

Jayne's mouth opened as a look of disbelief crossed her face. "But she's not intended for Rafe Sigur. And in Mayva's absence, I offer to take her place. I request to be mated to Lieutenant Rafe Sigur. This person should be put...in prison! Or killed! Or whatever you do with rebel trash like her!"

"Jayne!" her Galatian master said sharply. "Don't speak another word. Take your place and stay your tongue!"

Jayne looked around for someone to speak up for her, but the other consorts simply lowered their eyes.

Jayne finally moved to sit next to her sister consorts.

Karma looked over her shoulder and up at Rafe. "What did you tell them?"

Rafe's eyes lowered to meet hers. "I told them you are a fraud." Karma felt a wave of shame. "And the Collective knows and has already confirmed your identity." Rafe's gaze shifted to take in his brothers. "The commander has placed me in charge of the Galatian Exchange and I've been assigned the task of determining how far this deceit goes. In the meantime, they are feeding the human press information that my consort is the daughter of Arabian royalty."

"But she should be put in prison, not rewarded for her crimes!" Jayne appealed.

"Enough of these trivial human matters!" another queen snapped. "We tire of Earth and wish to return to our home! The ceremony will commence! Take your sexual aids, human consorts!"

Jayne looked around but didn't speak. The consorts stood and moved across the room, where there was a familiar lever built into the wall. One of the consorts pressed it and a tall, double-sized panel slid open, revealing another large room.

The lights were dim, but she could clearly see seven platforms, each shielded by sheer drapes. Each platform was piled high with cushions. Karma looked over at a nearby table, which held a silver pitcher and seven silver goblets. Seven frighteningly long syringes lay on a platter, appearing every bit like turkey basters.

While Karma took all of this in, the others were looking out the door where they had just come from. Karma turned to see what they were looking at.

The males were stripping out of their skirts and vests.

They were a sight to behold, and the consorts were frozen in place staring at their first sight of real-life, nude Galatians. Even Karma couldn't stop herself from staring at the six ten-inch-long, flaccid penises. Six, because Rafe was the only one not getting undressed.

"Oh my Guardian..." one of the consorts said wistfully. "Do you see their pricks?"

"And they're not even hard yet..."

Madeline slammed her hand to close the panel. Once it was closed, she spun around to Jayne.

"You are so treacherous, Jayne! You agreed you wouldn't interfere!"

"She's going to die tonight!" Jayne said while pointing at Karma. "And I'm the only one that did anything that could have saved her life!"

"Don't fight, you two," someone else said. "We're in this together now. You heard what Lieutenant Sigur said. They don't care."

Madeline gave Karma a sympathetic look. "Jayne is right. You're not going to survive this."

Karma shook her head. "I *already* survived it."

Jayne's mouth opened and then closed before she finally spoke. "That's impossible. You didn't have the elixir! You're lying."

"I don't have to lie to you," Karma replied. "We mated last night, and as you clearly see, I'm all right."

Jayne suddenly glared at her. "That's why he rejected me! You got your hooks into him. You planned this!"

Karma frowned. "Don't be stupid. Nothing I did had anything to do with you."

"But..." Madeline looked at Karma in confusion. "They taught us that the first time with a Galatian was the worst possible pain imaginable...and you did it without elixir?"

Karma shrugged. "I had no elixir, but I'll tell you what I know to be a fact; the first time always hurts. But sex hurts a whole lot less if you enjoy the experience."

Everyone watched her, and for once, they listened, so Karma continued. She gestured to the pitcher of Twilight juice. "If you drink and shoot numbing cream up inside of yourself, then I guarantee you will have a lot more pain than I did."

"You're a liar!" Jayne said. "They are too big for our bodies. There's no way you could possibly do it!"

"I didn't allow him completely inside."

"But you wouldn't have been able to stop it. They're animals. They can't control it!" someone replied.

Karma gestured to the table. "You won't be able to control anything if you're sedated and you let them take you from behind. You have to stay alert. You have to control how far and how quickly they enter you. And you have to find enjoyment in the act." Karma looked at each of them, including Jayne. "Do what you want, but they know how to give you pleasure, if you let them."

"But..." Madeline was blushing furiously. "How do we...?"

"Touch them," Karma smiled, remembering Rafe's reaction when she gripped him. "They like being touched...and they like tasting us." Her cheeks burned again.

"Titus does touch my skin, all the time," someone said slowly.

"Kendrick does too! He can barely keep his hands from my skin."

"What should we do?"

They were all looking at Karma for direction. Karma turned and opened the panel. "Follow me."

Chapter Fifteen

Once the door to the mating chamber closed, Ragna turned to Rafe and reached for the buckles of his rigging. The others were already undressed and had offered themselves to the queen they had been bound to.

"No, Ragna." Rafe spoke.

"If you want to undo your own rigging, then be quick about it. I've waited for this minute since learning you were to be a part of this year's Exchange."

Rafe refused to meet her eyes.

It had been so many years since he'd experienced the touch of his Galatian bound-mate, he no longer knew if he even desired her. Besides, arguing with Ragna would be fruitless, even if he chose to point out it was she that had denied him for so many years.

"Don't tell me you are still angry? I desire you, Rafe—"

"For that, I apologize. But I am already mated to my consort. Therefore, you and I will need to wait...again."

Ragna grew quiet, and Rafe finally looked at her. She looked perplexed.

"You put your human in danger—"

"I didn't," he growled. "She did not want Twilight. She was fully aware during the mating."

Ragna blinked. "But she's not even a true consort!" She once again reached for his buckles, and this time, Rafe gripped her wrist to stay her hand.

"We mated," he said firmly. "I spilled my seed inside of her!"

Several others looked at them and Rafe drew her to the side, away from where his brothers should be enjoying their last encounter with their bound-mate for the next seven years.

For Rafe, seven years was not much time in the scope of things. Ragna had denied him for far longer than that. It had been more than ten years since they had last mated.

Bound at birth, they had enjoyed their first sexual encounters with each other upon coming of age. But when she did not bear a child within the prerequisite time, he was free to follow whatever career choice he desired.

It should not have been a surprise he would join the Guard, with his family history of valor. All of the males in his bloodline were warriors. But Ragna wanted something that for once, she couldn't have; his seat on the Interplanetary Collective.

Although a prestigious position only offered to a select few, Rafe would have easily secured a seat if for no other reason than he was a Sigur—a name synonymous with leadership.

The issue was that Rafe did not desire to sit on a board where he made laws. He desired to fight. Ragna withheld sex as a way to force his hand, but he was as stubborn as she. He cared for Ragna, but after ten years, he had long ago stopped thinking about her.

"Ragna." Rafe spoke in a low voice. "The law is clear. As long as we are assigned to Earth, Galatian Guards will be assigned a human consort. And after seven years of duty on this planet we can return to Galatia, to our bound-mate, and to focus on our

144

objective; procreation and the continuation of our species."

"I know the law!" she hissed.

"Then you know that in order to maintain our commitment to our humanitarian mission while here on Earth, we will treat our consort with no less respect than we treat the queens we are bound to."

"Your human stands in our place while you are here — I know this! But we have always helped with the transition. It's our duty —"

"She did not wish for your assistance."

The doors to the mating chamber opened and Ragna turned in surprise as the consorts followed the one she and her bound-mate were currently speaking of.

When they entered the room again, the Queens that had already begun to satisfy their lovers hesitated, unsure of what to do. They were supposed to bring their bound-mate to completion in order to assist with the transition.

After their first seed was spilled, the queen would escort her bound-mate to the mating chamber, where symbolically she would pass him onto his human consort who would, for a time, act as her.

This had been the way for generations — since the humans had first insisted they provide their human women as a concubine — at least until the queens stepped in to educate the humans. No queen would want their bound-mate to return to them after they had lived seven years treating a female as nothing more than a whore.

Ragna watched the brown human with suspicion.

When the door opened, Karma and the other consorts were met with a sight that caused some to gasp in surprise, while others could only stare as if mesmerized.

The Galatian males stood in a semicircle in complete nudity. Kneeling before them were the queens, who held onto their thick erections while busily mouthing and licking their pricks. The queens remained dressed, but their skirts showed their long, limber legs that were revealed by the pleats of their skirts. Their tails swished the air when not curling around or stroking the ankles and legs of their partner.

In addition to the skirts, the queens wore cloth vests wrapped around their waists, concealing relatively small breasts. Although they were each brown, their tones ranged from sepia to sienna. And yet the one commonality was their pale-whiteish chest and bellies with smaller, smoother scales.

This was their soft underbelly, Karma thought.

A variety of moans filled the large room, from soft groans to low grunts, and even one high-pitched wail.

Off to one side stood Rafe, who was speaking to one of the queens. It was the same one that had done most of the talking. Karma's eyes moved to them, wondering if she was a lieutenant as well, or at least someone with some form of leadership.

The room quickly grew quiet as all eyes fell onto the consorts as if they were intruders. When none offered to speak, Karma knew it fell on her. She took a nervous breath and spoke directly to Rafe, focusing on him and him alone.

"The—" She began to stutter, and paused to inhale deeply. "My sister consorts would like the pleasure of knowing their mates without the sedative." She looked around, confirming they were in agreement and when none objected, she turned back to Rafe. She took in another deep breath, embarrassed this intimate conversation was taking place in front of so many strangers. But if she understood the state of things, then this was her purpose; to act as a sexual outlet for the Galatian protectors, mankind's saviors. She steeled her resolve to continue.

"The consorts want to do…what we did yesterday." Rafe just stared at her without comment. Karma pushed aside her shame; shame of voicing her thoughts to those that had assigned themselves as her superiors, shame of speaking of intimate matters, shame for deceiving Rafe…

"They want to feel good; the way you made me feel good." Her voice had gone softer and then her eyes flicked to the males. "But they also want to make you—their mates—feel good. They want to touch you, explore you."

Karma's eyes lowered to look at the floor, no longer able to meet their unrelenting stares. Madeline moved to stand next to Karma.

"We are prepared to give ourselves to our mates in a different way; a new way. A way in which we too will experience pleasure."

Karma looked at the young woman who sounded so brave and so self-assured. Everyone listened when she spoke, because even though Karma knew for a fact Madeline was unsure, she spoke with confidence. The males began to speak using the clicking sounds of their natural tongue as they communicated wordlessly.

Karma once again looked at Rafe, who continued to stare at her. She wasn't sure what he thought. His color hadn't changed, and she was still unfamiliar with the Galatians' facial expression—if his even changed—which she didn't think it had.

He hates me, she thought.

But it was Rafe who put an end to any speculation that was going on between his brothers.

"It is true it can be done without Twilight, and can even be...pleasurable for both parties."

Karma allowed herself to breathe again. Still, no one moved. Again, this was going to be up to her.

She walked to Rafe, concentrating on no one but him. When she was just a foot from him, she stopped, waiting for him to retreat or look away.

He did neither.

Once again mustering her courage, Karma reached up and lightly pressed the pads of her fingertips to the softer scales of his chest. She vowed that if he turned her away, she would never reach out to him again. Yet she had to know if he still reacted to her touch.

Rafe's breathing changed, seemed to catch in his throat before he released it in slow, even measures.

Feeling encouraged, she ran her fingers down over the plains of his chest, discovering the nipples she hadn't recognized the night before. They were so pale and unlike the scales that covered even the palms of his hands. This was like the skin that covered his prick. Wondering if it was just as sensitive, she ran both thumbs over them.

148

His breath caught again and the nipples beaded into hard pebbles, appearing strange surrounded by the smooth, scaly texture of the rest of his chest. She looked up to see he continued to stare at her, but it no longer unsettled her. She now easily sensed his desire.

No longer as afraid, Karma forced her hands further down, and as they grazed his toned torso, the muscles began to shift, jerking slightly, as if sensitized to her touch. She reached the buckles of his skirt and confidently began to undo them, fully understanding how the garment wrapped around his waist, almost completely concealing the lower portion of his body.

When the buckles were undone, she began to unwrap the garment and Rafe finally moved, his hands next to hers on the belt — but not to stop her, to assist her. He finished unwrapping it and tossed it carefully to the floor.

Karma didn't try to hide where her eyes went next. His prick had taken on a life of its own, becoming erect, and was pointing upward between them.

She didn't remember it being so hard, with veins protruding from a shaft that was not much different than any other man's prick, only thicker and much longer. Even the mushroom-shaped tip had the familiar glisten of wetness as precum spilled from it.

Karma's eyes met his again and realized his stare was not one of anger or mistrust, but of focus. His entire attention was on her — from the moment she stepped into the room and with every movement she made, Rafe looked at nothing but her. That awareness made the breath in her chest catch and her body warm.

She looked down and moved to unwrap her robe, an invitation for him to touch her, but Rafe's hands quickly covered hers.

"No," came a low, guttural response. "For my eyes only."

She nodded in understanding. The queens had not disrobed, and although she didn't liken herself to one of the queens, she was beginning to understand the depths of the Galatians' dominance towards their females.

With eyes still locked onto his, Karma reached down and ran one fingertip over the head of his prick.

Rafe's eyelids fluttered as he shuddered, his mouth parting to take in short, hissing breaths.

Relief washed over her when she realized Rafe didn't hate her—or if he did, he desired her more. And for now, that was acceptable.

Using both hands now, she slowly rubbed his precum up and down the last two fistfuls of his shaft. With a boldness born of seeing his desire flame to life, Karma moved one hand to cup his testicles. They were smooth, but as big as ripe peaches, and she stroked them carefully but firmly. Rafe's eyes quickly closed and she saw his jaw clench as his breathing became rapid.

Knowing he fought to contain his control sent a jolt of electric desire to the swelling nub nestled between Karma's thighs. Still rubbing his prick and testicles while his body shuddered with uncontrolled jerks, Karma leaned forward and plastered her lips onto one of his nipples.

She flicked it roughly with her tongue and Rafe's knees buckled slightly. Stumbling half a step, he threw his head back and groaned loudly, his breath as fast as an ancient locomotive.

He must have tried to control his hands because he suddenly allowed them to grip her shoulders and he held her firmly in place, either to stabilize himself or to prevent her from ending the contact with his nipple.

Karma was lost in her own growing desire; his reaction, the copious amounts of precum now spilled over her fists—so she didn't become alarmed when she felt something gently wrap around her leg.

She released her mouth from Rafe's nipple and looked down and saw it was his tail. It twined around her like a snake, even though his tail was thicker than any snake she had ever seen.

She didn't mind the sensation and returned her mouth to its manipulations, only this time, focusing on his other nipple.

His tail twined and untwined, moving restlessly from one leg to the other until it slipped between her parted thighs and pressed its long, smooth length against her moist V. There it rubbed slowly, maddeningly, as it moved back and forth with calculated ease.

This time it was Karma that gasped and shuddered and when her own knees began to weaken, she reached out and gripped Rafe's forearms, her nails digging into his arm.

Immediately, she felt the sharp pain of his scales slicing beneath her nails. Rafe quickly grabbed her hands and brought her fingers to his mouth. His tongue explored the injury but instead of pain, Karma felt her core pulse to life.

Rafe flexed and instantly his outer, darker scales contracted until they were as smooth and sleek as the scales on his underbelly. Karma's mouth parted at the sight and feel of his tongue on her fingertips, bringing back images of his tongue in other places…

Rafe quickly lifted her, as if that had been the signal he wished for. He moved with long strides to the second room; the mating chamber.

Karma's arms and legs went around him, clinging to him—not out of a fear of falling, but because there was nothing but the desire to wrap herself around him.

She remembered then that she and Rafe had not been alone. But she didn't have to worry long about what the others might have thought about her unabashed actions.

Her sister consorts were doing similar things with their mates—some did even bolder things. One woman was on her knees, suckling the prick head of her lover while he cried out in uncontrolled pleasure. Nearly all of the consorts had disrobed and were having various parts of their bodies stroked, licked, or suckled, and they each seemed to enjoy it—save for one; Jayne.

Jayne was wringing and pulling on her master's prick but no amount of tugging brought it to life. It remained flaccid.

She's doing it all wrong, Karma thought fleetingly. But she knew it would not matter how expert her touch; Jayne's master no longer desired her. The consorts were wrong. Being Galatian didn't mean they were insatiable beasts that had no control. Just like humans they were aroused by attraction, and Jayne had destroyed that.

Her attention moved onto the queens who stood indecisively, looking at each other in confusion. But Karma saw with a glance that one queen stared at her and only her, and that was the one Rafe had been talking to, the one that acted as the head queen in charge.

This time, Karma had no confusion about the expression on a Galatian's face, as this was not one of simple interest or curiosity. It was filled with malice.

Chapter Sixteen

Rafe moved to one of the mating platforms. He placed his human on the cushions and then closed the sheer drapes around them. He wanted to disrobe her, and even though the gossamer material would not conceal them completely, it would let all know his mate was not to be gawked at.

With the drapes closed behind him, he gazed down at her, the hint of what lay beneath the delicate fabric of her robe enticing him as much as her nude body did.

Slowly, he reached down to move her robe to the side, revealing her breasts and darkened nipples.

I like when you touch me there, she had said.

He resisted because he would only get lost there. He wanted to explore more of her — before desire drove his actions. He looked at one leg, which had parted the robe and revealed the dark curls at her core. Forcing himself to ignore that as well, he looked at her feet and saw the glass shoes. He removed them and thought about destroying them, but simply dropped them to the floor.

Rafe studied her toes, all five separated, with no webbing, like her fingers. He sat on the end of the platform and ran the pad of his thumb over the paler sole of one of her feet and then the brown skin at the top. He traced the delicate bones and Karma shivered.

He looked over at her quickly. Was she cold? But he smelled a fresh wave of desire from between her thighs. Rafe grunted in satisfaction. She did enjoy being touched by him. He saw her teeth as they lightly bit at her own lip. He didn't know why, but it was the way his human expressed her desire.

He knew what else she desired, and he no longer wanted to deny himself or her. Rafe moved up the platform, between her legs. Bigger than her, he was still lean, and she didn't have to spread far to accommodate him.

Her chest rose erratically as she peered down at him in anticipation when his head drew closer to her core. And then he saw her eyes change as the brown nearly disappeared to reveal black, dilated pupils.

Rafe groaned and plunged his head home, his mouth wide as his tongue accepted the gift of her tender, moist flesh. She bucked and he shielded his teeth while lapping and rubbing his tongue against her folds.

Karma screeched and gyrated and then grabbed for his shoulders as if ready to dig her nails into him. But she flattened her hands instead, as if remembering how sharp clawing his scales could be. He wanted to tell her not to worry, he'd flattened his scales and they were now safe for her to touch, to explore, to even taste if she so desired. But he could only focus on her bucking hips and moans of desire.

His prick ached to burrow into her tight depths, but this one thing he would deny himself. Instead, he focused on discovering the many ways his little human desired to be licked.

There was only pleasure for Karma, no fear, no anxiety, just the sensations that caused her to soar to heights she had never imagined possible.

It was nearly more than she could handle when his tongue flicked her sensitized nub, but then he licked and rolled the long appendage until the pulsing within her depths caused her body to writhe.

And that is when she felt his fingertips on her breasts, capturing her nipples and as if from a distant dimension, Karma heard loud cries of pleasure erupt from her gaping mouth. The bucking of her body intensified until she was in the throes of a seizure. Never before had she reacted so violently with the release of a climax. Karma did not know what this big feeling was, but it eclipsed anything she had ever experienced sexually.

She eventually collapsed with the word *Rafe* still falling from her lips. She realized she had no idea how many times she had called his name and her eyes popped open to look at where he lay on his side, facing her.

It was too late to be embarrassed with him, but as the sounds of moans and shouts of pleasure, both male and female, filled the room, Karma realized the others had surely heard her.

But just as quickly, she knew no one worried about her mating as they were too preoccupied with their own.

"What thoughts are in your mind, little human?" Rafe asked after a prolonged silence.

"I don't know—so many things. There is so much of this world I don't understand—your world." Her words sounded ignorant even to her own ears. But Rafe didn't respond as if she was a lower life-form.

"I know the biology of humans, but there is much I don't understand of your kind, either."

156

Karma thought about that. "No one human is the same as another. I imagine it's the same for Galatians."

He nodded. "Why did you mate with me ahead of today's ceremony?"

Karma's face suddenly felt warm and she wanted to cover herself with her robe. But she knew it would just make her appear as guilty as she felt.

"I..." she began hesitantly. He waited. "I don't want to anger you, Rafe. But I don't want to lie to you either. Can we talk about this later, after...?" She glanced at the faint images of other platforms with their shadowy occupants in the throes of mating. But also, there were the queens. She could see their tall outlines observing from a distance. One of them would surely be the female leader, the one who had looked at her with accusation.

"We will speak after this ceremony," he confirmed resolutely.

Karma closed her eyes and whispered the truth. "I was afraid if I didn't have sex with you — mate with you — then you'd get rid of me when the authorities came after me. Or worse."

"You thought I'd beat you," he finished for her.

She nodded, body tensing as she waited for his explosion of anger.

She felt a slight touch on her chin and she opened her eyes and looked over at him.

"Let me see your eyes, consort."

He didn't sound angry. She met his eyes and he peered into hers so closely she could see the amber and green flecks within his.

"Are you reading my mind?" she whispered.

A yellow blush immediately colored his scales and he chuckled with amusement. "No. That's not within my power. But your eyes reveal much about you—how you feel and what you think."

She turned to face him. "Then what am I thinking?"

He gazed at her quietly. "That you wish to be something you'll never be."

His words stung like a slap in the face. Somewhere, in the deepest corners of her mind, thought had lain half buried, sprouting with life whenever she had to sacrifice a bit of herself to survive.

"Was it worth it, human?" he asked flatly.

She swallowed. "I mean…there wasn't much of a choice." Tears filled her eyes. "You live with this wealth—so many riches you don't even notice it. I eat scraps for breakfast each morning and I'm happy to get them!" Fat, hot tears fell from her eyes. "They say there's not enough resources in the world for the people that are left, but I see with my own eyes the rich take more than they need and the rest of us fight for the scraps, just so we can open our eyes for another day of hunger and abuse.

"Was it worth it?" she asked with a shake of her head. "It wasn't. Because poor, hungry, tired, and beat down, at least I still had my pride."

Karma grabbed her robe and pulled it closed and then turned onto her back, where she sniffed back her tears and stared up at the canopy above her. She wiped her nose and continued to sniff until her tears dried.

She felt something glide against her leg. When she glanced down, she saw it was Rafe's tail, gently grazing her skin from her ankles to her knees.

"Please don't do that," she said in a rush, afraid he would touch her intimately. She felt a jumble of emotions, but the least of them was desire to be touched by him.

His tail slipped back to the platform.

"Consort...Karma." She looked at him, surprised at the use of her given name. His expression softened. "You asked me what I saw when I looked into your eyes. I saw regret. That is what I saw. Despite whatever motivation brought you to this moment, I believe your actions were without malice."

She nodded quickly, unable to voice the gratitude she felt at his words. They weren't exactly the forgiveness she wished for, but it was more than she had expected.

His hands moved to her face and a finger touched one of the trails her tears had left.

"So many reasons for human tears," he said, as if to himself. "Sadness and joy, relief, pain, embarrassment. Tears are a reflection of human emotion—but it is a characteristic I do not like. I do not think I want to see these in your eyes again."

He spoke with so much seriousness that Karma could only raise her brow. "Rafe, I don't think that's something I will be able to agree to. Sometimes the more you try to control them, the faster they come."

"Then I won't tell you not to cry. But I hope you won't do it in my presence in the future."

She turned bodily toward him again. "Are you saying there might still be a future with me as your consort?"

"We are mated. It is done."

"Even if...if you hated me?" she hesitated.

"Yes. It is done. I don't hate you," he added quickly.

"Then..." Her heartbeat quickened in nervousness. "Why didn't you...?"

"What?" he asked while his brow lowered. His way of questioning, not his way of being angry.

She drew her lower lip into her mouth and bit slowly while she thought. Rafe cocked his head as he observed her.

"You didn't...cum." She blushed furiously, trying not to look at his erect penis that lay on the platform between them.

He grunted in acknowledgement. "I don't have to spill my seed in you to find pleasure with you."

"The consorts are losing their virginities tonight," she said matter-of-factly.

"I hear them," he said in amusement.

"You didn't want to...be inside of me?" She couldn't meet his eyes when she said those words.

"I will not."

She did look at him then, waiting for an explanation. When he didn't offer one, Karma came up with her own.

Until she revealed all of her secrets, he would not enter her. How could she blame him for that?

"I understand," she said. His only response was the blinking of his slitted eyes as he watched her. "Do you want me to...touch you?" she asked.

"You never have to ask me that question, for the answer will always be yes."

Karma smiled slightly and then reached down to stroke his mighty shaft. It was as rigid as metal, and so thick that if she closed her hand around him, her fingers wouldn't meet. His eyes slowly closed and she wondered how it was that he would bring her to pleasure without seeking it for himself.

"Rafe?"

"Hmmm?" He didn't open his eyes.

"How do you say...cum, in your native language?"

She knew he was amused because his tone changed to a yellow that was becoming familiar to her. He made a strange sound with his tongue.

"Was that it?" she asked.

"Yes." He sighed as her fingers rubbed the base of his prick.

"I'll never be able to say that in your language," she said wistfully.

Rafe's eyes opened. "No. But you will understand it. I will teach you to understand it."

His hand moved to slide easily between her thighs. He cupped her there for several teasing moments, and then his middle finger slid up and down repetitively, separating her folds.

Karma's touch grew bolder. She rubbed him, stroking his shaft, circling the head, prolonging his pleasure until he had completely stoked hers. And just when she felt as if she would fall off the edge of a cliff, Karma leaned down and quickly covered the head of Rafe's prick with her mouth. The sweet, salty taste of his precum flooded her mouth. The feel of his body as he finally lost hold on his control, now jerking against her, as well as the umami taste of his seed, caused her to suck hard for more of him to swallow.

The domino effect was immediate. His seed burst into her mouth like a volcanic eruption, causing her fists to pump his shaft harder and faster, which then caused his fingers to quicken the rubbing along her swelling nub until more of her juices pooled in his palm.

It circled through them, intensifying with each second until Rafe yelled out in his native tongue as he violently orgasmed into Karma's eager mouth. The sounds were repetitive, shouted over and over, and Karma soon realized she recognized one of those words. Cum; spoken in Galatian. He was telling her he was cumming.

Chapter Seventeen

"No! Please...I don't want to! LET ME GOOOO!"

Karma sat up quickly at the sound of the female's screams.

Rafe's tail went across her body in an instant, protectively. "Stay here!" he growled while leaping off the platform. He was joined by the other Galatian males.

Karma stayed put, but moved the curtains back so she could see what the commotion was about.

It was Jayne. Several queens had surrounded her and she was cowering in the corner. Her mate stood nearby, but didn't appear to be attempting to hurt her. What was she going on about?

Someone quickly climbed onto her platform. It was Madeline. She was pulling her robe on. A moment later, several other girls joined her.

"They're trying to send her back to the training compound," Madeline explained.

"Her mate rejected her," someone else said. She was nude, but covered her breasts with her robe.

Karma looked at them in surprise. "I didn't think a Galatian could reject his mate."

"Jayne messed herself up!" another woman said. "She really thought she'd get your mate from you."

Jayne was crying now. "No. Please, no! I don't want to go back..."

Karma flinched and closed her eyes, trying not to think about the many times she'd heard women crying like that from a back alley or abandoned building...

"They can't reject her once they mated, but she ruined that." A girl leaned forward and whispered, "Her master couldn't get...hard for her." The girl began to giggle. The others were talking over each other in excitement.

"I never heard of anything like this happening."

"It's never happened!"

"They keep saying how uncontrolled they are." The woman covered her smile with her hands. "But they are sexy."

"Oh, Guardian!" someone squealed. "It was sooo good!"

"Their tongues are so long!"

"Shut up, Aura!" They were giggling like children.

"It didn't even hurt. I stopped him before it went too far and he actually stopped."

Karma turned her attention back to Jayne, who was being pulled from the room by one of the queens who was trying to cajole her with soft words.

Karma frowned. These girls didn't care one bit about what was happening to their friend. She leapt up, securing her robe around her and then hurried to the hysterical girl.

"Jayne. Come here." She held out her hand and Jayne ran to her, clutching her like a toddler running to her mother. "It's okay. Nobody's going to hurt you."

Rafe nodded his head at the others to let them go. The queens stood down.

Karma was soon joined by the other consorts. "Come on. Let's get you out of here." She looked at Rafe to see if he'd stop her, but he didn't move. Karma led all the consorts to the door, still holding Jayne, who was just beginning to control her crying. She saw one of the

164

women reach out a hand to her Galatian mate. They touched fingertips and it surprised Karma at the show of intimacy.

Even if nothing else good happened this evening, this had been a good idea.

She led them to the elevator.

"I don't want to go back to the school," Jayne sobbed.

"We're just going back to my home for now," Karma replied.

Once in the elevator, the others comforted their friend and she was able to release her. She looked at the sniffling girl. Was the school so bad? At least they hadn't kicked her out onto the streets.

When they got to the penthouse, she let them in and led them to her bedroom. Dorf came out of his room and watched curiously before following them.

Jayne immediately climbed into Karma's bed and pulled the covers over her. The girls surrounded her, stroking her hair and speaking comforting words to her.

"This should have been my bed!" She began sobbing again.

Karma rolled her eyes, her sympathy for the girl evaporating. Some of the others seemed to think the same.

"Get over yourself!" someone snapped. "Karma's done nothing but help us!"

"Without her help, we wouldn't know how pleasurable it could be to lose our virginity!"

Jayne sat up slowly. "How many of you have mated?"

"Don't answer that," Madeline said with eyes that had gone wide. "What are you going to do? Kidnap one of us so you can seduce one of our masters? Is that what you have going on in your head?" Jayne looked away, her guilty expression giving away her intentions. "You'd do anything to get ahead. Leolo truly liked you, until you destroyed his ego—and you did it in front of the other Galatians *and* his bound-mate."

"I'm getting out of here." One of the girls headed to the door. "I can't believe I left Aki for you."

"But what's going to happen to me?" Jayne appealed to them.

"Jayne," Madeline said simply. "You're going to return to the compound and you're going to wait for the next lottery. I heard Leolo's queen say you'd get another opportunity—"

"Noooo!" Jayne wailed. She actually writhed on the bed in the throes of a tantrum.

"SHUT UP!" Karma finally shouted.

Jayne was so shocked, she closed her mouth and blinked at Karma in surprise.

"You're no different than a spoiled brat! After the way you acted, you're still going to get another chance. And that's a chance a lot of us can't even dream of!" Karma shook her head. "Get out. Get out of my bed. Get out of my house."

Jayne threw the bedding aside and jumped out of the bed. "Fine! I don't need you. I don't need any of you! I'll get Leolo back or I'll get someone better. But I'm not waiting for my number to come up in another lottery!"

Karma had never wanted to smack the hell out of a person more than she wanted to smack this girl. She had been charged with watching children that were three and four years old whose antics couldn't rival this grown woman's actions.

They followed her out of the room only to be met with the sight of Rafe and the other males. They were all dressed, looking very smart in their long skirts and dark harnesses. Dark boots could also be seen from beneath the skirts, and their tails swished about them anxiously.

The men were so quiet, none had heard them arrive, and Karma had no idea how long they had been out there—but more importantly, what they might have heard.

Jayne's demeanor changed the moment she saw them.

"Leolo!" She hurried to her master. "Please forgive my outburst. It was the stress!" She dropped to her knees in front of him. Leolo just stood frozen like a statue. He never even looked at her.

Rafe made a series of clicking sounds and then gestured with his head to the other consorts. His brothers moved forward to their respective mates. They hurried forward, checking their consorts, touching them, smelling them, and in one case, a male lifted his consort and cradled her in his arms.

Karma looked at Rafe, and even though he watched her, he didn't move forward.

Was he angry? She couldn't tell because his color hadn't changed, but he had to be. She'd orchestrated this walk-out instead of letting the queens handle it. *His* queen. Why did the others keep saying his queen?

"Take your consorts home," Rafe said. "We'll reconvene in the morning."

The women seemed relieved to be with their men, and if they even thought of Jayne, it didn't show. They giggled and snuggled against their mates, all hurrying to the door as if anxious to get back to what they had been doing before the interruption.

Jayne had come to her feet and was waiting for Leolo, holding onto his arm possessively. She was so fake. Karma realized her tears and shouts had also been manufactured.

Once the others were gone, Leolo looked down at Jayne.

"You are a consort no more." His voice was cool, chilly. "You'll be returned to your family home—"

"No!" Jayne yelled.

Leolo snatched his hand from her and then swiftly grabbed her by the neck. His movements were like a blur.

"You are a consort no more," he growled, and then lifted her from the ground by the neck. "Heed my words, human." She began to kick and gasp as her breath was cut short. "You have two choices. One; I break your neck within the next thirty seconds. Two; you'll return to your family home, at which point you will collect your lifetime of riches and live the rest of your days without want of any material item. You will be rich beyond your dreams—for having done nothing more than angering a Galatian!"

He dropped her. There was nothing but dislike in Leolo's demeanor. Jayne fell to the ground and rubbed her throat. Her expression was filled with something far from fear. It was filled with terror.

"Choose, human," Leolo said.

"I...I'll take the money." Her voice was a faint croak.

Chills ran up Karma's spine. She now saw what it looked like when a Galatian truly had no feelings for a person.

She looked at Rafe. For once, his attention was on something other than her. His tail, however, seemed to stay at attention.

"Karma." She jumped at the sound of Rafe's voice. "Get dressed; shoes and a coat. We're going to the city center." His eyes shifted to Jayne. "Find her something to wear. She won't be returning to her apartment."

Leolo turned and walked out of the room without another word.

They sat in the back of a limo, bundled in expensive wool coats. Champagne was a hand's reach away, and probably music she'd never before experienced. But Karma and Jayne sat quietly, neither daring to speak.

Rafe was in the front with the human driver. Even if they wanted to talk, there was no way to do it without Rafe's extraordinary hearing picking up their entire conversation.

But Karma had nothing to say, especially to Jayne. She could dislike her easily—but were they really all that different? They'd both done what was necessary to get ahead. She looked at the back of Rafe's head.

And they'd hurt others in the process.

Once in the city center, Rafe had military soldiers waiting to escort Jayne to whatever fate awaited her.

Jayne turned and looked at her once they were a few steps away. Tears were streaming down her face.

"I got everything I wanted, and I didn't have to fuck an animal to do it."

She began to cry again, but this time Karma thought her tears were real. Rafe began walking.

"Follow," he said simply.

She lightly bit her lip. His words weren't mean, but they still stung. She followed behind him, wondering if Jayne hadn't actually gotten the better deal.

Chapter Eighteen

Rafe stood watching Karma as she sat in front of the empty table. He'd cleared the room, even though the queens had insisted on being present.

He had politely advised that while the mating was their concern, this was not. They had backed down, for now.

He blew out a tired breath. "How many are involved in this conspiracy?"

She looked afraid, but didn't weep like the other. He wondered if she had been involved in some way.

"I don't know anything about a conspiracy."

He looked deeply into her eyes and believed her, but without Dorf, he couldn't be completely sure of her truthfulness.

"I want you to tell me about your involvement."

She nodded. "Of course." She folded her delicate hands across her lap. They trembled the smallest amount, but he was impressed by her bravery.

"Up until about a few days ago, I was one of the maids for Mr. and Mrs. Tolbert. One day after work, he made me an offer." She shook her head slightly. "I don't have many details. He didn't tell me much, just that one of the girls had gotten sick and because she was his responsibility, he needed to replace her." She swallowed. "I knew it sounded too good to be true." She inhaled and looked up at the ceiling. "But I also knew what it would mean to say no." She met his eyes again, but Rafe said nothing.

"I told him a person that looked like me could never be in the Exchange."

Rafe cocked his head. "Why is that?"

"You should know better than anyone," she replied. Her voice was even, but he could sense the change in her emotions.

"You can clearly see the consorts don't look like me."

"Yes. I have seen that."

"And you have seen they never have. Ever."

"And?"

Rafe saw her shoulders sink. "Mr. Tolbert assured me that once I went through the lottery, then I would be a consort, protected by the Galatians." He could see her jaw clench. "Only he left out a lot of details. I realized long ago he just needed me to take the focus off him for a while until he could get away."

Rafe opened and then closed his mouth. He wanted to go back to what she'd said about consorts not looking like her.

There was a lottery, and everyone that chose to participate got an opportunity to enter. Many hated the idea of being, what they called, a concubine to an alien. Others could not afford the price of the entry. And still others had no issues with the idea of alien consorts but had no desire to offer their children into servitude.

The fact that all consorts from all over Earth's provinces always had white skin, blond hair, and blue eyes mattered not to the Galatians. The human males in charge just assured them they were only getting the most beautiful humans.

172

But a human's idea of beauty meant nothing to a Galatian. Nothing was as beautiful as the queen of their species.

But she'd said he'd used her as a distraction so he could get away, and that's what he needed to focus on.

"Where did he go?"

"I don't know. He wouldn't tell me information."

"What about the one you replaced? Mayva. Do you think harm truly came to her like Tolbert said?"

She shook her head. "I really don't know. What I told you is everything I know. I'm nothing but a maid—well, I was a maid, and now I'm a pawn."

Rafe crossed his arms in front of him. "Is there anything else you have to tell me?"

"There is nothing else."

His eyes scanned her. His anger hadn't disappeared, but none of it was directed at her. She had been placed in a situation beyond her control.

"Karma," he said. "None of the blame falls on you. You didn't orchestrate this. This falls on the shoulders of Tolbert—and whoever else might have assisted him. That's the job I've been sent here to discover."

"Rafe…"

"Yes?"

"I told you I wouldn't lie to you, and I won't." She intertwined her fingers. Nervous.

"When Mr. Tolbert told me about becoming a consort and getting all the riches I could ever dream about at the end of seven years, it wasn't an offer I could refuse.

"People like me don't say no. We don't turn down our employers and we don't make waves. Because when you have nothing, it's easy to make you disappear."

"Are you saying you feared Tolbert would murder you if you didn't agree to his idea?"

"I'm saying Mr. Tolbert and others like him are powerful enough to get other people to get their hands dirty." She swallowed. "But I'm also saying I didn't have to go through with it. There was another way. I could have run, disappeared, and he would have never been able to track me down."

Rafe nodded in understanding, but waited for her to continue.

"I wanted to go through with it...even though I knew it was fraud. I just wanted a chance, even though it was a long shot. Deep down, I knew I might not get away with it." She looked at her fingers. "And I'm sorry."

He sat behind the desk. "Remember when I told you it was done?" She nodded. "You are my consort. But things are happening that have never happened before. And that means change." He stroked his hand over his lips. "I'm going to be honest with you, Karma. I don't know if Mayva was in on this plan along with Tolbert, but I need to find them."

"What happens when you do?"

"Tolbert will be dealt with by Galatian-human law. But I'm bringing Mayva back."

"What does mean?" she whispered.

"I have no answer for that."

The ride back home was quiet, even though this time Rafe sat in the back with her. She looked at the champagne and felt her mouth water. She was thirsty

174

and hungry, but knew she shouldn't have any booze on an empty stomach. This wasn't the hungriest she'd ever been by far. She'd once gone three days without food — back when her parents had first been taken from her...

She looked out the window.

"Are you tired?" Rafe asked.

She turned to him. "A little."

"We'll be home shortly. You should rest. I won't be able to join you. Too much time has gone by since Tolbert and Mayva disappeared and I need to find their trail."

"Yes." She looked out the window again just as her stomach began to growl and she squirmed in embarrassment.

"Karma. Have you starved yourself again?" he growled.

Today had been a long one, with too much anger that had gone unacknowledged. She felt anger swell up until it overflowed.

"When did I have time to feed myself, Rafe? After you stormed into the apartment demanding to know answers? During the ceremony while we were mating? Or while I stupidly helped a woman that clearly didn't need my help because she's being rewarded for being a privileged bitch?! In case you haven't figured it out, I don't hold any of the power in this situation."

Rafe's brow moved up and his color quickly became tinted with red. Red like danger? But she'd said what she'd said and she wouldn't take it back. She stiffened her back and waited for what would come next.

He chuckled softly. She'd just lost her shit, and he was no more intimidated than if she was a yapping puppy!

"I think you're wrong, little human. You hold more power than you realize."

They were in the kitchen, and once again the mysterious food was there on the counter; Galatian food for him, human food for her. All set up neatly in metal trays.

Today she didn't even try to be dainty. She ate potatoes with gravy and chicken, roasted pork, and sauteed vegetables. There was plenty of Rafe's kind of food, and some of it intrigued her, but for now she was just concerned with filling the emptiness within her belly.

Rafe just sat and drank something that looked like tea but smelled like warm swamp water. He did watch her, but right now, she didn't care. She had eaten half of her meal before she cared.

"Aren't you going to eat something?" she asked while using her fork to move her chicken around on her plate.

"I ate earlier, while I was out. Why didn't you eat while I was out?"

"I-I wanted to wait until you got home...so that...we could eat together." She whispered the last in embarrassment.

"Why?" Rafe asked in confusion. "We don't eat the same food. Besides, humans don't like the way we eat." He raised his hand and studied his fingers. "We have built-in spoons, knives, and forks." He spread his fingers, showcasing the webbing between them; built-in spoons.

She knew his talons were sharp enough to pierce and gut the scariest aliens. It was true he wouldn't need utensils to eat with, or possibly even weapons to kill with.

But as dangerous as those hands were, she knew they also had the capacity for gentleness.

"You didn't answer me," Rafe persisted.

"You want to know why I waited to eat with you?"

"Yes."

"Because...that's what families do." His head cocked as if he didn't know what she was talking about. "You do know what families are, don't you?"

"Families are for children," he replied.

"Well, that's silly."

"Why would I need a family when my purpose is to guard? Everyone has a job."

"You have a mother. You're her child."

"Yes. And I have a brother. But we don't eat together."

She speared another piece of chicken and placed it into her mouth. "You have a brother. Your parents had two children?" She had heard most Galatians never gave birth. It was the reason they'd gone to worlds that had a similar atmosphere to Galatia and had left their DNA in the hopes of recreating themselves. It was amazing a couple had managed two children.

"Different fathers," he replied while eyeing her plate of food. "Once two Galatians are proven fertile, many times, they go about sharing their gifts with others."

Karma frowned. "You mean they sleep with others?"

He got up and retrieved a plate. "Yes." He filled it with some of his food. If he touched some sauce, he licked his fingers, sending a little quiver shooting through her. "Procreation is a responsibility." He sat down with his plate.

"You're very smart—more advanced than us. Plus, you create new species. Why can't you fix your infertility?"

"Our queens are the infertile ones. Do you want us to wipe out our queens and remake them?"

"No!"

He chuckled at her response. The technology and science behind this went beyond all but the greatest minds on Earth. But to him, it was quite simple. He desired to change the subject. "It cannot be fixed." He scooped up something slimy and green with his first three fingers and then licked them clean with his tongue.

Karma stared, mouth going dry. "Uhm." She blinked and turned her attention from his fingers and tongue to his eyes. "What is meant by bound-mate?"

"A bound-mate is the queen I will be mated to for life."

"Oh. For life?"

He plucked a humongous, snail-like substance from his plate and slipped it into his mouth while it still squirmed.

Karma didn't care about the living snail he'd just devoured. *For life.*

The one that had stared at her with so much animosity.

"So, you're already bound?"

"Yes. Since we were children."

Karma sipped her drink, her arms crossing in front of her afterwards. "And they—your queens—don't mind sharing their men?"

He gave her a curious look. "The ceremony is her offering me to you."

"What?"

"So you can take her place while we're on Earth. Are you truly telling me you never familiarized yourself with any of this?"

"No. I had no time in the two days he gave me once he hijacked my life! I spent two days being plucked, scraped, scrubbed, and practically cleansed from the inside out! They took hot wax and peeled off my hair!"

Rafe's mouth parted. "I had no idea. But you didn't have the surgery. You would not have had time to heal if it was just two days."

"No. They didn't do that to me."

He tapped a nail on the table. His expression had suddenly gone serious. "Should anyone else ask you about it, you will keep this information to yourself."

Karma looked at him in confusion. "Okay. Why?"

He pushed his plate away from himself. "The queens don't have very many rules, but this is one of them. I'll make the arrangements for the surgery. Utilize Dorf to assist you with what you need to learn." He stood and headed out the door before pausing, but still not looking at her. "I don't know when you'll see me next. I need to locate Tolbert and Mayva."

"Okay..." she replied. For whatever reason, she couldn't stop looking at his tail, which was poised upward. It was as if the tip of his tail was the face he refused to show her.

And then Rafe and his tail left the room.

Chapter Nineteen

Karma didn't know how she had managed to come out on top after everything Tolbert had put her through. After Rafe left, she sat back in her chair and realized for the first time she had actually prevailed.

It meant that for now, this was her home; a real home with heat, food, and a bed that wasn't infested with Guardian knew what. There would be no more sleeping in a fleabag motel with three roommates who might or might not steal from her. There was unlimited food, and as much music as one person could listen to.

Then why wasn't she jumping up and down?

Karma came to her feet and began to wrap up the leftovers and then quickly washed the dishes. She moved to the front room, looking towards Rafe's den, remembering the way he swam as if he was more at home in the water than on land. She didn't know how to swim, but she liked the cavern effect of his den. Maybe one day he'd invite her to swim with him again.

She picked up the phone and called the front desk.

"Hello, Mrs. Sigur."

"Hello. Can you have someone come up and take the leftovers out to the news crew?" She'd seen them still hanging out there, waiting for sight of her—or maybe just anyone from the Galatian Exchange.

"I'd be happy to do that, ma'am. But the journalists didn't want the...um...human food. Only the Galatian selections."

Karma sighed. Ungrateful. "You know what? Forget the news people. Please find a way to get these leftovers to the folks at the train station."

"Uh, yes, ma'am! Even the um…Galatian selections?"

"Even the Galatian selections. I'm sure you don't know this, but when you're starving to death, all food is worthy food."

"Yes, ma'am."

"Thank you." Karma hung up and then returned to the kitchen. She uncovered the dish of squirming, giant snails that looked as if they were in a mud sauce.

She picked one up and it was fat and disgusting. She thought back to that time when she'd gone three days without food. Could she have eaten this? The answer was hell yes.

Karma dropped the slug back into its sauce. Eating living alien snails was not something she would need to do now. She washed her hands and returned to the living room.

Dorf had somehow managed to climb up to the top of a bookshelf and was watching her quietly. She hesitated and waved hello at him. He lifted a paw as if mimicking her motion.

She went to the music player and spent several hours doing nothing but what made her happy; listening to as many songs as interested her.

Later that night, she went to her large bathroom and filled her tub with enough water to swim in. Dorf even snuck in without her knowing until she'd been soaking in the steamy water (which never cooled) for so long she heard him snore as he dropped off to sleep.

When she went to her oversized bedroom wrapped in a large, terrycloth robe, Dorf stretched and followed her.

"Dorf," she said with a grimace. "May I have a bit of privacy?"

Dorf stared at her.

She sighed. "Please."

He made a huffing sound, but turned and left the room.

She'd have to talk to him about lurking. She knew he had come into the room and was watching when she'd brought the consorts back to her bedroom earlier.

She wasn't sure if he spied on her for Rafe—but there was no need for him to do that. She had nothing more to hide from Rafe or anyone else.

She put on a nightgown and got ready for bed, not forgetting the satin bonnet she'd insisted the ladies purchase for her when they'd gotten her hair care products.

She was exhausted, but reached for the remote control and turned on the television set. She didn't have to be afraid about what they said. There was nothing *they* could do to her.

She watched fifteen minutes of national news before it came back to her.

"There is still no new information on the newest consort of the Galatian Exchange. No one has been able to identify the brown-skinned beauty that has taken so much of the nation's attention.

"Faheem Abbar Nabih denies she is among his many offspring. There is still no word from the Galatian Exchange, which has declined all interview requests.

"Whoever she is, she is quickly becoming favored by the news crews. Yesterday, a meal was provided to those

182

that have been camped outside of The Washington at Newburgh Circle complex; home of the Galatians and their new consorts. It is said to be compliments of the newest consort."

Karma sat up in bed. She had no idea they would know she'd done it.

The news cut away to a man with a French accent. Pierre Lavigne, two-time Michelin star chef, appeared below his image.

"It is extremely rare to see authentic Galatian meals. Oh, we can sometimes recreate their dishes, but the food at The Washington hotel would be authentic; they came from another planet! You understand this means a Galatian meal wouldn't cost a thousand dollars for a plate, but a million! I myself would have gladly given away one of my Michelin stars for one of those meals."

The newscasters returned, chuckling. *"If only we were so lucky to get even a glimpse of Galatian food, let alone a taste."*

They moved on to another topic, and Karma turned off the television. Rafe was probably going to be mad. Why couldn't she just stop worrying about others and mind her own business?

Rafe's driver stopped the car at the large house. It was nice. So, this is where Karma had worked as a servant before becoming his consort.

He stepped out of the car along with one of the human military personnel that had been detailed to him. It was good the man had come along. Sometimes humans became overwhelmed at the sight of a Galatian—especially if it was their first time in the company of an alien.

They walked to the door and the human rang the bell.

A woman wearing a gray uniform answered. She had brown skin, but not as brown as Karma's. She nodded in the direction of Rafe but wouldn't meet his eyes.

"Please come inside. The missus is expecting you."

Rafe liked that she realized he was the one in charge and not the human soldier. They stepped inside and were led to a room filled with books. The library. The books appeared more decorative than useful. Rafe looked around. The room was furnished in the manner humans found pleasing, with textured walls, bright fabrics, and an overabundance of baubles.

Mrs. Tolbert didn't leave them waiting for long. She wore an expensive wool suit jacket and skirt. Her short-cropped hair was perfectly coiffed in a halo of platinum curls that framed a face that had aged gracefully. She was a beautiful woman that had probably once been considered stunning.

She hesitated a moment at the sight of the seven-foot-tall lizard man wearing the pleated leather skirt, harness, and short sword at his side. She then straightened her back and marched straight to him. Ignoring the human military escort, she held her hand out to Rafe before quickly lowering it, as if she remembered *what* he was.

"Mr. Sigur—"

"Lieutenant," he corrected.

"Uh...of course. Lieutenant. Would you like to have a seat, a refreshment?"

Rafe glanced at the chairs with no space for a tail. "No. Thank you. I appreciate your time today. I won't keep you. I'd like to ask a few questions about your husband, and then I'll be on my way."

"It's me that should be thanking you. A famous Galatian Guard such as yourself should have no problem locating Heinrich."

"You know who I am?"

"Who wouldn't? You're a celebrity. You located those alien pirates that have been selling our human men."

"I didn't work alone."

"Yes, but you were the head of the team."

He found his notoriety to be annoying. Having a reputation was good in battle, but not so good when news cameras and microphones were shoved in his face.

"Can you tell me the last time you saw your husband?"

"That's hard to say..." She hesitated. "You have to understand, Heinrich leads a very busy life. Whenever there's a North American Exchange, he's constantly in the office dealing with one fire after another and I rarely see him. No disrespect intended, but the Galatian Exchange is a disaster."

"How so?"

Mrs. Tolbert rolled her eyes. "The girls are completely inept." She shook her head. "I mean, it's understandable, considering their lack of moral judgement. They're taken from their homes and sent to live in that...that...consort school. I'm going to be completely honest. I don't agree with the lottery. I think it's heinous."

"Are you a rebel?" Rafe asked.

She looked shocked and clutched her chest. "Oh, my goodness, no. I'd never!"

"Then I have no issues with your opinions," Rafe said. "But you say the Galatian Exchange is a disaster?"

"It is. Heinrich has to constantly go into the office for every little hiccup. And you can't trust any of the staff to know how to handle anything. It's almost like Heinrich is running the entire thing all by himself!

"So, to answer your question, I rarely get a chance to talk to him, let alone see him. Probably the last time was the day before the Exchange." She crossed her arms in front of her.

"What do you think happened to your husband, Mrs. Tolbert?"

She shook her head and looked distressed. "I can only imagine he came across something he should not have. I don't have to tell you, the lottery generates a great deal of money. I think my dear Heinrich saw something he shouldn't have…"

Mrs. Tolbert retrieved a handkerchief from the sleeve of her jacket and then dabbed at the corners of her eyes.

"Are you okay, ma'am?" Rafe asked.

"Yes. I'm just so worried."

"I understand. Just a few more questions and we'll be on our way." Mrs. Tolbert nodded. "Do you have any idea where your husband might go?"

She blinked in confusion. "Heinrich would never leave us. He pursued me for years. You see, I was a beauty queen—local, but I could have gone national. Heinrich loves me—and of course, the children."

"But if he had to go into hiding—maybe because he was in the wrong place at the wrong time, where do you think he might go?"

She nodded. "No place obvious. He would avoid our vacation homes, and I doubt if he would approach any of our friends. I just don't know, Lieutenant."

"Did your husband vacation or have to travel out of town within the last year?"

"Of course. His job takes him all over, due to the lottery. We always vacation together as a family, though, and always the same places."

"May I see a picture of your husband?"

"Of course." She hurried out of the room and returned a moment later with a framed photo of Heinrich, along with her and two children. Rafe retrieved a mobile phone and took several snapshots of the photo.

"Thank you, ma'am. One last thing. I understand you had a maid that also recently disappeared."

"Yes. She stole my pearls!"

Rafe's tail came to attention. "When was the last time you saw her?"

"Well, it was before my husband disappeared. You're not suggesting Heinrich had something nefarious going on with the maid, are you? Because he would have no interest in someone like her."

"Why is that?"

She looked at him as if he was crazy. Rafe decided it was probably the most genuine expression she'd worn during the entire interview.

"She's the help—and frankly, not much to look at."

"What's her name?" Rafe asked.

"I don't remember. I put it in the police report. Why are you asking about her? Girls like that come and go. I wouldn't have even reported her missing if it wasn't for my pearls!"

"I see. I appreciate your time, Mrs. Tolbert. If you think of anything, please call the Exchange and ask for me."

"Thank you, Lieutenant. Please find my husband."

"Oh, I will." Rafe nodded and turned before pausing. "By the way, how are your financial needs being met in the absence of your husband? Forgive me for my bold question, but as I'm now in charge of the North American Galatian Exchange, I'd like to see that your family is taken care of."

Mrs. Tolbert exhaled a relieved breath. "Thank you, Lieutenant Sigur. I've already been in contact with the Exchange for that very reason but I've gotten nowhere. No one is answering questions and frankly, I've been treated like a criminal, as if I'm the one—I just mean, Heinrich was the sole provider for me and my children. And with him gone…"

"Yes," Rafe cut to the chase. "Has Mr. Tolbert taken any funds from your bank account?"

Mrs. Tolbert looked away. "Every red cent. I don't know how we're going to manage. He didn't even leave enough money for the children's school fees. The academy won't keep them if they're even one day late."

"I'll make a call and have funds wired to you immediately. You will be set up with a new bank account—for your safety. The Exchange will continue to support you and your family, Mrs. Tolbert."

Mrs. Tolbert was so happy she reached out and gripped Rafe's arm before she seemed to remember his arm was covered in sleek scales and not skin. She quickly drew back.

"Thank you so very much, Lieutenant! You can't imagine how worrisome this has all been!"

"No. I'm sure I can't. However, we at the Galatian Exchange take care of our own. But...in order to preserve the nation's trust in the lottery, we would need to handle any bad press before it's raised. Do you understand, Mrs. Tolbert?"

She nodded slowly. "I do. Of course, I would never theorize about any possible mis-dealings within the Exchange."

"Thank you. As the Galatians are now in charge of the investigation on your husband's disappearance, you can contact your police services and withdraw your request for their help."

"Of course," she readily agreed.

"Also, you should withdraw the complaint against your missing maid. It would only bring unwanted attention."

"Of course. I'll do it immediately."

Rafe nodded once and left the room.

"Oh, Lieutenant," Mrs. Tolbert called after him before he reached the front door.

Rafe stopped and turned his head slightly but didn't look at her. "Yes, Mrs. Tolbert?"

"To preserve the uh...sanctity of the lottery, what should I tell friends and family about Heinrich's disappearance?"

"Tell them he ran off with his mistress."

Rafe and his escort continued out the door. Once back in the car, the man turned to him. "Lieutenant, you should have seen the look on Mrs. Tolbert's face after that parting shot. She knows more than she's letting on."

"Oh, I saw it." Rafe's tail remained motionless at his side.

Chapter Twenty

The bedroom door opened and Karma woke up without moving, feigning sleep.

It was Rafe. He moved quietly in the darkness and stood by the four-poster bed for a moment before going into the bathroom. He was only gone for a few moments and when he returned, he climbed into bed beside Karma. He sighed tiredly and she listened to his even breathing.

"Do you still have Mrs. Tolbert's pearls? Or did you pawn them?"

Her head snapped around to look at him. "What?"

"She filed a police report you disappeared with her pearls."

Karma shot up in bed.

"I never stole from her! At least not her damn jewelry!"

"And what did you steal?"

"Food—I ate while I was on the premises. That's it!"

Rafe turned his back to her, his tail moving up between the two of them as if standing as a sentry.

"I took care of it. The warrant will be dropped. But if you have those pearls, I'd like you to return them to her."

"I told you I don't have her pearls!"

"No," he said coolly, "You said you were no thief, not you didn't have her pearls."

She stared at his nude back, hurt he'd think so little of her. "I'm not a thief, Rafe, and I never took Mrs. Tolbert's pearls."

He finally turned. "I believe you. Mrs. Tolbert lied about many things, but she wasn't lying about her missing pearls."

"How do you know what she's lying about?"

"Humans are easy to read. It's not foolproof, but I hear the changes in your heartbeat, in your breathing, and even subtle scent changes. It helps me spot the lies—even when someone is pretending to be sleeping."

"I wasn't...fine," Karma said weakly. "I just wanted to see what you were going to do."

"You can just ask." When she didn't respond, he continued. "You think I don't trust you. But you don't trust me. Sleep, Karma. Or think about those words. In either case, I am going to sleep now."

Rafe turned his back to her again.

She did think about his words, and sleep took a long time to return. When she finally began to drift off, she thought she felt his tail resting against her belly.

The next morning when Karma woke up, Rafe was gone, but she wasn't alone. Dorf was reclining at her feet, staring across the bed at her.

"Jesus!" she yelped in surprise.

Dorf stood and stretched with long, sinewy movements and then sauntered over to her. He sought her hand and bit it.

"So...you think I'm a pervert?" Dorf's thoughts came to her.

"What?!" Karma sat up, careful not to remove her hand from his mouth lest she injure herself. "Why do you say that?"

"You bid me leave your room when you thought I'd see you nude."

"Oh, that." She relaxed some. "It's nothing personal, Dorf. I'm not used to being naked around others of the opposite sex. You are a he, am I right?"

"I am no more interested in seeing your skin bags than you are of looking upon an unclothed bird or cat. Do you find birds and cats sexually appealing?"

"No." She sighed. "I'm sorry for offending you. But how do you know that you seeing me nude wouldn't offend me? We don't know each other, Dorf, and that's not something to be mad about."

He huffed, still gripping her hand. "You are right, human—"

"Karma. Stop calling me human. You make it sound like an insult."

"It isn't. And it's not your fault you are ignorant. I will remember you missed your essential training. And I will remember to use your true name. Karma."

"Thank you. Did Rafe return to his den?"

"No, he told me to tell you he will be working. He also said not to wait to eat like a family, for he will be out for the rest of the day."

"Oh." She looked at Dorf for a few moments, thinking this was truly the strangest sight she ever thought she'd see; a one-way conversation with an alien creature that had his teeth sunk into her hand. "Is this the only way you communicate?"

Dorf released his grip on her hand. He began to speak rapidly, but it was in a strange language. He bit her hand again.

"I am only able to truly speak in languages I have learned to speak, and I'm not very fluent in many human ones. When we speak mentally, you understand me in your manner of speaking and I understand you in

193

my manner of speaking—it transcends actual words. My language is melodic. It's why I sing.

"The song I sang for you is the only language I have mastered; Icelandic. Iceland is where Rafe and I became acquainted."

"Rafe speaks Icelandic?"

"Rafe speaks more languages than I can count. But we communicate best without words. Words are not natural to either of us—sounds, inflections, tones, vibrations—that is our language. Does that make sense?"

She nodded. "It does. It sounds like a beautiful way to speak."

"Your words are beautiful too, but limiting. It is why I sang the song using human words."

He suddenly released her hand and then jumped off the bed. She saw him slip out of the room a moment later.

She felt as if he was sad and that made her feel bad. She didn't ever want to do anything to make someone else feel bad.

She got out of bed and got dressed for the day. She wasn't sure what the day would hold, so she wasn't sure how to dress. As far as she knew, there would be no more ceremonies, and since Rafe wasn't due back until tonight, she didn't have to dress to be pleasing to him.

Her wardrobe was not nearly as large as her rich employers' but she had more clothes and shoes than she'd ever owned in her life. She decided on gray slacks and a soft-gray cashmere sweater. She had several pairs of heels, but bypassed them for soft, suede slippers.

She liked the looks of her short Afro and didn't have to do much to it. Next, she examined her jewels. There were several pretty pieces, but much of it was too flamboyant. She did search for Mrs. Tolbert's pearls, just in case Mr. Tolbert accidentally slipped them into her trunk…

No…he wouldn't accidentally slip them to her. If he slipped them to her, it would be with a purpose—like to get her out of the way if she had decided to decline his proposal. The best way to get a person like her—with nothing or no one to stand up for them—wasn't to murder them. No; that was too messy. It would be to discredit her and send her to prison.

Karma cursed under her breath and then pushed past all of her new clothes in her closet until she got to her old woolen coat. She quickly dug through the pockets and immediately, her fingers came into contact with the smooth, cool jewels.

She held them in her hands, examining them. "Mr. Tolbert, you dirty dog…" she whispered.

She left her room with the necklace and marched straight into Rafe's den. Once she entered, she went directly to his closet. She placed the necklace with his weapons, looping them across the handle of one of his swords.

By the time Karma had breakfast, Dorf still hadn't emerged from his hidey-hole. If he didn't come out soon, she'd ring him and apologize again—for whatever she had done this time. It had to do with the music, more specifically, his singing. She didn't understand, but it seemed as if she needed him more than he needed her.

This time when she went into the kitchen, her meal was not waiting for her—and neither was Rafe's. The kitchen was state-of-the-art, so there was a vendor that shot out all kinds of food. But the refrigerator and pantry were filled with everything she could imagine wanting to eat, and she could actually see those items. So, she indulged, making herself scrambled eggs, bacon, sausage, and had a scone and Danish.

She ate every bit of it, and became curious about what had happened when the news people stationed in front of the hotel didn't get the million-dollar-a-plate leftovers that they thought they were entitled to.

She went into the living room and perched on the sofa and then turned on the large-screen television.

She didn't even have to wait. The very first image was of a crowd of people at the train station.

She leaned forward, frowning. She didn't understand what she was seeing. It was almost like a mob! People were struggling, shouting, nearly coming to blows, and it wasn't just the normal guards trying to keep order, but the Military Police was out!

She suddenly realized that the people in the mob were dressed too nice to be the homeless one usually saw in the depot. They were rich men and women dressed in furs and acting insane, grabbing for boxes.

Oh my Guardian! It was the leftovers she'd had boxed up for the homeless. The rich people of the city had come in droves for the leftover food! They were snatching it from the hands of the homeless, beating at them even!

"This was the scene yesterday evening when a shipment of leftovers from The Washington hotel was distributed to the homeless at the Cross Town Train

Depot. Hundreds of people showed up vying for the Galatian meals, which are estimated to be worth thousands, if not millions, of dollars."

The shot moved from the near-riot to various chefs who proclaimed the value of the Galatian meals.

"Seventeen people suffered non-life-threatening injuries—all were squatters or homeless. In other news..."

Karma jumped to her feet. "NO!" she screamed. "They take everything! They didn't even want the damn food!"

Dorf came hurrying out of his home, for once not moving in slow, lazy movements.

"What?!" he yelled in heavily accented English.

Karma ignored him and picked up the telephone and dialed the front desk. "I want every bit of leftover human food you have, and I want it packed up and ready to go in fifteen minutes!"

"But, Mrs. Sigur, the Military Police have given us strict rules not to deliver any more food to the train station. In fact, we are under orders not to distribute any leftovers outside of this hotel."

"So, are you telling me you're just going to throw the food away?"

"Yes, ma'am—"

"That's bullshit! You're not going to throw away all of that food when there are people starving right here in this city!"

"Uh...our orders—"

"Who is giving you these orders?"

"Management."

"Doesn't management work for the Galatians?"

"Uh...yes, ma'am."

"Who is the superior Galatian in this facility?"

"Lieutenant Sigur, ma'am—Mrs. Sigur."

"Hmmm...Mrs. Sigur." Karma tapped her foot angrily. "And you're telling me you can't do what I ask?"

"No, not at all. My apologies, Mrs. Sigur. We will have the human food boxed up and ready to be delivered—"

"I'm coming with you!"

"But, that's not possible. Lieutenant Sigur is not present, and you must always be escorted."

"I've seen all the Military Police stationed in this place. Assign me however many Military Police you want, but I won't take no for an answer. Do we understand each other?"

"Yes, Mrs. Sigur."

"Good." She hung up the phone and felt a bite on her ankle. "Ow!"

Dorf began speaking so rapidly she could barely keep track. "Are you insane, human? You cannot go out without Rafe. It's unheard of! He would never allow this! The dangers that await a consort are unthinkable! You could be kidnapped, held hostage—"

"Dorf! I used to be one of those starving people. This time last week that could have been me kicked and punched for a damn box filled with leftovers!"

"But you don't understand the danger—"

"It's you that doesn't understand. You live this cushy existence in a high-rise apartment where every one of your needs are met before you even know you need something! You have no idea what it means to have nothing or nobody! You have no idea what it is to go without!"

Dorf released her ankle and looked up at her.

"If you go, I go." He spoke in his strangely accented English.

Chapter Twenty-one

~Galatia~
The Queen's Council

Ragna had never bowed down to anyone; not her mother, her father, and not to the great Rafe Sigur. He was the only one she hadn't ever been able to quite wrap around her finger, but she knew when the time was right, he would be just where she wanted him.

It was Queen Amalia she was concerned with. No one got to the status of Most-Exalted without some form of trickery. No power was ever gained by kindness and honesty—although that is what the masses would like to believe when it came to their rulers.

She marched into the council chambers followed by the six queens whose bound-mates had completed the North American Exchange.

It was worse than she had thought. All fifteen thrones were occupied. These fifteen females represented one of the most powerful entities in the known universe; The Galatian Queens Council.

The thrones were heavy stone boulders whose seats had been made smoothed and concave to accommodate a seated Galatian as well as their tail. Each throne was positioned on a platform that overlooked the large council cavern. Of course, Queen Amalia's throne was at the forefront.

"Come forward," she said. "All of you."

Ragna and the others came forward, stopping once they reached the platform, and then bowed low.

"Explain this report we hear about the North American mating ceremony," Queen Juana demanded.

Amalia gave her sister council member a brief look and Juana knew it was her one and only warning to back down. She could easily be replaced—not by vote, of course, but due to an untimely death—poisoning being the most popular method of replacing someone that had raised the Most-Exalted Queen's ire.

"Queen Ragna, are you reporting that you could not verify that intercourse took place?" Amalia continued.

Ragna and the others rose. "Queen Amalia, none of my sister queens were able to verify the completion of intercourse."

"What!" Amalia roared, coming to her feet. "How is this possible?"

A wave of fear fell over Ragna. "In the report—"

"Don't speak to me about reports, girl! What happened?"

"Lieutenant Rafe Sigur's consort interrupted the ceremony to show her sisters how to…seek pleasure from the act."

The other members of the Queen's Council looked at each other in confusion, low whispers being exchanged.

"Pleasure?" Amalia said, but to herself. "Who thinks of pleasure when getting their insides ripped in two? It's why we produced the Twilight Elixir for their comfort."

"There is no doubt the humans have long been curious about the act of mating with our kind," another member of the council spoke.

"But they should have been taught the act is dangerous and potentially deadly—"

"Which is factual," someone else interjected. "We've covered countless deaths of consorts — at great financial cost to our treasury."

"Financial liability is the least of our concerns," Amalia stated firmly. "What happens if the human population loses their trust in our endeavors? Our control is just an illusion."

Ragna bowed. "There is another thing. Rafe Sigur admitted he had mated with his consort prior to the ceremony."

Amalia appeared confused. "And she was able to speak of pleasure to her sister consorts? That's impossible! Not even the surgical procedure can make the loss of their virginity pleasurable."

Another bound queen stepped forward. "Most Exalted and Queen's Council members. I witnessed my bound-one mating with his consort. They faced each other —"

"What?" others called out in alarm.

"But the consort used her hands to control his...entrance into her. When it became too painful for her, she stopped him and he complied."

There was much murmuring among the council queens.

"Then the mating was not completed," someone decreed.

Amalia had remained silent, but she finally spoke. "It is a mating if the males deposited their seed." She eyed the Queen that had recently spoken. "Did he?"

"He did. Twice."

Queen Amalia's skin began to tint purple. "Who of you witnessed your bound-mates complete the copulation with deposit of their seed?"

Only two stepped forward.

"Useless!" Amalia shouted as she sat down again. "If the males did not embed every inch of their pricks into those human whores, then we cannot assure the surgery was successful! And I don't have to tell you what that would mean for you and the rest of us Galatian females. We will no longer be necessary! You will fix this!"

Ragna bowed. "Respectfully, we cannot decree the males embed their consorts…with every inch of their pricks."

Amalia stood slowly and stepped down from the platform.

She approached Ragna, who stood her ground, although it took every bit of her courage.

"Ragna," Queen Amalia said. "You are the bound-mate to Lieutenant Sigur. In time, you will sit on the Queen's Council—you might even become Most Exalted." Ragna didn't look at her queen and did not respond. "You stand to lose a great deal should we lose control of our hold of these matings."

Ragna's tail stayed poised at attention, raised to eye level—ready to strike if necessary.

Queen Amalia looked amused but turned her back and returned to her throne. "If your bound-one mated with his consort before your arrival, you didn't get an opportunity to pleasure him—and for him to pleasure you."

"None of us were able to complete the act," Ragna replied defensively.

"Since you've lost your control on your bound-mates, and as you say," she glared at Ragna, "you cannot force them to embed their pricks into their consorts, I suggest you confirm their surgery was successful."

"Yes, Queen."

"I want all of the issues with the North American Lottery cleared up immediately. Find out how the brown one infiltrated the Exchange. Determine who her allies are. Also, maintain contact with the one that was displaced. She may cause problems. Make sure she understands her future wealth can only be guaranteed if she remains in our good graces."

"She's a difficult one." A queen stepped forward and spoke. "However, Lieutenant Sanchez—my bound-mate—wishes to be removed from the Exchange. He has lost his taste for human females."

"I don't blame him," a council queen said. "The hair and the skin is incredibly disturbing." She sighed. "But males will put their pricks into anything."

"Don't forget, these laws were the ideas of the queens," Amalia said. "We may not like it, but our predecessors realized generations ago that if we didn't control our men's pricks, then we would lose our hold on our race." She turned to the younger queen. "Are you ready for the final mating with Lieutenant Sanchez, or do you want him returned for another opportunity in the Exchange?"

"I wish for him to be returned to me," the queen spoke hopefully.

"Then it is done. But you may be sorry for what you request. Our males are bores, and you will have to relinquish your current interests to serve him. But if you are sure, then it is decreed." She waved her hand dismissively. "You are dismissed."

Ragna wasted no time leaving the council chambers with her bound sisters following close behind her.

Amalia is a fool; an idiot.

She focused on pacifying the humans instead of permanently removing them as a distraction. The males of their species focused on protection and honor. But it was the queendom that kept them all alive and thriving, despite their reduced birth rates.

If Amalia realized her outdated ideas would someday result in the end of the Galatian race, then she might realize the only remedy was the demise of the human one.

Amalia was weak. She did not see that many of the queens grew tired of their men being assigned to Earth instead of focusing on populating their own world.

It wasn't just the humans that had rebels. It was the one trait she did like about the humans—their total lack of gratitude. It made it so much easier to dream of the day when they no longer mattered to anyone but interplanetary slavers.

Rafe's consort was one she would like to keep living long enough to see her on a harem planet servicing every alien scum that needed their prick handled.

But the human race had been protected from such realities. They still had no idea what the universe held beyond their meager galaxy.

Rafe's brown one was more dangerous than any of them realized because she didn't just mindlessly follow. She had gotten too close to the inner workings, and already she had destroyed generations of tradition.

Just like the other consort that had discredited a Galatian male by vying for his superior. Both should have instantly been punished, but were benefiting from their treachery. If she had her say, things would be much different.

Amalia was right about one thing; she would someday become Most Exalted. Ragna had already been working very hard to move up in power. After her binding to Rafe, she would force him onto the Interplanetary Collective, making them the most powerful figures in Galatia.

She would then have Amalia's position on the Queen's Council — as well as her head.

Karma stared at the hybrid bird/cat creature that had just informed her he intended to follow her out into the world; a world filled with whores, pimps, scrubs, and poor, desperate people — as well as the very rich people that mobbed for food they didn't need.

"Dorf...I know the streets and how to protect myself. I wouldn't know how to protect you. I'm just beginning to learn there are many things we humans have no idea about — and you're one of those things."

Dorf reached forward and sank his teeth into her ankle again — this time being much gentler.

"Do you know how to fly?" he asked, and she wondered how she could hear his sarcasm when he just spoke to her mentally.

"No."

"I do. It is *I* who may not be able to provide *you* much help, but I will certainly be able to help myself."

She raised her hands. "Fine. Let's go." She hurried to her bedroom and got her new cloak and then changed into hard shoes that were fit for the outdoors.

They left the penthouse and arrived in the lobby, where she saw the frantic hotel staff scurrying about. Several soldiers came to attention at the sight of her.

One stepped forward and marched to her. He had more stripes on the shoulder of his uniform than the others. They were all geared up as if preparing for battle.

"Mrs. Sigur. I'm Staff Sergeant Jeffries. I will be leading the mission, and I will be your direct point of contact. I will remain at your side at all times, ma'am."

She wanted to tell him that all they were going to do was distribute food, but she didn't. She remembered the way the rich had mobbed the poor, and how the paparazzi had nearly accosted her at the Galatian Exchange Ceremony. Besides, with the military accompanying her, Rafe might not get so angry...although that last was doubtful.

"Okay, Sergeant Jeffries. I would like to handle this as quickly as possible."

"Yes, ma'am. That would be optimum. Follow me, and I'll lead you to our transport."

She and Dorf followed him to the back of the lobby and through several corridors. Each contained soldiers she had never before spotted. This place was a fortress. There was no way anyone would ever be able to get in.

Karma's anger diffused some as she saw all it took to keep them safe. Could it be true that she didn't understand the possible threats against her just because she was a Galatian consort?

Of course, she knew some people celebrated all things Galatian, including the consorts, just as there were those that hated them. She had never fallen into either category. None of it was a part of her reality. Again, she wished she had paid more attention to the national news. Hadn't there been several attempted kidnappings? And she remembered long ago, a retired consort had been murdered, prompting new rules that upon retiring, consorts would live out their days under the protection of the military.

As Karma followed along with the sergeant, she had another thought. Why was it so hard to share some goddamn food with people in need? More importantly, why was there so much excess? News reports never matched reality. There was a worldwide crisis because alien attacks had destroyed so much of the Earth's resources in order to control them.

But the sacrifices the world leaders were asking people to make were sacrifices being made only by the poor.

The rich gave up nothing.

Karma's shoulders straightened as she marched along with her military entourage.

Chapter Twenty-two

"Mrs. Sigur, you will need to wear these." The sergeant passed her an earbud. She pressed it into one of her ears, thinking it fit nicely, and wondered if they could get her better headsets for her music player.

They were riding in an armored truck with two soldiers in front while she, Dorf, and the sergeant rode in back. Two news trucks had followed them from the hotel—most likely suspecting there might be another food delivery. But although the sergeant received reports about them, he didn't seem concerned. No one could tell she was in the truck due to the blacked-out windows.

Dorf stared out the window, intrigued, as if he was trying to see everything at once. She wondered how much of the Earth he'd been exposed to.

"Mrs. Sigur, we will arrive at our destination in twelve minutes." The sergeant had seemed relieved she didn't want to go to the train station but to her old apartment complex; the one where she had lived with her mother and father.

She remembered the working families that tried so hard to maintain some semblance of a real life. Both of her parents worked two jobs and they still struggled.

"The entrances will be secured, giving you time to enter." She returned her attention to him. "We will then distribute the food—"

"I want to help with that," she interrupted.

Sergeant Jeffries missed only one beat before replying, "Yes, ma'am."

She was making their lives difficult. Karma stared out the window again, remembering a time when she had been happy in her home with her mother and father.

No child should ever see their mother's broken, dead body, or hear their father's screams as he was dragged off to die as an alien's slave.

No child should spend three days without food because no one had enough to share...

They drove to the back of the complex and parked. Military police swarmed from their vehicles and set up barricades before the news trucks could follow. Armed guards moved to the front doors of the building, ushering nearby stragglers to move along or to go inside. The same happened in the back entrance, with the exception of soldiers carrying crates of food inside.

They all waited tensely for the order to be given to allow her inside.

"The intercoms are non-operational," she heard a tinny voice through a walkie-talkie. Well, she could have told them that. If they wanted to tell people about the free food, they would have to knock on doors. This was a nine-story building, and she had no idea how many units there were per floor. This would not be a quick mission.

Sergeant Jeffries was looking at a handheld computer with an image of the interior on the screen. "Negative. There will be no door-to-door distribution. Set up the distribution point in the lobby. How many stairwells? Two, and the elevator is operational. The elevators will be utilized for those needing reasonable accommodations only; the front stairwell is to be used by those receiving, and the rear stairwell for those that have received. This mission begins now."

Sergeant Jefferies turned to her. His face was calm as he spoke. "I will exit the vehicle first, and you and Sir Dorf will follow. Soldiers will be on either side of you until we have safely entered the building."

Karma nodded. Dorf nipped her hand and she gave him a distracted look.

"Rafe is going to be angry with you," he said calmly.

His calmness renewed her nervousness.

"When is he not angry with me?" was her wordless response.

Shaking loose from his grip, she prepared for the sergeant to exit the vehicle. When he did, Karma concentrated on not tripping and staying close as he rapidly moved toward the building. She didn't even look around, too afraid to even push back her hood so she could see more than what was directly in front of her.

Once inside the building, she counted seven soldiers moving up and down the stairs, setting up boxes and busily preparing as if for the next world war!

She looked around in worry. *I did not expect it to be this big of a deal...*

The sergeant pressed one hand to his ear and looked distressed. "Copy. There are not enough soldiers present for maneuver. Only one floor at a time, starting from nine. I'm aware it will take longer. Make it happen. Out."

"What's happening?" she asked.

He sighed, looking stressed for the first time. "The people don't want to come out. They're afraid, and don't trust our presence. And this mission needs to be completed in minutes, not hours…"

"They'll have to see my face."

"Mrs. Sigur." Sergeant Jeffries was prepared to object.

"Like you said, the sooner this happens, the faster we can get out of here."

He finally nodded and spoke into his walkie-talkie. "Secure the elevator for Mrs. Sigur."

He put away his walkie-talkie but then pressed on his earpiece. The sergeant frowned and his face grew pale.

Dorf had been watching as well. "I think…" He didn't even bother to bite her as he spoke aloud. But she had no trouble understanding him.

"What do you think?" she prompted.

"That something is about to happen…" Dorf replied softly.

The front doors swung open and her head swiveled around. The soldiers stopped what they were doing and came to immediate attention.

Through the double doors swarmed six Galatians, although *swarmed* wasn't exactly accurate. They moved rapidly and with so much precision it was as if they flowed through the doors.

They each seemed to see her at the exact same moment and moved to circle her. They faced outward, their tails completely enclosing the circle with her, Dorf, and Sergeant Jeffries in its center.

They didn't move. They didn't say anything. They didn't even look at her, staring straight ahead, even if straight in front of them was a wall of beat-up metal mailboxes.

It had all happened so fast, but Karma realized instantly she recognized these Galatians. They were mated to the consorts. And this wasn't the first time she'd seen this happen. It had happened at the Exchange Ceremony the first time she'd met Rafe and the paparazzi had swarmed them. Galatian Guards had encircled him, keeping anyone from getting too close. Even when he walked, the circle surrounding him moved too.

The sergeant seemed to snap out of his alarm and picked up the walkie-talkie again. "Initiate plan C. Alpha, move toward the stairwell — forward."

He began to walk to the stairwell and to Karma, it seemed as if he would end up walking into the back of one of the Galatians. But without seeming to acknowledge the sergeant's intent, the six Galatians moved forward in perfect precision.

She and Dorf followed, and anyone watching would have seen the strangest sight as some Galatians walked backwards, some walked sideways as they moved to the stairs in perfect unison.

Once at the stairs, one of the Galatians made a clicking sound and the circle surrounding them tightened by a few feet. She could reach out and touch the scales on the back of the Galatian directly in front of her.

The sergeant began walking up the stairs with the rest of them in tow. Once on the first floor, she saw the military police had exited the elevator with a box of food.

There was another set of clicking sounds and the circle once again widened, giving her several feet of movement.

This was incredible to her. No wonder the Galatian Guards were considered the most powerful tactical military force in the universe.

They reached the first door and Karma reached out to knock on the door, but Sergeant Jeffries was quicker and rapped on the door before she could.

She craned to look around the backs of the Galatians that were in front of her.

"You'll have to move aside for them to be able to see me," she said.

The Galatians ignored her.

Okay, so they weren't going to move aside.

Karma inhaled past her annoyance and then pushed back her hood. "Hello?" she called. "I'm here to deliver food if you'd like it. I can leave it here on the floor but...I know how things work here. Once we leave, someone's going to take it—plus, I don't know how many people you—"

The door swung open. An older couple peered out at her, their eyes moving from the Galatians to the sergeant and then back to her.

"Just the two of you?" Karma asked. The man nodded slowly. One of the soldiers passed them two containers.

"I hope you enjoy." Karma smiled as they looked at her in surprise. She made to move to the next apartment but the woman spoke.

"You're just going to give it to us?"

"Yes, ma'am," Karma replied.

The woman blinked in surprise. "You're the consort..."

"Yes, ma'am," Karma nodded.

"And you called me ma'am?"

"Yes, ma'am. I was raised that way."

The woman smiled for the first time. "Thank you. Thank you very much."

Karma nodded and moved to the next apartment.

This time, they didn't even have to knock. Everyone had been watching from the peepholes in their doors and had seen the exchange with their neighbor. One by one the doors opened, and door by door, Karma greeted the occupants of her old apartment complex and delivered food.

Some were so thankful they had tears in their eyes as they accepted the meal. Some explained they thought they'd have to go to bed hungry — again. She saw some with little children who stared with awe up at the Galatians. She loved the way they accepted their own individual meal boxes, hugging them to their small chests once they realized they didn't have to share their box with the other members of their family.

If she had any doubts, they disappeared at the sight of those little faces and the relief their parents wore. Despite all the trouble it had taken to orchestrate, Karma felt good about what she was doing.

Dorf remained quiet, not biting her or speaking aloud. He seemed curious, and did what he did well; staying unobtrusive. For some reason, people saw Dorf but didn't seem to realize he was an alien, apparently taking him for a large cat. Of course, if you were starving, why would you look closely at the big, white cat that accompanied the first Black consort and the first Galatians they had ever seen in person?

The entourage went from floor to floor, and somehow, the word spread and it became easier as the people left their apartments and lined up on their own for their free meal.

"It's so good to see one of *us* win the lottery," a woman said.

"Bless you!" An old woman's hands shook so much she could barely accept her box, and one of the soldiers actually carried it into her house for her.

There were times when a face looked familiar to Karma but she never revealed her identity. It had been so many years since any of them had seen her—she'd just been a child, after all. But it surprised her that no one had figured out who she was. Not just the people from the building, but what about her roommates, or the people she had worked with since being an adult?

Did makeup and fancy clothes really cause her to look so different?

Rafe found a seat in the canteen, having been assured there would be no other Galatians around. He had selected a level on the satellite station where the air was more carbon-based, which meant his comrades wouldn't be likely to show up. The other aliens present kept their distance, because Galatians were notoriously bad-tempered.

Rafe was extra tired and cranky, and not in the mood to talk or joke around with his comrades. It was the first time all day he'd had a moment to himself for a quick meal. The food on the satellite station was marginally better than the trash they served on Earth. But at the moment, he was hungry enough to even eat beef or pork, and the idea of that had always disgusted him.

It annoyed him that the one thing he had looked forward to in taking a consort would never occur, and that was having authentic Galatian meals prepared by someone trained in their preparation.

Well, he couldn't lie. He had also looked forward to regular matings; but even that hadn't turned out as planned, since his consort hadn't had the surgery. He needed to contact the surgeons about correcting that but had just been too busy.

Besides, mating with Karma had been oddly pleasurable, even without the complete penetration. Mating was always good, but even better when his partner enjoyed it as well. Ragna had treated mating like a reward she dished out to him when she got her way. And even that hadn't occurred in years.

But Karma was different. She might have had ulterior motives each time they mated, but he knew she enjoyed it. It bothered him that, despite knowing she was a fraud, he still felt attraction for her.

He bit into an egg, crunching on the soft bones of the groh while he considered his dilemma.

It would be so much easier if he could ignore her, but even last night, when he should have slept in his den, he had climbed into bed with her. And then to make matters worse, he observed her all night, even while he slept—which is why he was tired and cranky now.

He was drawn to her, not just because of her looks; although he liked her looks a great deal. Perhaps because she was brown like the queens, which he considered the standard for beauty in all the universe. But he was also captivated by her large, brown eyes.

All humans had eyes bigger than Galatian eyes, but hers made him feel something he had long ago lost; innocence.

Rafe had seen fear, hatred, anger, and even defeat in the eyes of humans. But he wasn't used to what he saw in Karma's eyes. Maybe because they were emotionally connected, he could feel every thought he saw reflected back at him through those eyes.

He didn't like it, but it drew him.

His communicator sounded and he gladly pushed back the remainder of his food while he retrieved it.

"Yes?"

"Get back to Earth. Now!" It was Drago, one of his brothers from the Exchange. Rafe was on his feet and heading out of the room before he'd even asked his first question.

"What happened?"

"Your consort has left the compound."

"WHAT?!" he roared. Alarm caused his body to move with a speed that seemed impossible for a being of his size, yet his sinewy muscles optimized his rapid movements.

"We just found out, and we're on our way to her," Drago said breathlessly, as if he too was running. "She's been sending out food to the poor humans."

"I already got that report. Where is my consort?!"

Rafe didn't want her doing anything to bring attention to herself, but didn't completely object to her giving out food. Still, he had intended to talk to her about the investigation and keeping her identity a secret. And now she had left without his or his men's protection! Rafe cursed.

"I'll ping you the location." Drago disconnected.

As Rafe rushed down the corridor, he couldn't stop wondering what had possessed her to do this. Was she trying to run away from him? Just because he hadn't coddled her and her human sensibilities? How could she think she could ever flee from him?!

The blood literally raged through his veins, causing him to revert into the warrior that scoured galaxies for his enemies, the beast that dismembered his foe with nothing more than his talons and sheer hatred.

He rushed into his transport and began the flight back to Earth. He was angry, but what he felt went beyond that. It was hard to identify because it was an emotion he rarely experienced. It was almost like fear — yet that was impossible, because Rafe Sigur feared nothing...except the image of Karma kidnapped, attacked, or murdered.

Chapter Twenty-three

There was enough food for everyone, with a few boxes left.

"Mrs. Sigur." Sergeant Jeffries turned to Karma. "We've serviced the last of the residents."

"I know, Sergeant. But we have five boxes left, and I want to give them to a certain human family in this building."

For so long, memories of this place had represented nightmares and horrors. She could barely think about the good times with Mom and Dad without being overwhelmed by visions of their murder and kidnapping. Sometimes those thoughts would give her so much anxiety, she had to force herself to forget her parents' faces.

But being back here today allowed Karma to realize that memories might hurt a little, but it felt good to open up and allow herself to feel. She had allowed herself to remember things that didn't hurt. This was closure.

"One of my men will take the leftovers to the apartment—"

Her stomach dropped. "No. I need to do it—"

"Mrs. Sigur, I appreciate what you've done here today—I believe we all do. But we must disband. The word is already spread that you're here—"

"Then we'd better get to the third floor immediately."

One of the Galatians turned his head slightly, and then came a low ticking and clicking sound.

Suddenly, they began moving again to the stairwell. Karma, Dorf, and the sergeant were forced to follow, as they were still within the protective circle formed by the Galatians.

Karma had no opportunity to object—even if she dared to do that. It just didn't work like that with the Galatian Guards. She kept silent as they went down several flights. They moved quickly, but smoothly. When they reached the third floor, the Galatian that had been doing all the clicking sounds—the one apparently in charge—turned his head slightly and spoke.

"Which door, ma'am?"

With relief, she replied with the apartment number, amazed it came to mind so easily.

They moved in that direction, and once they reached the familiar apartment, the sergeant rapidly knocked.

When the door opened, a man stood looking at them in surprise. For a moment she saw her daddy's face, even though this man was a completely different height and weight.

Her worried, tired daddy worked so hard just for them to have this battered apartment complex to live in, and deserved so much more than to be another no-name victim.

"There's…" Karma had to swallow back her emotions as the man transformed once again into an unknown stranger. "There's extra. I'd like you and your family to have it."

His face brightened. "You've done so much for us, Consort. Bless you!"

"How many people live with you?" Karma tried to see around the broad backs of the Galatians for a glimpse inside the apartment.

Her heart began to pound when the small front room came into view. That's where her mama died...

"There's four of us," the man replied. The soldiers passed out the last of the boxes while the man's family came forward to accept them. When she saw one of the children was a little girl that looked about the age she had been when she had last lived there, Karma's eyes began to shimmer with emotion.

"Take care of yourselves," she whispered. She then turned to the sergeant. "We can leave now."

If she thought things moved quickly before, they were basically running now.

Sergeant Jeffries was back to talking through his walkie-talkie to his officers stationed outside the building. "Secure the exit!" he commanded, and then turned to her and spoke in a gentler voice. "Please pull up your hood, ma'am."

She did. The Galatians clicked, and the circle of scaled bodies grew tighter—enough so they were touching on all sides.

"Dorf? Are you okay down there?" Karma asked when she felt his wings flapping.

"My legs aren't as long as yours."

"Jump up and I'll carry you."

With a rapid flapping of his wings, Dorf flew into her arms. His downy, white feathers were softer than she had expected.

They moved rapidly out the back door. She couldn't see where she was going but didn't need to, as she was virtually being carried along by the Galatians. The firm swoosh of their skirts as they marched, along with the thumping of their boots, filled her ears—even more than the sound of the distant crowd that called after them.

Finally, they reached the transport and the Galatian circle opened in front, allowing for an open pathway into the vehicle. Once settled in her seat, Karma looked out the darkened window at the crowd of people that had gathered behind the police barriers.

Why were people making this into such a big deal? Okay, the military and Galatian involvement was understandable in light of the crowds. But why? She still had Dorf in her arms and she unconsciously stroked his soft fur/feathers while he too stared out the window at the crowd.

They drove to the backdrop of walkie-talkies and commands about coordinates, traffic, and crowds.

She felt a soft nip on her wrist and looked down to see Dorf staring up at her.

"Why were those humans half-starved?"

"Because they're poor and can't afford the high prices for both food and shelter."

"But what about the subsidies given by the government?" Dorf asked, sounding confused.

"Welfare? The law says only families, the old, or disabled qualify for that, and it's just a bunch of vouchers and some food that should be in a compost bin!" She remembered her mom being too afraid to cook the meat because it smelled bad or had maggots in it. It was nothing but the food grocery stores could no longer sell. The vegetables were the same. The only thing worth anything was the powdered milk and eggs, the dried beans and rice, flour, and sugar. Many old ladies baked bean empanadas they'd sell from their kitchen windows just to survive.

When you got too old to whore, you got on welfare and sold empanadas and tamales...

"Those people in the apartment were half-starved..." Dorf said, and Karma understood he spoke more to himself than to her.

"Mrs. Sigur," Jeffries said. "I have Lieutenant Sigur on the line. I'm connecting you now."

Before Karma could react, she heard Rafe's low, angry voice in her ear through the earpiece she still wore.

"Karma. The military police are bringing you back to the building. I will be there to meet you and Dorf at the rear entrance, where I'll personally escort you to the apartment. You are not to give any more orders to, or make any more demands of, my men or anyone else. Do you understand?"

Karma's body went rigid at the controlled anger she heard in Rafe's voice. He didn't yell or threaten, but a flash of fear rocketed through her all the same.

"I understand," she said.

"You have to press the earpiece for him to hear you," Sergeant Jeffries prompted.

She had to shake loose Dorf's grip on her hand in order to do it, and then she replied again that she understood. Rafe disconnected without another word.

Dorf was watching her and she gave him a shaky smile.

"I guess Rafe's not happy with me."

"I warned you."

Rafe paced the short corridor as his skirt swished loudly about his ankles and legs. His tail whipped from side to side, cutting through the air. Soldiers that stood at attention grew more and more wary as the minutes passed and the Galatian grew more anxious.

As a soldier, Rafe had seen more than enough dead and torn bodies. But his concern had little to do with what he knew concerning the effects of battle, and everything to do with what he knew about the rebels and their hatred of everything alien.

If only human rebels were like Tybernees or their Malnamanian henchman. Then they would be able to visibly see their enemy. But the human rebels wore the same face as any other human. Their numbers were impossible to determine, because they were the people that walked down the street or worked in the market. They cleaned houses and were the ones who stayed in the background, watching and waiting for an opportunity to strike.

And when they did, they hit with a vengeance, bombing and attempting to destroying Galatian outposts—although they would find it much harder to destroy the Galatians within them. It was the reason many outposts were now positioned in outer space, and why Galatians did not make themselves easily accessible to humans and their curiosity about the *friendly* aliens.

Something like the Galatian Exchange was always a danger, and why the human military kept a strong visual presence—while the Galatian Guards kept a nearly invisible one.

Humans supportive of the Galatians and their efforts to protect Earth were known to abruptly disappear. In some cases, their executions were filmed, or their mutilated bodies discovered with anti-alien propaganda.

Keeping these execution-style killings out of the public eye took much effort, and finding the assailants took manpower. The human soldiers were very good at tracking down and handing out swift justice to these terrorists. With the end of sovereign rule and Earth's inclusion in the Interplanetary Collective, control of these matters was much easier to manage.

Loss of their perceived control spurred these attacks, but the Galatians knew this bloodthirsty behavior wasn't all due to the loss of their government rule.

Humans murdered each other—sometimes for no other reason than utter curiosity—gaining nothing from the act. But it seemed these psychopaths had found a common enemy in their hatred of all aliens, as well as their supporters.

Rafe had seen more than his share of human-on-human crime in the name of keeping the sanctity of the human race intact. The rebels spared no one; neither man, woman, nor child.

Karma had put every person in that building at risk.

Finally, the building's emergency doors swung open and military police swarmed inside.

Rafe watched without moving until he saw Karma and her escorts. She was completely concealed in her cloak, and carrying Dorf. His Galatian brothers shielded her on both sides and his tension finally eased. He hadn't trained these human soldiers and didn't know their worth. But when it came to the Galatian Guards, trust came implicitly. Rafe was thankful his brothers had been present, or he would have torn through the city to get to Karma.

This building was a fortress, and nearly impossible for a rebel to breach the security protocols put into place to protect the consorts. But once outside of these gates, nothing could be assured.

Rafe's blood seemed to surge when he saw Dorf in her arms. He'd gone out amongst the humans too. His jaw clenched as he stepped forward to take possession of them from his Galatian brothers.

"Thank you. I will take them to the safety of our suite." He spoke in his own language.

Only then did the Galatians guarding Karma and Dorf relax, allowing their tails to drop from the rigid attention they had maintained.

Karma pulled back the cloak, revealing her face, and he knew then she was safe. He didn't look at her with his eyes but turned to face the human standing at attention by her side. He never ended his observation of her, though. He saw her swallow, and the sheen that covered her face, as well as the wariness in her dark eyes.

"Your name, officer?" he commanded to the soldier by her side.

"Staff Sergeant Jeffries, in charge of this mission, sir."

"I want a full report by o six hundred."

"Yes, sir."

Rafe finally turned to face Karma. "Put Dorf down." Karma hesitated, and then gently set the little Japoxillian onto his feet.

"Rafe—" she began.

Rafe turned. "Follow."

Even though his back was to her, he again observed her every move and saw when she briefly exchanged a look with Dorf before she quickly followed. Dorf had to flap his wings and hop in order to keep up with Rafe's long strides, although Karma easily kept up despite her much shorter stature.

Rafe exhaled a long breath and slowed his steps so as not to punish his long-time friend. He suspected Dorf had only gone along to keep tabs on his consort.

Everyone in the lobby discreetly went about their business, trying not to watch as the trio entered the elevator. Rafe sent the elevator to the penthouse while Karma stood quietly behind him.

At least in their time together she had learned that much.

When the door opened to their home, he pressed his hand to the security panel and the front door opened.

"I didn't know it would be this big of a deal," she said softly as they walked into the room.

"But you saw the soldiers, did you not?"

"Well...yes—"

"Then don't lie to me."

Dorf moved to recline at the top of the bookshelf with a soft flap of wings that sent him flying.

Rafe saw Karma look at Dorf as if surprised a creature with wings could fly.

"I don't understand why you would do such a thing," he spoke. "Explain yourself."

Karma nodded and undid her cloak. Once it was removed, she clutched it in her arms as if it was her armor.

"We have so much extra, Rafe. There is so much food in this place that goes to waste every single day."

He cocked his head. "And what does that have to do with you?"

He saw a small frown form across her brow. "It has everything to do with me! This food doesn't get recycled. It doesn't get sold or even given away. It's tossed out like garbage—"

"Karma, I'm not going to explain to you the disparity between the rich and the poor. You have seen with your very own eyes that the rich can afford more and they can afford better—"

"But that's no excuse for us to waste these leftovers when people are starving—"

"You could help those people without jeopardizing yourself, Dorf, and every single individual that went out on that mission with you today! There is a reason you don't leave this compound, consort! There is a reason we have taken strides to keep trained military as security in every location you travel to.

"We have a team that maps out the security *days* in advance. Every single human has to be screened. Every possible way to infiltrate an area has to be secured. Yet you used your position as my consort to force the security team to do your bidding."

"It wasn't like that, Rafe."

"You are lying," he said angrily.

"I'm no liar!" She surprised him by yelling back. "Stop calling me a liar! I'm sorry I...I just didn't understand how big of a deal this was! And by the time I did, it was really too late. We were already out of the building and on our way with the food."

"The food is of no consequence to me! Give it all away for all I care! You have used my power to endanger yourself and you're too foolish to understand that!"

He pointed to the front door. "The other consorts may have been trained in many things you did not get the privilege of learning, but understand that while you

229

serve as my consort you do as I will, and if I did not give you direct instructions to leave this compound, you should have never left!

"So let us make this clear. Your purpose is to fuck, cook, and meet my needs. Nothing more. You can think in seven years! Do you understand?"

Rafe's heart was pumping so rapidly he felt like he was on a chase. But Karma's previous anger disappeared. He could see it and feel it—maybe even smell the absence of it. And in its place was…nothing.

"I understand." She watched him, not quite meeting his eyes, looking at his throat or chest but not his face. "And I apologize. I won't do anything like that again."

Rafe's tail swished. That is what he wanted to hear. "You're dismissed. Go tend to your human needs while I tend to mine."

"Yes," she said with a nod and then quickly left the room with her cloak still clutched to her chest.

He watched her go to her room and quietly shut the door after her.

His anger had suddenly sifted away. He remembered Dorf and looked up at the top of the bookshelf.

"Well, what do you have to say?" he asked in Icelandic.

"I warned her not to do it," he replied in the same language. "Perhaps this tongue-lashing will serve her well." He stretched and got comfortable again. Rafe turned for his den when Dorf continued. "But while you may have secured her safety, I think you're the one that may have lost the most this evening."

Rafe paused and then entered his den without responding.

Chapter Twenty-four

Karma went into her room and sat on the edge of her bed. She was still clutching her cloak without even realizing it.

Who was she to think, to have will, to want?

Rafe was right; she had no significance other than to serve him. The other consorts had not used their platform to do anything beyond what was expected of them. They understood their roles, and now she had to do the same. Her likes and dislikes didn't matter.

Just like when she was a maid, it didn't matter if she had to clean the toilets or serve as a nanny for her employer's children, she did what she was paid to do. And she couldn't deny that being an alien's whore and servant paid well.

She got up and hung up her cloak and then used the bathroom. She was tired, but it wasn't very late. Of course, a person that woke daily before dawn in order to get across town to her job didn't gage her day by what time appeared on a clock. Her body told her when it was time to wake up and when it was time to sleep.

But for the rest of the country, it was just past dinner and their evening was just beginning.

Back in her room, she picked up one of the telephones and pressed the button she remembered belonging to Madeline's home.

"Engström residence."

"Madeline?"

"Karma? Is that you?"

"Yes."

"Oh my Guardian. What have you done?" Madeline's smooth, cultured voice rose anxiously.

"Too much," Karma replied tiredly.

"It's all over the news! For days all they've done is talk about you, and they know it was you that went to the apartment building in the ghetto! Why would you do that? Drago ran out of here before even having dinner—"

"Madeline, I need your help."

"I'm not going to help you escape whatever punishment Rafe set for you. And don't even think about asking me to help you escape!" she hissed quietly into the phone.

"Remember when we said if I help you enjoy your first mating, then you would help me?" Karma replied.

"Yes, but—"

"I'm not asking you to help me escape. I need to know how to take care of Rafe. How do I serve a Galatian?"

"What? Is that all? I told you, there is no manual on this. We learned over the course of years."

"What did you learn?"

Madeline sighed. "How do you expect me to just tell you over the phone what took me years to learn?"

"Madeline! I risked myself to help you all the night you lost your virginity!"

Madeline cursed softly. "I know. Look, you pleasure them sexually, prepare their meals, oil their scales, tend to them when they are shedding their old ones, and tend to their home—just like a wife, I guess.

"They have celebrations, and there are special meals you have to prepare, like when you attend Galatian events. Best of all, you must always look good doing it—

233

like back in ancient times when they had 1950s housewives." Madeline chuckled, but Karma remained completely still.

"I don't know anything about Galatian meals." *Or 1950s housewives.*

"That is what takes the longest to learn. It won't be pleasant, but I guess I can show you a few things. Has Rafe had his dinner?"

"I don't know."

"What? That's something you have to know. Know your master, Karma. Know what he needs, what he likes, and at the most basic, figure out if he's hungry!"

"Okay," Karma replied quickly.

"Well, Drago finished his meal in seconds and said it reminded him of his home. I can give you the leftovers. There's plenty and...I know how you feel about leftovers."

Karma suppressed her groan at Madeline's attempt at a joke. "I would appreciate that. Because of how I got where I am, Rafe hasn't had the benefit of a true consort, and I really want to understand my role."

"Hmph," Madeline said. "I'll help you, but I want you to tell me everything about how you got here. Everything."

"I'll do that, but really, there isn't much to know."

"I'll pack up the leftovers and you can get them in a few minutes."

"No. I can't leave. Rafe hasn't given me permission and I don't dare ask him."

"Sounds like he was mad."

"Sounds like you don't need me to tell you just how mad."

"No. There are certain things you don't do to a Galatian, and one of those things is to jeopardize their property. You are that property."

"I get it. Believe me, I get it."

"Okay, I'll bring it up through the maid's entrance in the kitchen. I'll see you in about fifteen minutes. I don't have a key, so you'll have to open the passage for me." The phone went dead.

Karma quickly checked the mirror and saw she looked far from good. She sat at her vanity and quickly applied face powder, eyeliner, and finally, lip color. She spritzed her hair with oil sheen and then hurried to the kitchen to meet Madeline.

She didn't see Dorf, who had probably gone into his cubby, or maybe he and Rafe were in Rafe's den exchanging notes. She was just happy not to see either of them.

Madeline arrived soon after and knocked lightly on the panel that served as a hidden entrance. Had Karma not seen one of the maids caught in the midst of utilizing the secret door, she probably would have never known about it. It did cause her to wonder how many other hidden entrances this home had.

Madeline scurried in and set several covered dishes on the kitchen counter.

"This should be enough for two meals."

Karma removed the lid from one of the covered dishes. It was inky-black tendrils in brown sludge. She squinted. Was something moving? The tendrils were moving!

"Feed him this first, before they die. Keeping those things alive is no easy feat. The stew can't be too hot and it can't get cold, so you just have to leave whatever is left over on the counter — covered, so it doesn't escape."

"Escape?!"

"A lot of the food escapes. And you don't want to see some of those things crawling in your bed. Galatians prefer living food. So, by the time it gets to Earth it's half dead, if not completely unusable. This building is the only one in North America that has a working Galatian farm. Oh! You'll have to learn to harvest from it."

"Okay." She replaced the lid. "Can humans actually eat this?"

"Yes. It's not appealing, but it's not poisonous either."

"Have you tasted it?"

Madeline blanched. "Each and every dish I've been taught to prepare I've had to taste. But no. I don't eat any of it. Look, I have to go before Drago misses me. He likes to have his scales oiled before we mate." She tried not to smile, but Karma saw something that surprised her. Madeline actually liked Drago. The girls had made it seemed far-fetched that liking their masters was part of the equation.

"I'll call you tomorrow once Rafe and Drago leave for work and we'll begin our lessons then." She hurried back to the hidden panel but paused to gesture to the leftover food.

"It should stay alive for two days but after that, it's best to just get rid of it. It goes in the compost. I'll show you where tomorrow."

Karma followed her to the panel. "Thanks again. I'll see you tomorrow."

She stared at the closed panel for a full minute before she forced herself to turn around. Karma marched out of the kitchen and walked to Rafe's den. She thought she could hear him swimming, but it was hard to tell due to the gentle sounds of the waterfall separating the cutout from the living room to his personal space.

She knocked on his door.

"Come," he said.

She pressed the lever to open the door. Rafe was indeed in his pool. She stepped inside and was immediately met by the dank smell of dark, wet places. It wasn't altogether unpleasant. There was something in the smell she liked, although she didn't know what it was—it was like smelling the rain, or the grass after it was freshly cut. The den smelled like that to her.

He looked at her, waiting, and she remembered to speak.

"There is a meal for you in the kitchen if you're hungry."

"Have you eaten?" he asked without leaving even a beat after her words.

"No. Not yet."

Rafe floated at the far end of the pool, half submerged with his arms spread and resting on the cavern rocks that were situated on either side of him. He quickly submerged himself beneath the water and reappeared a split second later at the edge of the pool closest to where she stood. A human could not have swum as quickly and without barely causing a ripple in the water.

"Prepare yourself a meal as well," he said, not bothering to wipe away the water that streamed over his pale-green face and into his slitted, topaz eyes. "And then we will discuss what I found in my ammunitions room."

The necklace. Karma had forgotten she had placed the string of pearls on one of his swords.

She had sworn she was no liar, but in leaving the pearl necklace, she understood she appeared as both a liar and a thief.

She didn't even bother to explain herself. Karma nodded and left the den.

Rafe floated in his pool, deep in thought. He assumed Karma would have avoided him. But she had faced him fearlessly. He did wonder if he had been too harsh, as Dorf seemed to insinuate, which caused him deep reflection.

One moment, Karma defended her actions while acknowledging what she had done wrong. But then in a split second, she barely seemed to be present. Had he stamped out the spark of fire from her? He hadn't been able to stop thinking about her reaction. But why would he care when he was right and she was wrong? And by that token, why should he care about the thoughts of a consort that had only gotten her position by cheating and lying? He had gotten what he wanted, and that was all that should matter.

He knew there was more to her tale than simply being a liar and a cheat. Yet it still annoyed him because while he had felt an immediate attraction to her the moment he had seen her at the Exchange—noticing and appreciating her complete contrast to her sister consorts — it seemed she had only seen him as a means to an end. That was confirmed when she admitted to mating with him before the ceremony in order to secure her position as his consort.

He shouldn't allow anything about her to affect him so strongly.

He felt secure she had learned her place. And yet that thought still didn't mollify him.

Rafe left the pool and then dressed in a comfortable wrap. He went into the kitchen still barefoot and saw Karma standing behind her chair, waiting for him.

He studied the table filled with many bowls as he took his seat. Karma began removing the coverings from the bowls. He perked up as he recognized each dish and then gave her a quick look. Where had these come from? Someone with knowledge of Galatians had prepared this.

He piled a platter with food and raised it to drink the broth. It was delicious. He gave her another suspicious look.

"Where is your meal?" There was no human food on the table.

"I thought I'd try some of your food."

Rafe laughed. He laughed so hard he had to lower his dish before he spilled it and the mofreka went scampering across the table.

Karma didn't smile. She simply picked up a spoon and ladled some broth into her bowl. She spooned it into her mouth.

His laughter quickly died. His mouth fell open and he stared at Karma in surprise, preparing to jump up the moment she began to vomit. But she didn't. Her eyes grew wide and a moment later, began to water. She swallowed audibly and completely shocked him by lifting her spoon for a second bite.

"What are you doing?" he asked, causing her to pause.

"Having a meal with my mate."

He stared as she forced down another spoon of broth.

"And how do you like it?"

She picked up a bottle of cola and drank half of it before answering. "I don't much care for it."

"Then why—"

"But I am here for seven years and in time, I'll get used to eating what you eat."

Was she trying to throw his words back at him? She wasn't going to shame him because he'd put her in her place.

Rafe picked up one of the large, fat mofrekas. Its tentacles quickly wrapped enticingly around his fingers—they were, of course, the tastiest part of the creature. He brought it to his mouth and bit it in half, being sure to capture any of its juices. He chewed, savoring the taste while Karma stared in awe. It was likely she'd never seen anyone consume living food. And if that was the case, then perhaps he should assist her.

He held the dying, squirming creature out to her lips. It wouldn't be alive much longer.

Karma swallowed dryly while staring at the thing gripped by his fingertips.

"It's better while it lives," he prompted.

Her eyes met his. "Do I chew?"

"You should, or you might choke. As you become more practiced, you can swallow them after just one or two bites."

Karma gripped his hand as if that was the only way she could follow through. She closed her eyes and then quickly took the remains of the mofreka into her mouth.

Now Rafe was even more surprised. He had not expected her to accept the challenge. Karma chewed rapidly, her eyes growing even wider. She swallowed with great effort and once it was down, she hesitated and then smiled proudly. She chuckled a little.

"How was it?" he asked slowly.

"Actually...it wasn't bad. It was strange moving around in my mouth but once you get past that, the taste reminds me of..." She shook her head. "Asparagus and bacon."

She reached into the bowl for another mofreka. Rafe actually sat back and watched, amazed as Karma bit the sea creature in half and chewed it daintily. She then popped the other half into her mouth while nodding.

He shook his head. "Enough. Another consort prepared this meal for her mate yet you take pride as if it's your accomplishment. Let's discuss the pearl necklace you had in your possession after insinuating you had no knowledge of it."

Karma folded her hands on the table and her animated expression dimmed.

"Okay," she said simply.

"Okay? Is that all you have to say?" Rafe asked in annoyance.

Karma opened her mouth, seemed to think better of it, then closed it. She simply nodded her head in response.

"Speak freely, consort," he demanded.

Karma was looking at him, but not his eyes or his face. She looked at his neck or shoulder, but not his eyes.

He needed those big, brown eyes to look into his. Not just because he could read her better that way, but because he missed the way he felt when their eyes locked, as if there was an unspoken exchange.

"Karma," he finally said, gentler. Her eyes moved to his and immediately Rafe felt a current of excitement that sped up his heartbeat and seemed to cause his blood to race through his body. "Speak your truth."

Rafe reached out and touched her chin.

Chapter Twenty-five

Karma didn't know what the point was in Rafe's request. Speaking her "truth" when it meant nothing to anyone but herself was fruitless. Rafe sought and understood facts. And the facts he had lain out before her was truth.

Besides, he was her master, not her mate, and she had to stop thinking in those terms even though *mate* was a term used to loosely describe their relationship.

But when she looked into Rafe's eyes, she couldn't stop herself from thinking back on a time before he hated her. When he first saw her at the Exchange, he had looked at her as if she was a unique jewel. He'd defended her from the beginning, when others treated her like one that had risen above her station.

And now he too treated her like that. Owners, just like employers, didn't really want the truth unless it validated their own beliefs.

What did it matter? Give him what he wanted so these next seven years could run smoothly.

"You're right. I took pride in the food I served you even though I didn't prepare it. I was proud I was able to serve my ma — my master food that would be pleasing to you even though I don't yet have the knowledge to prepare it with my own two hands.

"But while I suppose it appears all I did was take something someone else had put so much effort into preparing for their mate...my truth is I did what I was supposed to do to make sure my master had a well-prepared meal regardless of whether I could do it or not.

You said I was to take care of you, and I made sure to do that." Rafe's head tilted but he made no comment, so she continued.

"I disagree that I took pride in eating your food. It wasn't pride as much as self-preservation."

"Self-preservation? That's not something you ever need to worry about. Your welfare was secured from the moment I claimed you."

"My truth, my words…" she gently reminded him.

"Continue."

"Food is not a simple pleasure for many of us. And while I can't speak for those that have faced starvation in other parts of the Earth, here in my city, there is no place where families can set up farms — even a small illegal one. So, when there is no food, choices become extremely slim.

"As a child, I knew when we had soup it was because the food was so rotten my mother had to boil it to make it safer to eat. I didn't know what food without rot tasted like until I was an adult and worked in the homes of rich employers. Then, kindly cooks would serve us leftovers.

"Whenever that happened, it was like a feast — even if it was just a chicken drumstick some child had failed to strip clean of its meat. I'd devour the bits of cartilage and crack the bones so I could suck the marrow from them, and that child's garbage was a good day for me."

Karma shook herself slightly because she had gotten lost in her memories.

"As for Mrs. Tolbert's pearl necklace, I found it in my old coat pocket. I guess it is convenient I located it right after our conversation, but I was thinking about Mr. Tolbert and how he was desperate for me to enter the Exchange. At the time, I knew even though he had given me options, I had no choice in the matter.

"I know the stories of the many people like myself in prisons or worse, because they are throwaways. If I didn't take his offer, he wouldn't allow me to continue walking around freely, knowing his plans. So, I checked my coat pockets—the same one I had worn to our meeting. And sure enough, he had planted his insurance that I'd be sent away and discredited.

"I knew, deep down, there was really no way to win, but I had to find a way to..." She swallowed, her voice now just a whisper. "To get to the finish line alive and well. Self-preservation. That's what everything is about—not making it seven years until our contract is complete, but making it to the next day, the next hour."

Rafe leaned forward until his face was close to hers. She saw the movement of his nostril opening as if he was smelling the air around her. He stared so deeply into her eyes, she dared not move. His topaz, slitted eyes were like magnets that made it difficult to look elsewhere.

He finally sat back in his seat. His scales had taken on a yellow blush of color. It was one she didn't recognize—not the purple of his annoyance and anger, a color she was well familiar with. And happily, it wasn't the red of his rage, which she had only seen once.

Then what did it mean?

"I now understand your truth, Karma. And I feel sorrow you suffered so much. I don't understand how it's possible when there are so many programs that have been put into place in order to provide housing and food."

Karma shook her head. "I'm alive. In that case, their efforts were successful."

He inhaled deeply and made several clicking sounds with his throat and tongue. He suddenly slammed a fist on the table and his scales moved rapidly from the sunshiny yellow to bright purple.

She had managed to piss him off again.

His hand reached out and he touched her chin. "I understand your truth, Karma, and I apologize for not understanding sooner. I allowed my emotions to taint my actions and I directed my...frustration in the wrong direction." His voice became a low, threatening growl.

"I will remedy this folly. Know that I will get to the bottom of why the humans under our watchful eyes have suffered so much. Protecting our charges is one of our life's missions—my life's mission—and I had no idea. I had no idea."

He stood and headed out of the kitchen, pausing long enough to turn his head, although once again he didn't look at her while his back was turned. Only his tail seemed to have risen, giving Karma the impression it was his tail observing her, although that was ridiculous. Tails didn't have eyes.

"I will be busy handling several matters. My Galatians are at your service in my absence. Determine what humans you will feed and have the chefs in the building prepare true meals for them. Not leftovers."

Karma's heart lurched. Did she actually hear what she thought she had?

She jumped from her seat and ran after him as he entered his den. He was already pressing the panel for his closet and had removed the wrap from the lower half of his body.

"Rafe, wait. Are you giving me permission to go out?"

His head swung in her direction as he hung his wrap on its hook. She saw his complete nudity, and although her mind was on something important, another part of her mind recalled the pleasure he could give her—when and if he chose to.

"No! Hear me well, Karma. No one but me escorts you from this building! Ever! Do you understand?"

She nodded quickly. "I understand. I just—"

"My men will be in charge of the mission. The soldiers will carry them out. But you will stay here in this building."

"Okay." She nodded. She suppressed a smile. He was allowing her to feed the poor and right now, nothing else mattered. Well, except for him. He hadn't eaten much, and his needs had to come first.

"You're leaving now?"

He reached for his uniform skirt. "I have things I need to take care of."

"I...haven't oiled your scales yet."

He stopped and looked at her.

"That's one of my duties, isn't it?"

Rafe looked from her to his uniform. He nodded once and returned it to its place in the closet.

Karma remembered cutting her hand on the scales on his back during their mating. Her cheeks warmed as she recalled the pleasure he'd given her that had caused her to scratch his arm and then the way he had quickly licked the injured tips of her fingers, easing the pain.

Her core began to warm and tingle.

"You'll have to tell me how. This is something I know nothing about."

She wasn't staring at his prick, but saw it jerk slightly. Was oiling his scales a prelude to sex? She hadn't meant to be so presumptuous as to initiate sex with him! She almost told him when he reached for a jar from his shelf and unscrewed the lid.

"Dip your hands into it and take a liberal amount. Rub it in your hands until it warms."

He then surprised her and turned his back to her and went down on his knees with his head lowered. He was now in a position of total submission before her.

"Begin at the top of my head and rub your hand over every inch of my face, head, neck, and shoulders." His voice had become low, like a rumble of thunder in the distance. The sound plucked at her, sending soft vibrations throughout her body.

"Uh, will they cut me?"

"No. I flattened them. That should have never happened and it won't happen again." He sounded ashamed, maybe embarrassed.

The oil had warmed between her hands and she rubbed them over the top of his head. The scales were flat, and as her hands moved down and then up, they felt smooth over her fingers.

Rafe's scales weren't cold and rough the way she would have imagined. They were warm because his body was warm. She rubbed her hands over his face. His eyes were closed and he lifted his head to accommodate her.

She studied his serene face as she rubbed the oil into it. There was something so noble about the Galatians. People called them humanoid because they were only a step away from them genetically. They shared so much of the same physiology. It wasn't difficult for her to find beauty in Rafe.

The lack of protrusions—ears, lips, nose—didn't detract from his beauty, it enhanced it. He was as smooth and beautiful as any exotic sea creature she'd ever seen in a book.

Her fingers moved over his mouth, his chin, and then down his neck, caressing the oil into his scales. She could feel his Adam's apple and detect the air he breathed into his alien lungs.

Her hands moved back up to the top of his head where they explored the spikes that began and then traveled down his tail. She circled her fingers along the largest one, which was the size of the tip of her finger.

Rafe sighed in pleasure and she took note that he liked his spikes rubbed. She spent a few minutes rubbing each of them before she had to get the jar from his hands to apply more.

She saw his erection had grown so massive it hovered before him like a club! He didn't seem to pay it any attention as his eyes remained closed.

Karma rubbed oil between her palms and put her attention back to her task; applying the oil. She focused on his shoulders next. The muscles beneath the scales flexed at her touch. They were hard, yet limber. She applied more pressure there and felt as much as heard him sigh. He wanted his muscles here rubbed. She used the heel of her hand and applied pressure.

Rafe trembled and then while still kneeling, he lowered his body until his head touched the polished stone floor. Karma could now use her weight to apply pressure to his muscles of his upper back and shoulders. She was now his masseuse, and in a sense, his master.

She kneaded and rubbed, working her way down to his lower back to where his tail connected to his spine.

His tail swished along the floor, reminding her of the tail of a cat expressing its contentment. It wasn't the only thing that expressed it.

She could hear a humming sound emanating from him. Was he…purring?

While it was obvious he enjoyed this, it also gave her an opportunity to do something she'd wanted to do for days now; to explore his body.

She moved her attention to his tail. Beginning at the thicker base, she rubbed the residual oil there. The muscles of his glutes flexed. Tail or not, Rafe had an ass. How could he not when his thighs were so massive with muscles?

Her hands moved down his tail, circling each spike. It remained still for her as she worked the oil into it. When she finally reached the end—it was easily six feet long—Karma used only the tip of her finger to circle it, just like she would circle the head of a penis she was trying to entice.

She didn't know what to expect, but not for the tail to slowly encircle her body from behind. The tip moved up to stay at her face level as if it had eyes to stare at her with.

She stared back, just as helpless to break the contact as she would if Rafe was watching her with his topaz eyes.

The tip of the tail stroked her cheek and then unraveled from her. Rafe came up on his haunches, slowly stretching his long, lean body and then he moved to lay on his back.

Her eyes took in every inch of his perfect body, from the talons on his feet to the eyes that watched her with an intensity she couldn't identify.

His prick had grown so thick it surged with a pulse that must mimic his heartbeat. Clear precum rolled slowly from the head and was making its way down his shaft.

Karma's mouth flooded with desire to taste him. Having a man's prick in her mouth had never been her favorite sex act, but she wanted Rafe's pale-green prick head in her mouth. She wanted to wrap her hands around his throbbing shaft and stroke him until he spilled his thick cum into her mouth...

Rafe's eyes closed slowly, as if he had read her every thought. And strangely, Karma knew he had.

She drew in a slow, shuddering breath and then once again dipped her hand into the jar of oil. After rubbing her palms together and getting them slick, Karma moved to his chest, ignoring his prick.

His chest was perfection. She found the tiny nipple buds and used her thumbs to circle them.

Rafe sucked in a sharp breath and his body arched. He looked at her in surprise and she moved her thumbs from his nipples. His body once again relaxed and he breathed in deeply. He didn't seem to know his body would react the way it had. So, Karma did it again. She circled his nipples with her oil-slickened thumbs, this time flicking roughly.

As if an electrical current had shot through him, Rafe's body once again arched and this time his groan of pleasure grew in intensity. His eyes closed as his head was thrown back.

"Karma..." he groaned. He suddenly sat up and grabbed her around her waist. "Pleasure me now!" His hands moved over her clothing as if he wanted to rip them from her body yet he restrained himself, as if not wanting to be the brute he'd been thus far.

She put her hand on his chest and pressed him back until he was lying on the floor.

She pleasure him? He gave her power to control his pleasure...

Karma stood and stripped out of her clothes as Rafe watched her with reverence. His eyes followed each movement of her hands as they undid buttons or slipped material from her body, revealing brown skin that glowed with its own natural sheen.

When Karma stood nude before him, she stared into his eyes, seeking to read his desires. And then she knew. She stepped across his body until one foot was planted on each side of him. His eyes moved from hers to the spot between her legs. His eyes seemed incapable of moving anywhere else; not until Karma lowered herself to her knees with her pussy across his face.

Rafe's hands captured and held Karma's thighs, locking her in place. His mouth was wide open and her pussy fit into it perfectly.

The aroma of her desire cloistered around him, filling his nostrils and tantalizing his tongue.

He lapped at her, seeking every drop of her slick juices. They ran freely from her tender opening and greedily, he wouldn't wait. His tongue slipped inside of her, stretching and burrowing deeper into her opening.

Karma cried out and her body began to spasm with the sudden onslaught of pleasure. Rafe's tail moved to position itself behind her and when she arched back, it was there to capture her, preventing her from collapsing completely.

Rafe's tongue filled her and knew what to do to cause more of her delicious juices to flow. He used his tongue to fuck her, allowing it to roll and dip and flick in a manner no human appendage could ever achieve.

Karma screeched and her hands locked onto his legs, her nails trying in vain to dig into them. Rafe's tail moved to twirl around her neck, its base still supporting her body, but the tip was free to lightly stroke her nipple.

She choked out a loud moan. The tail moved to the other nipple, teasing until it peaked as hard as the stones in his pool, and all the while Rafe tongue-fucked her hard and fast.

His own senses seemed overwhelmed by Karma's taste, sounds, and aroma. He drank of the elixir that ran copiously from her body and when he felt her clitoris had thickened, elongating against the base of his tongue, he knew she had only moments before she would give him all of herself.

"Cum, my little human. Cum." He spoke these words not in English, but in his Galatian tongue, for he swore he would teach her to recognize the sound of those words, and that was a vow he intended to keep.

Karma's body froze for just a heartbeat—the calm before the storm.

In the next second, she screamed out meaningless words as her body grew rigid. She began to writhe over him, her hips pumping uncontrollably while her hands clawed at his legs.

He greedily refused to unlatch his mouth from her pussy but did loosen his grip on her thighs. He was rewarded with a fresh flow of her female ejaculate, different than her slick lubricant; this was thin, yet even more fragrant. Rafe lapped and sucked hungrily as he felt her collapse, her only movement several feeble spasms.

His tail moved her carefully while he lifted her knees so she was able to lay prone on top of his body. Her body now trapped his throbbing cock and while it was sweet agony, he didn't want her to move.

Rafe closed his eyes and stroked the silky skin of her legs and thighs.

It took her a full minute to come around, and whether she was passed out or just paralyzed from the intense orgasm, Rafe wasn't quite sure.

Karma rolled her head from one side and then to the other as if testing her capacity to move. He grew amused, observing her through his tail, which hovered just over her face. She blinked rapidly and then looked at the tip of his tail.

"You're watching me with your tail, aren't you?"

"In a manner of speaking."

She studied it closely. "How is that possible? There are no eyes…"

"Our biology is not easy to understand, but we have neurons in our tail that allow us to perceive our surroundings even better than your human eyes. Do you know the word *photoreceptor*?"

"No."

"No matter. It is possible to see without eyes. Just as it is possible for a reptile and mammal to exist in one body, like a Galatian."

He continued to stroke the delicate skin of her legs as he spoke.

"That feels nice," she murmured. She wiggled her backside, feeling his hard erection. "I was supposed to pleasure you, and once again you beat me to it. I'm a novice," she explained cheerfully.

"Far from it," he said lazily. "You just know that what gives me pleasure happens to be mutually beneficial to us both. I like to touch you, and taste you."

"Mmm," she murmured in pleasure. "That is mutually beneficial. But, Rafe?"

"Yes?"

"I like to do the same..." His prick gave a hard throb from between them. "I like when you use your tongue and the way you touch me. But I also like when your prick is inside of me. I know we don't fit, and the first time it hurt, but we can try to go further..."

He sat up slowly, causing her to sit as well. He liked that she didn't try to hide her nudity and he longed to touch her breast—to flick the nipples with his tongue...

He forced himself to look at her face. "Even when I don't require it, you still want intercourse?"

"Your tongue," she smiled. "It's like a prick, but I still want..." she exhaled an embarrassed breath, never having to speak words like these aloud. "I'd like to have the real thing."

He sighed. His erection had become so hard it ached. He wanted nothing more than to bury himself into her tight, little opening. He even had to close his eyes to stop himself from picturing it. He swallowed and looked at her again.

Was there anything more enticing than the one that makes your heartbeat quicken confess how much she desires to be fucked by you?

He used his thumb to lightly trace her lips and then her jaw. "I cannot do that again. It's too dangerous. I didn't understand your condition the first time but now that I do, I won't risk you. One slip... No."

She appeared to think about his words. "You said I can have the surgery that allows me to accept you fully."

His brow dipped. "And you would willingly allow this, knowing you'll never be able to bear children?"

She hesitated. "Isn't it what you require?"

He quickly shook his head. "I've never made that a requirement as a condition of being my consort; only as a condition for intercourse."

"But you will never be fully satisfied until happens," she said. "And satisfying you is my only purpose — at least for now."

It was his turn to consider her words.

"That pussy of yours is beautiful and delicious...but that's not the only thing about you that can give me full pleasure. Have you forgotten so easily?"

Chapter Twenty-six

Rafe's words caused Karma's skin to warm. How was it possible to be so thoroughly satisfied one moment and then the next to crave more? Sex had created in Karma something she had never before experienced to such a degree.

Lust.

It wasn't merely sex that made her heart quicken and her core swell. What she desired was sex with an alien; sex with Rafe.

It was his artful use of his tongue and the magnificence of his prick; the way it glistened and pulsed, all for her. That much was certainly true. But it was also in his eyes, and the way they followed her every movement as if trying to decipher a puzzle.

He didn't always get it right, but she could tell he wanted to.

He wasn't human. He wasn't emotionally supportive, and he certainly lacked manners. Yet Rafe was still a better man than many of the human ones that had crossed her path.

She gazed into his strange, alien eyes—eyes that over the last few days had become pleasing to her.

"I haven't forgotten the other things that give you pleasure." She was still sitting on his taut, muscular belly, his prick so hard behind her his shaft rested comfortably along the crack of her ass cheeks.

Slowly, she turned so she was sitting on him but facing his lower half. She felt his hands move to her hips and then his thumbs grazed her ass.

Karma could not believe the beauty of his prick, and for a moment, all she could do was gaze at it. It had taken on an angry purple tint and it throbbed and pulsed, reminding her of a volcano preparing to erupt. With each pulse he ejected a small stream of precum that glided down his length, drenching his tight balls and the floor beneath them.

She had teased him enough, and had denied herself far longer than she could bear. Karma wrapped both hands around his prick; one near the base, the other at the center of his length. And still her hands didn't touch…

Rafe's body tensed and his breathing paused. She leaned forward and licked and sucked the head, delighted by the umami taste of his seed.

He inhaled a shuddering breath as if her touch was both agony and pleasure. She felt his hands on her hips tighten, although not enough to cause pain. His thumbs rapidly circled and caressed her ass, exploring the crack briefly before squeezing her buttocks.

She came up on her knees slightly as she continued sucking and lapping at her treat, giving him access to more of her lower half. He was quick to locate her vulva and stroke it as gently as one should stroke a kitty.

His precum offered a wonderful lubricant for her fists, but she reached for the jar of oil and quickly slathered his shaft with the slippery substance. She massaged it into him as she sucked and licked, not neglecting his testicles.

Rafe's tail writhed against the floor while his hips bucked up to meet her seeking mouth. A groan rumbled from his chest like a beast's wild cry, growing in intensity with each hard stroke and twist she applied to his shaft.

"Ka-Kar-!" He tried to call her name as his legs quaked and his muscles tensed and released. His breath seemed incapable of remaining in his body as he gasped and then sucked in ragged breaths.

His fingers had momentarily forgotten their task of pleasuring her, but when he remembered, he plucked at her clitoris as if it was a guitar string.

And for a moment, Karma too forgot what she was doing. Her eyes clamped shut and Rafe's prick slipped from her lips as she held onto his shaft as if for dear life.

And when she did that, Rafe's tail stiffened and his body hardened and the last of his control was torn from his grasp.

She heard him cry out his special message to her using his strange language; an alert, or maybe a warning, because a moment after exclaiming he was cumming, a torrent of semen flew into the air in rapid pulses.

Karma quickly covered him with her mouth and heard Rafe's sudden hiss of agonized pleasure. Cum soon filled her mouth, gliding from her lips and down her chin. Her fists moved rapidly up and down as she milked his shaft, coaxing more of his seed into her mouth.

Rafe pumped his hips responsively, fighting to control his thrusts so as not to hurt her. Karma was unsure how long this lasted before the spurts slowed until they had become a continuous stream that flowed into her waiting mouth, and then how long after before he pulled himself up to a sitting position and wrapped his arms around her body. He gently lifted her and sat her on the floor, causing his prick to slip from her grasp.

She blinked, drunk and dazed by the sensory overload. Rafe came to his feet in one graceful movement with the aid of his tail. He effortlessly lifted her into his arms and walked to his pool.

Karma quickly wrapped her arms around his neck as he eased them into the water, not seeming the least bit unbalanced by the addition of her weight. He didn't stay on the shallow edge of the pool, but moved to where the water ran deep. At the same time, he artfully twirled onto his back so he was now her raft.

Karma didn't know anything about swimming, but he hadn't allowed the water to touch even an inch of her face so she relaxed, with her back against his chest.

He swam slowly, but only stayed in the lukewarm portion of the pool. One hand always held her securely in place while the other streamed water over her body to wash away his seed.

After a few moments of this, Karma was able to close her eyes and enjoy the feel of Rafe's body as it supported her from behind. She could feel his prick between them. It wasn't hard but it wasn't soft, either.

He kept them afloat with slight movements of his limbs while one hand or the other stroked her wet skin. They swam like that in quiet contentment until Rafe guided them back to the edge of the pool.

He lifted her effortlessly until she was sitting on the pool's lip, her lower body still submerged in the lukewarm water.

Once he was sure she was safely in place, he ducked his head beneath the water and when he reemerged, he was all the way on the pool's far side, where steam rose into the air.

"Rafe?"

"Mmm?" he grunted while rolling and twisting like a sea monster.

"How can the water be boiling hot over there and still nice over here?"

Rafe disappeared beneath the water and suddenly emerged right in front of her. He held out his cupped hands and when he opened them, there was a palmful of water captured.

"Touch it."

She reached out and touched it. It was very warm, but not hot enough to burn. It was much warmer than the water her body was resting in.

"That's a hot-water spring," he gestured with his head. "While this is salt water. Both are continuously pumped into this pool so they never mix."

She gave him a confused look. "Is it an alien thing?"

"Estuaries aren't exclusive to Galatian bodies of water."

She gave him a confused look.

Rafe pointed to the hot spring. "Do you see where the water meets? They are different colors."

She saw what he said was true. One side was blue, while the other was green. "Why did I never see that before? But how is it possible the water isn't mixing?"

He climbed up on the ledge to sit beside her. "Because one side is salt water while the other is fresh water; the difference in their density keeps them separated. Without the pumps, this pool would eventually turn brackish. But on Galatia, the natural pull of the tide allows for a body of water to be both fresh and salt."

She looked at him in awe. "You're really smart." It made her feel very small in the face of all he must know.

He seemed disinterested in the compliment. "You know this information now, so by that token, you're also smart. Having learned something doesn't make you smarter than someone who hasn't been taught the same thing."

He climbed out of the pool. "Come. I have business I have to attend to." He took her hand and helped her out of the pool.

Karma thought about how he had stormed out in the middle of dinner after she explained the truth about the government aid that went to the poor. She was curious about what he intended to do, but knew it wasn't her place. Fucking her master didn't make them equal. She still had to maintain her station.

"Do you want to finish having dinner before you leave? And I think you washed off the oil I just applied..."

He cocked his head and gave her an amused look. "You've taken good care of me, my consort, and it hasn't gone unnoticed. But you've brought to light some matters I can't leave unaddressed, even for a few more hours of pleasure with you." He sighed.

"I want you to wash in your own bath. My pool has many health benefits, which we can discuss at another time. But the salt water is harsh and your skin too fragile, and I like it just the way it is."

She hid a smile and reluctantly left Rafe's den. She liked this Rafe; the one that talked easily and made her

262

feel desired. She just wished they could spend more time talking...and, well, mating.

Rafe got dressed and then went into the living room where he paused, listening for sounds of his consort. Her bath was running, which meant she would wash her delicate skin. He would love to watch; not for sexual reasons, but out of curiosity. Her flesh had begun to pucker and it seemed painful, especially due to the harsh salt water and the natural bacteria that existed in his pool. Humans claimed puckered skin didn't hurt, but to the best of his knowledge, no Galatian had ever done a study on it. And without a Galatian study in place, Rafe didn't necessarily take a human's account as accurate.

He saw Dorf on the top shelf of the entertainment center, lazing quietly.

"Dorf. I need to investigate some things and I don't know when I'll return."

Dorf deftly dropped to the ground with the use of his wings. Afterwards, he clamped onto Rafe's tail.

"Which matters are you going to investigate? Your consort's claims about misconduct towards the poor, or the misconduct within the Galatian Exchange?"

"Both must be addressed. I am tasked with locating two missing people and this Earth is vast. A human taskforce will be much more efficient in infiltrating areas I cannot, so I need to handpick my men — ones have been trained by our Guards." He sighed. "But I must speak with Commander Einar about my seven-year mission."

Dorf sent him a questioning emotion.

"Karma's claims of corruption in the North American government need to be investigated."

"They aren't just claims. I've seen it with my own eyes."

"What did you see?"

"People living in hovels, half-starved, and many sick with illnesses I could smell. I could *smell* their sicknesses. And the children...dressed in clothing that didn't provide enough protection against the elements. Of course, they would get sick! It was easy to see many of those your consort served would have gone without eating today if she hadn't provided a means for them to do so."

Rafe sent a wave of discontent to their connection. He folded his arms before him.

"I can appreciate my consort's wishes to help the needy, Dorf. What I can't accept is her hands-on approach." He began to pace, causing Dorf to release him. He stopped, realizing he and Dorf were no longer attached. He sighed and stayed in one place.

Dorf reattached and cut through Rafe's internal tirade.

"Rafe. You and I have been friends for many years — since Iceland, before you ever became decorated in the Guards and before anyone spoke your name with reverence." Rafe looked at his friend. Dorf had been assigned to him, to assist as an interpreter. For many generations, the Japoxillian have been friends with the Galatians and for high-ranking guards, the Japoxillian's unique abilities became invaluable. This allowed them to be the only aliens besides Galatians to enter the Galatian Guard. But for Rafe and Dorf, it was more personal. Rafe was his friend when the Japo needed him most.

"You have been a good friend, Dorf," Rafe replied, quieting.

"As you have been to me. So, hear me well, Rafe. I have known love and I have lost it. I would have never said this to you if you had simply been mated to any of the other consorts. They have been conditioned to never stand out. But not the brown one. You are getting a human that has not been taught to conform, and who doesn't know why it might even be an expectation. The only conditioning she will receive will be from you. Bear in mind what you wish from your consort, because you have a unique ability to actually get it."

Rafe touched his chin. Dorf spoke of love and concubines in the same breath. They were never meant to fulfill that emotion. He could never love anyone but a queen, yet the one he was bound to did not fill him with love or desire. After years of rejection, Ragna had become nothing more than a requirement, like being forced to be mated to a human while grounded on Earth instead of pursuing his lifelong dream of battling space pirates.

But in this, Karma was not at fault. Even though she was not supposed to have been his consort, it was wrong for him to treat her as if she was an inconvenience.

Rafe looked at Dorf, knowing he had picked up on his thoughts.

"I...agree that I've misdirected many of my frustrations to my—to Karma. But I don't..." He shook his head. "I've never had to be...understanding of the females' needs."

Dorf gave him an amused response. "You first have to stop being like a chauvinist and show her the same consideration you would one of your Galatian brothers."

"A chauvinist!" he roared out loud. "How can you call me that when I grew up in a queendom?!"

Dorf had made sense until that statement. There was no way he put himself before females when he fully accepted the laws and the many rules put forth by the queens. The only purpose male Galatians had was to serve and protect, and they did so with pride.

Dorf released his tail to laugh. He actually fell to the ground. When he spoke, it was in Icelandic. "Your queens are the deadliest beings in the known universe. They're smart, cunning, and they can fight just as well as you can."

"How can you call me a chauvinist when I know this about our—"

"You are until you realize it is *you* that should be walking behind *them*."

Rafe just blinked at Dorf. How could a warrior speak of such matters to an intellect?

Dorf straightened himself, flapping his wings to put his feathers in order. "Rafe, if you do nothing else, use Karma's knowledge." He walked to his door and stopped to look at Rafe. "And tell her what your intentions are. She is just as curious as I am." He went into his home, shutting his door soundly behind him.

Rafe didn't like that Dorf had pointed out flaws he hadn't been willing to recognize. But he had to admit they were accurate. He sighed and returned to his quarters, where he removed his rigging and sword and donned a comfortable wrap.

Whether or not he completely agreed with Dorf, he had to admit that the two had to speak—he needed to speak to her. And while locating Heinrich and speaking

266

to his commander about government misconduct was important, so was his relationship with Karma.

Relationship. He paused to think about that.

Galatians mated for life. Ragna was his intended, and the only "relationship" he'd ever had despite the fact that he'd had many lovers. But what he had with her felt far from a relationship.

No one forced the males to serve their queens. They did it because someone had to run Galatia while they were out battling and discovering new worlds. They didn't come home only to change the way their queens operated. And after decades of this, Galatia evolved into a queendom. Afterwards, new rules and laws came into play, but it took nothing away from the males to submit to their queens.

But submission only went so far. And Rafe would be damned if he allowed Ragna to force his hand in matters that affected his lifelong dreams. While she couldn't force him, her unspoken ultimatums had left their relationship lacking.

Rules about consorts and about human interaction had never meant anything to him — until now. Now he was mated to one, and he didn't want the same thing with Karma that he had with Ragna.

It surprised him to realize he actually did want something from Karma. Dorf had wondered what he wanted to condition Karma to become. He found he respected more qualities in Karma than he found in others, male or female, and that included himself. No. She wasn't the one that needed to change.

Chapter Twenty-seven

The living, squiggly thing Karma had eaten earlier had found its way out of her bowels with explosive intent. Her bathtub was filling with warm, sudsy water while she sat on her toilet reevaluating her decision to consume alien food.

She would have to search the cabinets for something to help her stomach. She was just grateful she hadn't experienced this attack of bowels during sex.

"Oh my Guardian! I would just shoot myself," she muttered. "He already thinks I'm a hot-ass mess." By the time she was finished with the toilet, her tub was full. But before sinking into its soothing depths, Karma carefully grabbed the old-fashioned music disc of *Songs in the Key of Life* and then inserted it gently into the music player she had recently discovered beneath the television screen situated at the foot of her tub.

She sighed contentedly as she sang the familiar lyrics. Her mind drifted back to a time when her mother had played music like this on an even older music player where large, black discs rotated on a box with a needle fit into its groove.

As a child, she didn't understand how so much sound was captured in a flat, black disc, and perhaps that was the root of the magic Karma found in music.

The music player had been passed down to them from her grandparents and their parents, along with several record albums. When Karma was old enough, she and her mother would go scavenging and if they found a record, they raced home and danced to its music, even when it was opera and not meant to be danced to. Daddy used to look at them as if they were crazy, and even though he never joined them, he would hide his smile.

One day, the music player and all the albums she and her mother had collected were gone. No one mentioned it, and when Karma asked about it, her mother brushed it off. But that day, their refrigerator had food for the first time in a long time, and she had a store-bought pair of shoes...

Karma never mentioned music or the music player again. And when she got old enough, she went without in order to purchase her own.

There was a knock on her bathroom door and Karma jumped and pulled herself from her reverie.

She looked around, unsure if she should gather the bubbles closer to conceal her nudity or if she should get out of the tub and quickly don her robe.

"Who is it?" she called quickly.

"Rafe. May I enter?"

Rafe? "Yes," she called, still unsure if she should get out.

The door opened and Rafe came in, no longer dressed in his uniform. He wore a long cloth wrapped around his lower half that put her in the mind of pictures she'd seen of Polynesian men that lived on distant islands. His feet were bare and he seemed more relaxed dressed in this manner.

He looked around and she suddenly remembered she had just recently lit the bathroom up!

Oh my Guardian...Galatians could smell a fart in the wind!

"Um, I'll get out," she said while preparing to stand.

"Don't. I'll get in with you." He unwrapped his skirt and hung it on a hook behind the door.

Her mouth opened in awe, but she settled back down, wondering if there would ever be a time when the sight of a prick that dangled a full foot long would ever seem normal.

Rafe padded to the tub, his movements so graceful they seemed almost effeminate. It was just that he didn't stomp, he swayed, reminding her of a snake that hypnotized its victim.

He stepped into the large tub and used his webbed hands to stream fragrant water over his head and shoulders.

"I thought you had left," she said.

"I very nearly did. But I wanted to stay."

Karma looked surprised. "I'm happy you did." She suddenly realized his wanting to stay might not have anything to do with her. Maybe he wanted to interview her more, or chastise her again.

"Why did you want to stay?" she asked tentatively.

He cleared his throat. Usually, he was very quick to respond, his thoughts and words moving much quicker than hers. But this time, he took his time in replying.

"I wasn't ready for our connection to end."

"You weren't?" she asked slowly. So, the magnetism she'd felt right after their time together wasn't just one-sided. She hadn't wanted to leave him but when he had insisted he had more important things to do, she had to remind herself who and what she was.

"No, I wanted to stay with you. So here I am." He looked at her and then moved to sit directly in front of her, right in the center of the over-sized tub. "Also, there is another matter. I owe you an apology. I have not always been considerate of you, which is bad enough. But I also failed to explain that I welcome you in my life."

Karma was struck dumb by Rafe's words. She almost wondered if the food she had consumed earlier had some type of hypnotic properties. This felt so unreal. There were many times in her life she had dreamed of hearing words like this from someone that didn't just want her for a momentary thrill.

But coming from an alien that had yelled at her more times than not, it seemed unbelievable. Was she missing something? Karma thought carefully before responding. "I am happy to serve as your consort and to bring you pleasure."

Rafe's scale tinted pink. Pink? What was that emotion?

He reached out and traced her jaw with the side of his finger, not allowing his talons to touch her.

"You misunderstand. You see, being given a gift of a consort is supposed to be a grand achievement after years of service. No longer being required to battle and being given the gift of a woman to meet all of one's needs is a reward for most.

"But you see, I never wanted to settle down on Earth. I am best suited to be a warrior. Being stationed on Earth is no reward for me; not when I have so much more I can offer the Galatian Guard.

"Having a consort felt the same. I expected an emotionless servant whose thoughts and needs were something I'd never have to consider because contractually, you serve a mutually beneficial purpose.

"But I didn't get that type of consort. I met you; a person that showed me you had worth beyond being my servant. So, when I say I welcome you in my life, I mean as an individual I want to know and understand.

"You are not what I expected, Karma. Of course, that makes sense now." She looked down, but he gently lifted her chin until she met his eyes again. "You are not like other consorts. Your individuality shows through. Your unique qualities are…" He paused as if searching for the right words. His expression cleared. "Desirable."

Her heart felt as if it would pump out of her chest. His words were so welcome, especially after going so long without another living individual in her corner; no one to praise her when she prevailed or hug her when she was afraid. These words that settled into her very core could very well be her undoing—if she allowed them into her heart.

She closed her eyes and then opened them and met his. "Thank you. I appreciate you saying those things — and you don't need to apologize to me. I did a lot of things wrong— "

Rafe dropped his hand. "The apology was owed to you. The other words I spoke could have stayed unspoken. Yet, I hope this will be the beginning of something new…for me at least."

"Something new?"

This time it was he that looked elsewhere. The pink tone of his scales deepened and after a moment, he met her eyes again. "I want a meaningful relationship."

Karma was unsure what she could say. She was a servant and he was the master. He could say and even mean those words today. And then tomorrow, he could chastise her for some unknown reason. This was a potential minefield.

She'd already made the mistake of thinking being Rafe's consort was more than he wanted, such as expecting him to eat his meals with her like a family, and thinking they should cuddle and have deep conversations after sex.

She had been put into her place more times over the last few days than she had been in the near-year she had worked for the Tolberts. Rafe's words were beautiful, and she desired for them to be real, but words weren't enough. There could be no true trust between a master and a servant. Even if he asked for it using the sweetest words possible.

Karma nodded her head and averted her eyes. "Yes. That would be nice."

"Do you want to get out of the bath now? I should like to have a meal with you...but maybe you should stay with your own food today. I don't think my food was good for your digestion."

Oh my Guardian!

Karma's eyes nearly popped from her head. He had smelled it!

"I think I'm just going to lie down." She stood up and clumsily climbed out of the tub.

"Would you like me to lay with you?"

She wrapped an oversized towel around her body. "Maybe tomorrow?"

He nodded. "Of course."

After Karma left the bathroom, hurrying to her bedroom, where she firmly closed the door behind herself, Rafe palmed his face.

He cursed in Galatian. He had truly messed that up. He slipped beneath the water and stayed there for a full five minutes.

Chapter Twenty-eight

Rafe had no sooner opened the front door when Dorf appeared from his apartment.

"I thought you were going to work things out with your consort?" he asked in confusion.

Rafe looked over his shoulder. "She obviously doesn't want that. She hid in her quarters."

"Rafe —"

"Tell her I'll be back tomorrow, in time to share a meal." And with that he left the apartment.

He wasn't angry. It wasn't her fault he had taken so long to realize that what would truly give him pleasure wasn't found between his legs. Besides, what good would it do to force his attention? Especially when giving her time to adjust to his statements also allowed him to follow up on several important matters.

Karma had brought several issues to light, but his first responsibility was locating Tolbert and the missing lottery winner. He was in the process of coordinating the CCTV across the city and wanted to personally review them. He had already reviewed footage of Tolbert's daily routine while in the office.

The man had been a constant visitor to the consort school, but those visits had increased over the past year, culminating into almost daily trips within the last month. Rafe had conducted interviews with the instructors who had been tasked with questioning the students. It had gone nowhere. Even if the humans knew anything, they weren't keen on giving up their own—which made it a strong possibility Mayva had been a willing participant in her disappearance.

The lottery winners were to be protected at all costs. Therefore, strong-arming them was out of the question. He couldn't rely on the consorts-in-training or any human. This had to be done his way.

Rafe got into a truck that easily accommodated his size. With blacked-out windows and military plates, he was free to drive around the city at will. But he had never been much interested in the human world. North America interested him no more than Iceland, the European Union, or any other place he'd been on this planet.

But as he drove to the military compound where he had stationed himself, Rafe couldn't help but to actually observe the people milling in the streets. The people heading to and fro looked like average humans. They dressed appropriately for the weather, in wool coats and boots, with hats pulled low on their heads. He saw no homeless, and it was impossible to tell whether anyone was hungry. But this was Newburgh; the working-class part of the city. The Heights was where the even wealthier lived.

Cross Town is where Karma had been raised—along with others that were considered underprivileged. He thought it was a bad choice of words. *Poor* was more appropriate, but not on government paperwork.

Rafe took an impromptu detour. He had never had much of a reason to travel to Cross Town, as his business basically occurred on the outposts, the military compound, or in the Galatian consulate.

As he drew closer to the outskirts of Newburgh, it was obvious the homes had given way to apartment buildings and then housing complexes, and then the parked cars seemed to disappear unless they were rusted-out older models. Finally, he began to see bars on the windows of the few shops and trash littering the ground.

The people he saw were vastly different than those he had seen earlier. Older men and women sat on benches huddled in groups of two or three. They weren't waiting for buses, as bus service had ended years ago.

Were they huddling for warmth?

His imagination might be getting the better of him. Anytime he saw gaunt, drawn faces, he imagined starving people. Some people just wore their struggles on their faces, and it didn't mean they had no means to obtain proper food and housing.

He didn't doubt Karma's words about widespread neglect, but he wouldn't be able to identify it by just driving down the streets of Cross Town.

He thought about the first time Karma had sent leftovers out to the train station.

He had witnessed the near-riot as the rich tried to take food from the hands of the less fortunate. He hadn't actually thought much about why there were so many poor in the train station. Maybe because the authorities referred to them as scrubs, giving the impression they were just shiftless.

It bothered him enough that Rafe turned his vehicle and headed to the train station.

He parked in the military lot and when he got out of his vehicle, the soldiers present came to attention. A soldier came forward.

"Staff Sergeant James Shu at your service," he saluted.

"At ease," Rafe advised. "I'm here to visit the depot."

"Yes, sir." The man moved to retrieve his walkie-talkie. "I'll advise the guards of your visit and I'll escort you."

"Escort me, but don't advise anyone of my arrival." The staff sergeant's eyes instantly became uneasy before he caught himself. "Lead the way." Rafe gestured forward.

They walked into the facility and through an office where several guards were laughing and talking. They instantly came to attention at the sight of the seven-foot-tall, green alien. Rafe ignored them as he headed out of the office and into the train station.

Rafe stopped at the entrance of the second level before heading down old cement stairs that led to the trains. Only staff would use the upper level and unless the people on the lower platform looked up, they wouldn't see the staff sergeant and Galatian Guard.

Rafe saw a group of guards dressed in long wool coats and hats gathered in the nearby guard's shack. They were laughing, eating, and drinking from thermoses.

Several others roamed through the crowd of men, women, and children that stood waiting on the platforms. The benches appeared to have been removed, and a few people were sitting on the cold tiled floors in corners, as if trying to stay out of sight. They jumped to their feet at the approach of a guard and then quickly moved to another part of the platform.

He was surprised to see an older man struggling to his feet. But when he didn't move quickly enough, he got hit in the chest with a metal baton.

The staff sergeant moved to take a step forward, but Rafe held out his arm to stop him.

"Stay," he said simply.

A Black man reached out to help the one who had crumbled back to the floor while holding his chest. The guard then hit the younger man across the knuckles. Rafe could clearly hear the sharp cracking of the man's bones and the loud cry as he held his broken hand.

After that, things moved swiftly. Rafe saw several men on walkie-talkies hurrying from the guard shed. Several looked up at him and the staff sergeant.

So, someone from the guard's lounge had informed the others they were being watched.

The guard that had struck the two men had a gleeful look on his face until his fellow guards surrounded him and obviously told him he was being watched. The abuser looked up and met Rafe's cold eyes. The man paled and was then led away to the guard shack.

Rafe had seen enough, and he had only been there a mere minute. He turned to the staff sergeant. "See about the two injured men. I want a report from the hospital about both men, and the bill will be covered by the guard that injured them. I also want a full report of the disciplinary actions the guard will incur for the unwarranted abuse. And I want the full report on my desk, Lieutenant Rafe Sigur, within twenty-four hours."

The staff sergeant's face instantly paled. Perhaps all green-scaled aliens looked alike to him, but he certainly recognized the name. He gave a rapid salute.

"Yes, sir!"

Rafe gestured with his head. "Deal with that. I'll see myself out." Rafe walked out and had returned to his vehicle within minutes.

His plan to spend the next several hours reviewing video at the military compound ended. He was going straight to Commander Einar's office at the satellite station.

Handling Tolbert wasn't a matter of life or death, but this was.

Karma curled up in her bed. She didn't even want to listen to music. She went over her entire conversation with Rafe once he'd shown up in the bathroom with her.

I want a meaningful relationship...

She tried to think of every possible meaning behind that statement. It was obvious she and Rafe didn't see one thing in the same way. Maybe she didn't understand what he meant with that statement.

She was already having sex with him, so that was not what he was asking for.

He was bound to a queen, so he wasn't asking for anything long-term.

He was her master, and had certainly corrected her attitude and she, in turn, had sworn to submit to his will.

So, what was left? What else did he want from her? Love?

She closed her eyes and sank deeper into sheets that were softer than anything she'd ever touched. She lived in luxury. She was warm and safe during a time when so many were cold and homeless. She wanted for nothing, and Rafe was a considerate and gentle lover.

But loving him was out of the question.

Rafe Sigur scared her.

He was quick to anger, and his potential for violence was obvious. He was an intergalactic warrior; one of the top hunters of intergalactic pirates. Who was she to question him, to dispute him, when her inclusion among the consorts had been a matter of trickery?

She knew he regretted his harsh words to her, and maybe all he wanted was her forgiveness. She held nothing against him. But who she gave her heart to; who she loved? That just wasn't something he—or any male—could force.

She had nearly drifted off to sleep when her door opened. Karma's eyes popped open thinking Rafe had returned, but a moment later, the small creature with the pristine, white feathers leaped quietly onto her bed.

Dorf sat at the foot of her bed, observing her.

Karma sat up and turned on the lamp next to her bed. She rubbed her eyes and then held out her hand to him.

With a short hop and a flap of his wings, he landed next to her hand and bit on the meaty side pad.

She was getting used to the fact that a bite like that from another animal would have certainly caused pain, and it would have probably left blood—but not with Dorf. She barely felt anything more than a bit of pressure and a shot of adrenaline.

Dorf's gentle, soothing words flooded her mind. "Rafe has left for the remainder of the evening. He said he will return to have a meal with you tomorrow."

At the mention of his name, her heart leaped.

Dorf flinched.

"You shouldn't think that way, Karma. Rafe means you no harm. There's no reason to fear him."

She sighed in annoyance. "Why do extraterrestrials think they know more than humans know about their own thoughts and feelings?"

"Are you angry at me or angry at Rafe?"

Her shoulders sank. "I'm sorry, Dorf. I'm not mad at you; and don't you dare go telling Rafe I'm mad at him! The last thing I need is for him trying to decipher my thoughts."

Dorf huffed between the teeth embedded in the side of her hand. "Believe this or not, I don't share any of our communications. But you are a frequent topic of conversation."

Her brow quirked up. "How so?"

"Do you really need to ask? His newly assigned job centers around the reason you replaced his rightful consort. Even when we aren't directly discussing you, we're discussing how your current position affects him.

"Now, Karma. In regards to me knowing more about your feelings than you do, bear in mind that I not only read your thoughts, I can also read your emotions. But they are your emotions, before you ever share them with me. Individuals are oftentimes conflicted by varying feelings. I cannot help that I can cipher through them much easier than you can."

She sighed and rubbed her eyes with her free hand. "Oh my Guardian! Fine, Dorf. Please tell me about my conflicting emotions."

"You feel fear, and rightfully so. But you don't directly fear Rafe. You fear your unknown circumstances. Does that make sense to you?"

After a moment of thought, Karma nodded. "That's probably right."

"You're also attracted to Rafe. And not just sexually, although there is that. But with you, sexual attraction would not come first—it would come after you feel a connection— "

"Okay, that's enough!" She pulled her hand away from him. "I am not discussing sex with you!" she hissed.

He tilted his head to the side and she remembered his command of the English language was limited. She offered him her hand again.

"Dorf, you know everything about everybody you sink your teeth into. How about telling me about yourself?"

"My story is in the lyrics of the song you heard me sing."

It was her turn to tilt her head at him. "So that disc cover wasn't just a picture of any random Jaxo...Jaxop..."

"JaPOxillian," he replied. "No. That is me on the music cover, as that is my song."

"It was...very sad. What's it about?"

"It's about loss, Karma. An emotion I have witnessed in you. But I didn't need to connect with you to do it. You listened to my song and you cried. You see, among my kind, our emotions are...they can be overwhelming. And when we feel something so deeply painful, we can only deal with it by sharing it in song."

Karma was embarrassed now. She realized the song she had played repeatedly had been one that represented his pain. Had she known, she wouldn't have played it in front of him.

"I'm sorry for whatever loss you suffered. I just want you to know you have the most beautiful voice I've ever heard. When I hear you talking in my head, it's always very nice. But it's nothing like hearing you with my own ears."

There was a thoughtful silence before Dorf continued. "I created that song after my wife died."

"Oh. I didn't realize..."

"Japoxillians mate for life. When we find someone, they have to be our soul mate. There's no other way when you experience the other's every thought and emotion without loving them with every ounce of your soul.

"Just like your planet, ours has been under frequent attack by the Tybernees, despite our inclusion in the Interplanetary Collective. Because of our unique communication skills, we are prized throughout the universe." Dorf paused for a few moments. "My wife was kidnapped, and I joined with the Galatian Guard to find her. Almost all of the Japos that joined the Guard did so for the same reason. I was assigned to Rafe's unit—well before he was a decorated officer. Back then, we were under the command of others, and I was the unit's interpreter.

"Rafe always made locating my wife a top priority. There were times when he was assigned one mission, but continued searching for my wife. He didn't just do it because I was his friend and teammate. He did it because, as a Galatian, he has a strong sense of...preservation—not just his own, but for others.

"Galatians are protectors—it's embedded in their very being, just like my emotions are buried in mine. I would say it has to do with their imminent extinction.

They've crossed galaxies to reinvent themselves. But they will die out.

"But it is my story I tell, and not Rafe's, so let me finish it. Three years after I joined the Galatian Guard, Rafe heard about a small but dangerous rebel force that was much too informed about the various interplanetary life-forms not to have a Japoxillian in their possession.

"We're too valuable to risk. I kept telling myself this as each year passed without word of my soul mate. When we finally infiltrated their compound, Tili was there among them. I saw my Tili for the first time in three years. But as the last of the Tybernees rebels was cut down by the Galatians...that final Tybernees, with his dying breath, took my Tili's head."

Karma felt a stab of pain at those words. It was so much like her own story, her heart ached for them both. Dorf released her hand slowly.

She wasn't sure why she did it, but Karma reached out tentatively and stroked his soft feathers. After a few moments when he didn't object, she stroked his wings, his back, and the top of his head.

Dorf stood and she thought he was going to walk out of her room and retreat to his own quarters. But he moved to sit next to her, his warm body resting against her side. Once settled, he tucked his head against his wings and closed his eyes.

Karma reached over and turned off the light. She then lay down and snuggled against Dorf's downy feathers.

Chapter Twenty-nine

When Karma awoke, she was alone in her bed. She lay there in a way she could never afford to do before becoming a consort.

She tried to see things from outside of her body — as if she was a stranger looking at her life through a magical window. In this home lived three aliens, each from different planets, and with different backgrounds. But in so many ways, they were each very much alike.

Ultimately, they all wanted acceptance.

She got up and dragged herself out of her bed and then got ready for her day. She dressed in slacks, ankle boots, and a cashmere sweater she thought made her look like a rich woman. She headed for the kitchen, peeking into the living room for sight of Dorf. He was nowhere to be seen.

Sighing, she thought about how nice it would be to have his company while she ate breakfast. She liked Dorf, and that wasn't an easy thing for her. It had been a long time since she had trusted someone enough to truly like them.

When she saw the covered dishes of alien food still in the kitchen, her tummy flip-flopped and she nearly lost her appetite. Thankfully, a maid had apparently shown up and covered everything and set them back on the counter.

Doing her best to ignore them, Karma fried up some bacon, scrambled a few eggs, prepared skillet potatoes, and heated up a Danish to have with a cup of coffee with real cream. Once she had eaten every morsel of her meal, she checked the time. She was learning to sleep a bit later in the day, but it was still the crack of dawn.

Polite people didn't call this early. She decided she would do some cleaning. After washing the dishes she returned to her bedroom, only to find her bed had already been made up.

She smiled to herself.

"I'm not going to complain..."

She glanced at her vanity and was ashamed it was once again tidy and pristine. She decided that from this moment on, she would be the easiest client the cleaning staff ever had.

Karma looked out the window. There were still a lot of reporters out front. So that meant she wasn't going to turn on the news. And if they were out there doing their work, and she was awake trying to pass the time, then Madeline could surely get up if she was still asleep.

She called her, but Madeline answered in her usual, professional manner.

"Madeline, are you busy?"

"Oh, my goodness. Are you going to be the death of me?" Karma shrugged.

"Is your mate home? Rafe is gone and I have no idea what consorts do when they're not taking care of their masters."

"Drago is gone too. They usually head off for work early because Galatians don't sleep as much." She sighed. "There's plenty to do when they're gone."

Karma looked around. "Okay, like what?"

"Well, I was on the Internet looking at property in England. And once you move there's decorating, and then entertaining, and of course the Galatian celebrations to prepare for. We have plenty to do."

286

"England? That's so far away. Won't you miss your family?"

"You mean the people who birthed me and then pimped me off to a lottery in order to further their status?" She chuckled mirthlessly. "Yeah...I'll miss them a great deal."

"I thought...well, everyone wants an opportunity to win the lottery."

Madeline sighed. "I would have married some government worker and been just fine. But I suppose having my own money under my own terms is a better deal. I hear there's even a surgery that will tighten your pussy back up. But they lie so much. Look, come down to my place and we'll get started."

Karma got Madeline's floor and unit number and then jotted a short note to Dorf promising she wasn't leaving the building and explained who she was visiting.

Madeline was dressed in a flowing robe and fur slippers with heels. Her makeup was perfect and her long, straight hair flowed down to her butt, shining as if she had brushed it a hundred strokes.

They appraised each other. "They like when we're nearly nude. They don't want to see us in pants and sweaters. And always wear heels," Madeline said critically.

Karma cupped her chin, equally as critical. "Who told you this? Drago? Or your *handlers*?"

Madeline gave her a surprised look. "I mean..."

"Rafe hates heels. Did Drago tell you he likes all of...*this*?" Karma made a dismissive gesture towards Madeline, whose amazed look turned to one of awe.

"Your master told you he hated heels? He said those words? To you?"

"Yes. I think his words were, 'they're ridiculous.'"

Madeline began to pace while rubbing her hands together.

"Are you serious?" she asked, but the question wasn't directed at Karma, it was directed to herself.

It was then Karma realized Madeline might not be the best teacher in the ways of Galatians.

"What does your Japoxillian say?" Karma asked.

Madeline stopped pacing to give her a confused look. "Polo? Why would he need to tell me anything? I don't need anything translated."

"But he knows Drago, right?"

Madeline shrugged. "Yes. So?"

"Well, who would know your mate's likes and wants better than his Japo?"

Madeline thought about that. Karma could tell she was trying to decide whether or not to accept Karma's words and to reject years of training.

"But..." Madeline began. "Why would our instructors spend years teaching us proper etiquette if none of this is correct?"

"So they could keep their cushy government jobs?" Karma ventured while giving her an incredulous look. "I know if I had financial security, I wouldn't rock the boat—even if that boat was falling apart." She shook her head. Eh, that wasn't quite true. She had rocked the boat plenty. "Look, I don't know if they're teaching you right or wrong. I just know what I've seen with my own eyes." Madeline quietly nodded. "Maybe we should talk to Polo?"

288

Madeline gave her a doubtful look. "That still seems strange…"

"It won't hurt."

Madeline nodded, and led them to the far side of the much smaller living room. The apartment was still very luxurious, but only half the size of her and Rafe's home.

Madeline rapped on the panel that marked the entrance of the Japoxillian's home.

"Polo. May I have a word, please?"

Karma tried not to cringe. She sounded like a huge snob. Maybe she couldn't help it—just like she couldn't help wanting to help people who wouldn't go out of their way to do the same for her.

The door opened and Karma saw Polo step out. One Japo was apparently different than the next just the way no two Galatians looked the same. Polo was beautiful, as all Japos must be. He looked like a hybrid between a cat and a bird but had shiny, red feathers—the ones on the top of his head stood up like a mohawk. His cat head was leaner, as opposed to Dorf's rounder head. He was also taller, easily reaching above her knees.

Madeline offered her hand. "Polo, I'd like to ask you some questions about Drago."

Obviously, Karma couldn't hear Polo's response.

"Thank you. Does Drago think heels are ridiculous?"

Polo tilted his head, as if confused.

"Okay, never mind that. I dress a certain way in order to please Drago. Do you think he even cares how I dress?"

Madeline listened, and it was her turn to cock her head.

"What's he saying?" Karma asked.

Madeline held up her finger, indicating she should be patient.

It was nearly a full minute before Madeline finally spoke. She gave Karma a pointed look. "It appears that while Drago likes beautiful things, he couldn't care *less* about the way I dress or whether or not I wear makeup. He does, however, like my hair...and wishes I didn't shave...the other hairs."

Madeline closed her eyes in disgust, even anger. But Karma sensed she wasn't angry at Polo, or even her. But she was pissed. Madeline looked down at Polo.

"Thank you, Polo. That's all for now."

Polo released her hand and then gave Karma a thorough up and down look before retreating back to his room.

"What was that look?" Karma asked suspiciously.

"Curiosity, I'm assuming. You have caused quite a stir—even within these walls."

"I guess. Look...I think I'm going to just leave—"

"Wait! I thought you were going to tell me everything about how you replaced Mayva as consort?"

Karma shook her head. "I've helped you a lot, and you haven't really done much for me."

Madeline's mouth dropped. "What about the meal I sent to you? Didn't that help?"

Karma nodded slowly. "I bet you Dorf can get me a recipe book on how to prepare Galatian meals. You have nothing valuable to teach me that I haven't figured out on my own. The truth is, you need to *unlearn* whatever those fools at school for consorts taught you. Because the way I see it, they only taught you how to appeal to *human* males, not Galatian ones."

Madeline stared at the floor while shaking her head. "Mr. Tolbert said we were the cream of the crop. I can't believe I actually fucked him!"

Karma gave Madeline a hard look.

"Wait. You and Mr. Tolbert...?"

"Not just me. A lot of the girls. You know him. He put you up to this, so you and him were probably doing it too!"

"Hell no we weren't!" Karma exclaimed. "I was his maid, and I definitely wasn't his...type." Karma lightly bit her lower lip as her brow gathered. "Did he...force you?"

Madeline smirked. "No. Maybe the opposite. He had a prick, and we wanted to know what all the talk was about. What? I'm not the only one. A lot of us did. It's not like anyone would ever be the wiser. After the surgery, it's impossible to tell if we're still virgins. And there's no chance of getting pregnant.

"But it was barely worth all the trouble. His prick was too small to even feel." Madeline frowned at Karma. "That's what they really steal from us; being able to fuck like a normal woman when this is all over. And yes, we'll earn every penny they'll give us—even if all we do is sit on our asses all day looking pretty and picking out furniture for our mansions. Because at the end of the day, they took our uterus!" Madeline looked at a point over Karma's shoulder. "And I'd do it again, willingly, just to have my own money and my own life."

Karma didn't ask the question that burned to escape her mouth: what would you do if you knew they couldn't care less about fully penetrating their consorts? The surgery wasn't *their* requirement, but the requirement of their queens. And why would the queens care more about the male's level of pleasure than even they did?

That would be too cruel to discuss with Madeline. But when she returned home, she was going to ask Dorf a question she had thought she knew the answer to…because everyone knew Galatians and humans couldn't reproduce. But what if that was just another human lie…or in this case, a Galatian one?

"Stay for a while. Sit and have some tea with me. Or I can make you breakfast."

Karma nodded and followed the girl into her neat kitchen. For a person like her, used to keeping busy, having idle time on her hands was unusual. She wasn't sure if she liked Madeline, but she could admit to liking her more than she liked the other consorts. The others didn't exactly talk down to her the way Jayne had, but that was only because they were smarter, and knew not to burn their bridges. "Tea is fine. I had a huge breakfast," she said.

"I don't dare eat too much. If I gain an ounce, I'd be afraid of Drago losing interest."

"Rafe seems to want me to eat more. For some reason, he's obsessed with the idea of me being starved." Funny how many times over the years she had actually been in that state, which ended only after she'd met him.

Madeline watched Karma with interest before pouring them both cups of tea in the finest little teacups. Karma wondered if she had a set of teacups like these somewhere in her kitchen.

Probably not. She suspected Madeline's wealth had afforded her comforts Karma's poverty hadn't.

She stirred plenty of sugar into her tea and then a squeeze of lemon and finally a splash of cream. Her employers had the fine china, but she'd never seen any of them holding a tea party.

Madeline whisked her teacup away before she could drink it and then poured the contents down the drain.

"Let's do that again," she said as she took her seat. "I know you said you don't have much to learn from me when it comes to our mates, but if you want to fit in with the sister consorts, you have a lot to learn."

Karma frowned. "I've never thought I needed to fit in with those snobs—or you, for that matter." She knew she was being ugly, but Madeline had made her feel inadequate and she didn't like it.

Madeline smiled, as if her words just rolled off her back. "Oh, you will. It will be months before our final homes are prepared, and there will be several important Galatian ceremonies you will need to attend—with your sister consorts." Madeline paused in pouring Karma more tea. "Having us on your side is much better than having us against you."

Keeping her attitude in check was in her best interest, Karma decided. She wondered if any of the consorts actually liked each other—or if it was just an elaborate act of tolerance. She nodded slightly, mimicking the way she'd seen Rafe do when he seemed too preoccupied with such little things.

"Good. Now watch how I do it." She watched as Madeline used the tongs to pick up a sugar cube, which she dropped into her tea. She then used the fork to pick up a wedge of lemon. She didn't squeeze it, but just dropped it into the teacup as well. She picked up her spoon and instead of stirring in a circle—which Karma knew would have dissolved the tea the quickest—she moved her spoon back and forth without clanging the delicate teacup.

"You shouldn't dare clang your spoon against an item of fine Wedgwood china." She then placed her teaspoon facedown on the side of the saucer and lifted the teacup to her lips. "Delicious. Now you. Select two items only. And don't be a pig about it."

Karma resisted rolling her eyes. She selected two cubes of sugar *and* a wedge of lemon while giving her instructor a defiant look.

Madeline overlooked it. "And don't you dare point your pinky finger out. You'll look like a fool that's trying to be posh." Madeline got up and retrieved a tin of cookies, which she shook onto a serving plate. "Now we should have friendly conversation."

"About?" Karma asked after taking a sip of the too-sweet tea. It was still good, though. But next time, she would only use one cube.

"About the Galatians, of course. It's what brought you to my home."

"How old are you?" Karma asked abruptly. She looked like a teenager, but acted like she was middle-aged.

"Nineteen. Why?" Madeline asked.

"I thought you were older."

"How old are you?"

"Twenty-three."

Madeline took a cookie and bit into it. Karma mimicked her. "You used to be Mr. Tolbert's servant before coming here?"

"Yes. More for his wife than him. Until he asked me to join the Exchange, I didn't even think he knew who I was." But Karma didn't want to talk about herself too much. She did, however, want to know more about the girl she had replaced.

"Do you think the consort I replaced ran off with Mr. Tolbert?"

"Well," Madeline said. "Well, that's obvious. But if she had made an actual plan, she didn't tell any of us...not even me, and we were friends—at least, I thought we were."

"Maybe Mr. Tolbert kidnapped her."

"He'd be a fool to do that. You know what they do to men that have their way with a consort, don't you?" Madeline whispered the last, for once looking like a young girl as opposed to a kid playing the role of an aristocrat.

"I heard they are tortured."

"Their pricks are cut off!" Madeline stated while leaning close.

"Well, he had his way with you and a few others, so he didn't seem too afraid of that happening to him."

"Of course, he wouldn't be. He's the head of the North American Exchange. He can easily hide the information. We'd be the ones to disappear before he'd let his prick get removed."

"A missing consort looks like a big deal," Karma said as she thought about how much time Rafe spent away from home investigating Mayva's disappearance.

"It's happened. They're overwhelmed, commit suicide...or so we're told."

How tidy.

Madeline looked at the clock. "I need to begin the broth for Drago's meal. You may as well come with me and I'll show you how it's done." Madeline got up and headed out of the kitchen, leaving the tea where it sat. Karma followed anxiously. She still had more questions—mostly about Mayva. But right now, this was more important.

The two women left the apartment and went down the elevator to a level that was lower than even the lobby. The space was as big as a warehouse, but there was a courtyard that housed a large greenhouse to one side. Guards came to attention at their arrival, but it was easy for Karma to ignore them. Anytime she stepped out of the penthouse, she saw guards.

Barrels and boxes were stacked neatly on pristine metal shelves and a woman sat at a desk behind a computer. She was dressed in a neat, dark suit.

"How may I help you, Mrs. Engström?"

"I will need these ingredients." Madeline began listing a number of items—none of which Karma understood, with the exception of the word *sauerkraut*.

The attendant quickly jotted down the items. "Right away, ma'am," she said as she passed the list to a young man that had come to assist.

Madeline walked away, with Karma following. "Grab a basket." Once they had their baskets, the women entered the glass-enclosed courtyard.

It was beautiful. There was a rock garden, and flowers of every kind—many of which Karma had never before seen. There were stone benches among the greenery, and despite the cold season, the environment within the enclosed courtyard was comfortable.

This was a botanical garden. She knew that word from a field trip she'd attended with one of her employer's children.

She looked closely at some of the beautiful greenery as they hurried past. "These aren't...?"

"From Earth?" Madeline finished. "No. Galatian plants. I don't know why they even bother. I doubt if our mates will ever have time to come down to enjoy them. Come on, we need to get some fresh items from the garden."

Karma tried to take in everything at once. This was amazing. Why didn't she ever hear of the existence of such a place here on Earth? And why didn't they allow humans to come and observe it? It was just sitting here unappreciated, and that was disturbing. The rich took so much for granted.

They finally entered the greenhouse, where row upon row of exotic vegetation grew. The smell inside the greenhouse was warm and dank, with hints of sweetness. It was oddly tantalizing to her nose, which was more accustomed to the urban stink of exhaust and poverty than the earthy smell of living vegetation.

"Madeline!" They turned to see one of the consorts filling her basket with vegetables and herbs. Like Madeline, she was dressed in a thin, satiny robe that practically touched the floor. Not only was it not weather appropriate, it also left nothing to the imagination, as every impression of her nudity from nipples to hip bones could be clearly seen imprinted through the fabric.

She carried a pair of gardening shears, which she dropped into her basket and dusted her fingers before greeting Madeline with two air kisses, one on each cheek.

"Auras, how are you, dear?" Madeline turned to Karma. "You remember our sister Karma, don't you?"

Auras gave Madeline a quick side-eye at the phrase "our sister" but quickly straightened her smile and greeted Karma with the same air kisses.

"Of course I do. Karma. How have you been getting along?"

Oh my Guardian...I can't with this fakeness...

"I'm fine," she replied without a smile. "Madeline is helping me with the food."

Auras raised her brow at Madeline, who gave the slightest shoulder shrug. "Yes, of course you would need help with that. You never attended the consort training—at least not in North America."

"No need to get into all that," Madeline said. "Our sister is here now, and she's helped us with certain matters; and we should return the favor."

"Of course!" Auras leaned in to whisper. "Mating is nothing like they said it would be. Kendrick is so patient! Who would have ever thought!"

Karma looked at her pointedly and smiled for the first time. "So much better than Mr. Tolbert."

Auras nodded. "Oh my Guardian—worlds better!"

Madeline gave Karma a quick look but didn't say anything.

"So, what's for dinner?" Karma asked, changing the subject.

The ladies chatted, and Karma kept up by asking questions in the right places—even though most of the discussion was gossip about old friends still at consort school.

Karma placed the exact same things in her basket Madeline had in hers. The plants were strange, and she couldn't tell the fruit from the vegetables.

"Humans can eat these?" she interrupted, thinking about the creepy-crawlies she had consumed the night before and the upset stomach she'd experienced afterwards.

"It's not poison," Auras answered.

"But it's not very tasty, either."

"Madeline, you *must* have her taste each dish." Auras spoke while hiding a smirk.

These little micro-aggressions were so childish, but Karma decided she would play along. "I've had a taste. It wasn't the worst thing in the world."

"Having a bite of some leaves or fruit isn't the same—"

"I ate that thing that looked like a baby octopus."

Both women looked at her in surprise. "You ate a chifpod? While it was alive?" Auras asked.

"It can't be eaten after it's dead. The only way to safely eat it is alive." Madeline turned back to her. "What made you do that?"

"Well, you said you had to try every dish—"

"Not the creature!" Madeline exclaimed. "No one would dare eat a living chifpod!"

"They are so disgusting!" Auras said.

Karma shook her head. "The broth was disgusting— it was way too salty. But the chi-chifpod tasted pretty good."

"But the insides would have gushed out into your mouth!" Auras insisted with a look of revulsion on her face.

Karma shook her head. "It didn't."

Madeline just stared at her and didn't look revolted at all. Karma thought she saw something close to admiration.

Chapter Thirty

Back at Madeline's home, the two women were in her kitchen, cooking, with Karma following Madeline's steps exactly.

Things seemed different to her. Madeline didn't sound nearly as snobbish. In fact, their conversation didn't consist of any passive aggression from either of them. Madeline praised her when she chopped something perfectly, and they both screamed and then laughed when a spider-like creature dropped from the top of its container and tried to make an escape.

Karma caught it and carefully placed it back in its box while Madeline hid behind a chair.

"You'd actually eat that thing?"

"Uh...after the way my stomach flipped last night, I might have to wait a while."

Madeline returned to the stove to stir the broth. "You're braver than I. You are probably the bravest girl I've ever met."

Karma blinked. "Me?"

"Yes, you. You walked into all this without knowing a thing. You take control even when I can tell you're scared. You stand up for yourself, even in front of the Galatians. You spoke your mind in front of a queen. No one does that."

Karma thought about those words. She didn't feel brave. She just had to survive; but she didn't know how to explain that to Madeline.

After the broth was stewed, the vegetables chopped and spiced, and she was instructed to throw the living creatures into various dishes once everything was cooled, Karma headed to the door to go home.

"Thank you for your help. Even with a recipe book, I don't think I could have done all of this on my own."

Madeline smiled. "You're welcome. Um…if you want to come back tomorrow, we can do it again. You can pick up all the bugs and I can cook the broth." Karma grimaced. "I'm kidding," Madeline said quickly. "It was…fun having company."

"You could invite any of the sisters," Karma replied, a bit surprised at herself for opening that door. But they'd gone to school with each other so they had to at least have some familiarity there.

"If I want to spend the afternoon competing with them." She rolled her eyes briefly before allowing them to settle once again on Karma. "But there's no competition between us." Karma's back stiffened, but Madeline continued. "You're already above me. You're mated to the lieutenant, and that puts you at the top."

Karma tried not to look uncomfortable. She'd figured out her power when she'd forced the soldiers to do her bidding. She wasn't going to force a friendship between herself and the other consorts.

Madeline continued. "Besides, you don't put on airs, and I actually like you."

A chuckle erupted from Karma at the reluctant surprise she heard in Madeline's statement.

"Well…I might like you a little bit too. Let's do it again tomorrow."

"Good!" Madeline beamed. "We can cook in your kitchen, since yours is so much bigger."

"You just don't want the creepy-crawlies getting loose in your house," she joked. "But fine."

Karma left feeling good. She hadn't exactly made friends after becoming an orphan, and prior to that...well, it had been so long ago, she barely remembered what having a girlfriend was like.

When she got home, she had to put some of the dishes on the floor in order to open the door. She shuddered when she heard the soft scratching of crawling tentacles within one of the covered dishes.

When she opened the door, she heard the music of the *Saturday Night Fever* soundtrack. Her music was being played. Dorf jumped down from the couch and hurried to her in excitement.

"Wait, Dorf. I have to put this in the kitchen," she said when she couldn't offer her hand. He followed along behind her and after she had deposited the food onto the table (the other items had magically disappeared—probably because the chifpods had died), she sat down in one of the chairs and offered her hand.

"Karma! This music is fantastic!"

She smiled. "I know! I love it too! They call it disco."

"I know about disco!" he exclaimed, and then he shook his little butt.

Karma giggled. "Did you just dance?"

"Yes, I dance. How can one sing without dancing?" He gave her a curious look. "But why such old music? There are so many new artists using instruments that are far more advanced."

Karma eyes grew distant. "I love all music but music makes me think of the time period. The twenty-first century was the last one before everything went to hell."

Dorf listened intently finding it rare to engage with the young woman when her shields were lowered.

"I'm sure they didn't know it then when people were killing each other over their different beliefs and fighting over who should have more or less rights. They had no idea that they didn't have long before they'd lose their complete and total freedom. If I could go back in time, it would be to the twentieth century, dance all night at the discos and watch old fashioned sitcoms and eat fast food hamburgers..." Her eyes brightened.

"Hey, you know what we should do? You play one of your favorite songs and I'll play one of mine."

"Yes! I would enjoy that. But first, did you prepare food for Rafe?"

She looked over at the covered dishes. "Yep. I've been at Madeline's house for the last few hours and she showed me how to cook them. But please feel free to have some if you like."

"No, I can't tolerate Galatian food. It's much too...alive."

"Okay, so I'm not the only one."

"No. When I trained in Galatia, I had a terrible time with my digestion. Come. Let's play the music game!"

Karma could have lain on the floor all afternoon listening to music with Dorf. She had kicked off her shoes and when she needed the use of her hands, Dorf connected with her through a bite on her ankle. He was entertaining, and told interesting stories to the backdrop of good music.

But she hadn't forgotten about wanting to pick his brain about the queens and more specifically, about reproduction between Galatians and humans.

"What time do you think Rafe will come home?" she asked.

"Who can tell? But he did say he would have a meal with you, so he will come home."

"I hope he likes what I prepared."

"Even if he doesn't, he'll respect your effort."

She nodded. "Dorf? I've been curious about something."

"Yes?"

"Why do the queens allow us to sleep with their men? Shouldn't they be jealous?"

"That's a complex question. Perhaps you should speak to Rafe about it. Have you had time to gather your thoughts about him?"

She'd had time to digest Dorf's words about the nature of her fear. Rafe was scary, but deep down, she knew he wasn't out to hurt her. She'd placed herself in this position and it was up to her to make the best of it.

"I need to make it easier for us both and do whatever it takes to make this successful."

"Good."

"Rafe said the queens have issues with getting pregnant. But wouldn't it be possible for Galatians to get humans pregnant? Everything I hear says it's not because we're a different species. But they created us, so we can't be very different, right?"

Dorf had been relaxed against her leg as he had moved to attach to her feet. He changed positions enough to be able to look at her.

"I'm sure you know the Galatian race has been dying out. When they realized they would go extinct, they set out to find worlds comparable to Galatia where they could begin the process to create new life-forms using their own DNA.

"The idea being to not only recreate themselves, but to give themselves another means to procreate. Galatians have successfully created several comparable species and in time, have been able to produce hybrid offspring. But the occurrence was even more rare than procreation with their queens, and like in many cases of hybridization, the resulting offspring were infertile. Centuries of effort was in vain.

"But you asked about interbreeding between humans. It may be possible, but it has never happened, and it will never happen."

"Why is that?"

Dorf didn't respond for a long time. She began to wonder if she'd made a mistake in asking. Rafe had told her never to tell anyone she hadn't received the surgery, and she assumed that included Dorf. But what if Dorf could *read* it in her head? She began to panic, and made to move her foot from his mouth when she heard his response.

"One reason is because intercourse with a human female is impossible without the surgery — and you know how the surgery leaves a female; infertile and incapable of ever breeding.

"The surgery offers no assurance intercourse still won't result in death. Humans have died during mating. Your bodies were just not meant to accommodate a Galatian male. And a male human would never get close enough to a queen for that to ever be a consideration. So that is one reason. The second, and probably the most important, is the queens would destroy a hybrid offspring."

Karma frowned. "But why? The hybrids wouldn't even be able to reproduce—"

"I can only say it is what has happened in the past on other planets. But Galatians no longer procreate with any species they created. The queens won't allow it. They have to content themselves with caring for the life-forms they created and through you and others like you, their DNA will continue in some form, even when they become extinct."

"That's sad."

"Yes. The Galatians are not only warriors, but they are also caretakers."

The males obviously were, but she wasn't so sure about the queens. They would see their own species die out before allowing interbreeding between their males and others.

She understood why Rafe had warned her not to speak of the fact that she hadn't had the surgery, and it made sense why he refused to have intercourse with her again.

She had to decide once and for all if she actually wanted to carry on with her idea to have the surgery. She had seven years with Rafe, and although that wasn't forever, when her time with him ended, would she want to have a child of her own? She just had never thought that far ahead…

When the front door opened, Rafe took in the sight of Karma and Dorf reclining on the floor listening to music. She came to her feet and greeted him with a smile.

"Welcome home."

"Thank you." He took in her relaxed demeanor. "How did you spend your time today?" he asked, wondering if she had orchestrated more food deliveries to the needy. He hoped she had.

"I'm happy you asked about that, because I spent the day preparing a meal for you."

"You prepared it?" he asked.

"Yes, with the help of a sister consort. Would you like to have a meal now?"

"After I spend time in the pool."

"Of course. Is there anything I can do for you?" she asked politely.

He scanned her form, trying to detect her true emotions beyond her words. She said all the right things, and he didn't sense any fear.

"You can keep me company." He headed for his den and heard her follow. Once he had opened the panel to his closet, he stripped out of his uniform and shoes and placed them neatly in their place.

She stood by the pool with her hands clasped. "Would you like me to get into the pool with you?"

Rafe paused before climbing into the relaxing waters. "Only if you would like to do so."

She nodded, surprising him. "Yes." She shed her clothing, and Rafe enjoyed watching her reveal her nudity. Once she stood naked before him, Rafe looked at her, pleased at the sight of her flawless skin and bright eyes that looked directly into his.

He lifted her into his arms and then stepped carefully into the pool. He was conscious that she didn't know how to swim, but he could swim with her.

He held one arm around her waist and both of her arms went firmly around his neck.

"How deep is the water?" she asked with a bit of apprehension.

"This portion where the temperature is safe for you is approximately ten feet deep. There are areas much deeper, and it's shallow by the hot spring; but obviously, you wouldn't be able to tolerate the heat."

Her arms tightened reflexively. An amused yellow tint colored his scales. "Don't worry. I won't drop you."

"I know."

He swam around a bit and after a few minutes, she relaxed enough for him to float onto his back while keeping her safely atop his torso. She tensed, but after a second, smiled and relaxed again.

"Your home planet is made up of mostly water," she said. "Can you live in water?"

"There was a time when our kind had gills and we could live underwater, but as we made our way to land and then space, our gills were no longer needed and we lost them. This is after centuries, of course, but we still have an affinity for water."

"I see. It must be very exciting to travel across universes."

"It's part of my life, so I suppose I take it for granted."

"Do you think I could ever travel to space?"

"Certainly. But once you reached your destination, you might find you aren't very comfortable."

"Do you mean because we have a different atmosphere on Earth?"

"Earth has a unique atmosphere. There are many similar ones, but nothing exact. And your body wasn't formed to adapt."

Her eyes flinched and he found that curious. "Does that bother you?"

She met his eyes, but then looked away. "My father was kidnapped by Malnamanians."

"Yes," he said, now understanding her expression.

"They say humans can't survive more than a year with the Malnamanians."

He knew it had been more than ten years since her father had been taken. When humans were taken by space pirates, they were treated as disposable, for quick labor. Humans rarely lived more than several months outside of Earth.

He had been responsible for bringing home several trafficked humans. In this case, they had survived their months of kidnapping. But there was no way Karma's father would still be alive after so many years.

He ran his thumb down her back. "I'm sorry about your father."

"I lost my mother that day too."

"Yes. I am truly sorry for your loss."

"Well, thank you for all the Guard does to keep our people safe."

"It's the least we can do." He paused thoughtfully. "I've witnessed the poverty you spoke of."

She looked surprised.

"Did you go to my old apartment complex?"

"No. I went to the train depot. It was the place you first attempted to feed the needy."

"Yeah...that turned into a fiasco. So, you saw all the homeless?"

"As well as how they were treated by the soldiers."

"Hmph. They consider it sport to harass us when all we want to do is find a warm place."

"Yes! That's what I need from you; as much information as you can give me to help investigate and hold those responsible to task."

"Oh, I certainly can do that. And I have some more information about Mr. Tolbert and the foul things he was doing at the consort school."

Rafe's expression grew serious. "Shower in your bath and I will meet you in the kitchen." He swiftly but smoothly swam them to the edge of the pool, where he sat her on its ledge. She saw him disappear beneath its depths. It all happened in mere seconds.

Karma didn't try to figure out when and where he would emerge. She climbed out of the pool and gathered her clothes and then headed for her bathroom, where she quickly showered off the salt water of Rafe's pool.

She dressed quickly in one of the robes that had been placed in her trunk. It was as thin and revealing as Auras's and Madeline's, but unlike them, she had no intention of leaving the house in it.

Rafe was waiting for her in the living room. He was dressed in his own variation of a robe; a long, grass-colored cloth wrapped around his waist in such a way it gave his tail freedom to move without revealing his ass.

She saw his eyes scan her form in what she assumed was appreciation, but she did the same.

Regardless of being green and having scales, an individual that stood seven feet tall, with lean muscles running down their arms and torso, made an impressive sight. And since living with Rafe, Karma found she didn't notice the things that made them different as much as she initially had.

"We will have a meal while we speak of Tolbert." He went into the kitchen and took his seat at the large kitchen table that took up the far side of the large room.

He reached for a covered bowl but she stopped him. "Let me serve you."

A spark of yellow appeared across his face. She remembered that meant he was amused. He nodded, and she took the bowl that contained only broth to the stove, where she poured a small amount into a saucepot. She then diluted it with water from the teapot and heated it.

When it was warm, she poured the contents into a bowl and placed it in front of her chair. Rafe watched her curiously, but remained patient as she went about opening the lids containing the non-living contents.

She spooned the raw but dressed vegetables onto a plate for herself and then a larger amount onto a platter for him. Once his platter contained some type of salad, slices of a sweet fruit, berries that reminded her of cherry tomatoes, and pieces of edible sponge that were used to dunk into the broth, Karma finally took her seat.

Only one dish remained covered, and that was the alien spider creatures.

"You prepared this yourself?" he asked.

"Yes. Madeline, Drago's mate, showed me how." He stared at the bowl of watered-down broth in front of her. She quickly explained.

"I'm not sure how the broth will affect my system, so I had to water it down." She had tasted it, and did like the individual ingredients, and they seemed safe enough, but undiluted, it felt like drinking sea water...which, considering his water origins, might be to his liking.

He picked up his mixing bowl of broth and took a long drink while she waited expectantly.

"Perfect," he said.

Karma smiled and then picked up her bowl and drank from it as he had, ignoring her spoon. Rafe opened the lid from the bugs and didn't seem concerned when some began to escape.

Karma sat quietly, trying not to squirm or squeal. But he picked up the bowl and dumped the spider contents into his broth while plucking up the escapees and plopping them into his mouth.

He paused before placing the last spider into his mouth and looked at her. "Have some?" he offered it to her.

Eeeek! She nearly yelped aloud. "No thank you...maybe another time."

He nodded and ate it.

"Good?" she asked, noting his obvious enjoyment.

"Very. It's like being home again. Thank you, Karma. It has been a long time since I've had vrbein so young and lively." He slurped down half of his broth with half of the spiders, and she was never so happy to see something disappear from her sight.

"Now, what information do you have about Tolbert, and how did you come to receive it?"

She explained in detail about her conversation with Madeline and how Tolbert had been having sex with many of the girls.

Rafe's face moved from its normally still neutral tone to red.

"He violated the girls in his charge."

Or they just had mutually consensual sex—however one chose to look at it. But she supposed a Galatian couldn't see it any other way, considering their possessiveness.

"I think sex is a large part of what they are taught at the consort school. It's natural for the girls to be curious about it. And if he's willing, and they're willing—"

"Have you had sex with Tolbert?" he interrupted.

"What? No!" He stared at her without moving, but his red flush had grown deeper. "That has never been something I've done with an employer."

"But you were no virgin when you came to me."

Her expression stiffened. "I didn't realize it mattered…"

His eyes grew hooded as he regarded her. "You did nothing the way it should have been done and therefore, I can't hold you accountable, as I have already accepted you. It no longer matters in regards to the other consorts, either, as the matings have taken place. But for the others, the ones yet to be mated, their safety is of the utmost importance. None of their groomers should have sexual contact with them while they are in our care. I don't care how curious they are."

Karma bit her lip. "Okay." After a moment of silence, she picked up her fork and began to eat.

Chapter Thirty-one

Rafe watched Karma once again shut down. When he'd come home, he saw his consort's disposition had been much better; as if she was open and willing to accept him. He could sense it while they swam in his pool. And then watching her learning to eat his food made him feel hopeful, and also honored she did something most humans obviously found disagreeable.

His appreciation for his consort had grown tremendously in just minutes.

And then he had done it again. He had made a mistake.

He had not meant to become jealous of the idea that Karma had enjoyed sex with someone other than him. He had never thought to care what his human consort did before meeting him. There was a time when he had been jealous of what Ragna did with other males, especially when he was away or when she denied him. But although Galatians mated for life, no one discussed infidelity because in the end, producing a child was the goal. After a time, he was just happy Ragna was too busy to keep pushing him to join the Collective.

It was unspoken by males that while they were mated to their consorts, the queens had sex with whomever caught their fancy. He too had satisfied a variety of queens in his youth—and had enjoyed the attention of other life-forms throughout his years of travel.

But he did wonder if Karma would go to this past human lover when her seven years ended. He shouldn't be thinking these thoughts about what had happened before and what would happen after. Other Galatians never seemed to care.

But he wasn't like any other Galatian, and Karma wasn't like any other consort.

He could not keep showing her his anger while not expecting her to think it was directed at her. In truth, something was awakening in Rafe that made him think of things he had never before been concerned about.

But if she wanted to reconnect with her human lover after her time as a consort ended, then it was none of his concern.

"Karma." She looked at him. "My anger is not directed at you. If you have more to say, I would like to hear it."

She looked into his eyes and then returned to scooting her food around on her plate with a fork. "That's all the information I had to tell you."

He looked down at his own plate before looking at her again. "I'm sorry. I was jealous because I wondered if you had enjoyed sex with Tolbert like the girls you spoke of." He wanted to get up and leave the room when he was met with prolonged silence. Why was he trying to make her into something she so obviously didn't—

"If you ask, I'll always be as honest as possible, Rafe. I know what this looks like—me being your consort. But I've never been a sex worker. One day I probably would have been...but then this happened." She chuckled mirthlessly. "I guess I'm lying to myself because what is a consort if not the ultimate sex worker?" She frowned at him. "But I won't be ashamed for what I'm doing...and what others like me have had to do in order to survive."

He shook his head. "It was never meant to shame you. Being selected as a consort was always intended to be an honor. At least it is an honor for us. Maybe it feels different because neither mate has a say in any of this."

She watched him with interest as he continued, speaking of things he had never said aloud—not to his brothers, not to his family, and especially not to the person he was to be bound to.

"Some Galatians want to create families, some want power, and others choose the life of a warrior. I'm the latter. It was never my desire to reap the rewards of being bound to Earth and assigned a safe duty and a consort. I am a warrior, and that is my life's dream. There is so much more I can do to protect our charges. Yet they want me to be happy on Earth doing work any human can do. I know my job; how to hunt and how to kill. And while I understand human biology, I readily admit I don't understand the human psyche. This is not the assignment that is fit for who I am." Rafe could not believe he had spoken these words aloud.

"I have accepted my duties," he said resolutely. "Even though there are many things that give me misgivings—but that's another topic. What I would like you to know is, while I might say the wrong things, I mean you no ill will.

"I am accustomed to reacting, and that has saved my life more times than I can recount. But in our home, I am not at battle. I believe I would be best served in understanding my mate—and there is no one better for teaching me this than my mate. So, regardless of whether you accept my other offer, I hope you will help me to understand how to react to humans."

He noted her posture had become relaxed. She instantly lost her defensive stance and her eyes grew soft again. His heartbeat sped up hopefully. There was something to be said for baring your heart.

"Rafe, thank you. I didn't understand either. I think we both can benefit from understanding the other. I don't think it's just a Galatian-human thing. Every...couple has to work on their relationship."

He nodded his agreement. "You are right, Karma. And you have much more insight into how humans think. Is it your opinion that Mayva willingly left with Tolbert?"

"That I don't know," she said earnestly. "And Madeline said she didn't know either. I believe her." He rubbed his chin, and she continued. "But the girls know much more. I don't mind picking their brains." He gave her a long look.

"That would be of great help. Anything you can add would be helpful. This brings up another issue that pertains to you."

He had been putting it off but it wasn't fair to her, just because the entire situation annoyed him. "As you know, I've been investigating the missing consort and director, but I've also been assigned to replace Tolbert as the North American director of the Exchange."

Her brow moved up. "I didn't realize that."

"Yes. I hope once I locate the missing individuals, then we'll be able to relocate wherever you wish. I apologize for this inconvenience."

She blinked at him and tilted her head in confusion. "This all seems so weird to me. Why am I the one who gets to select where we live? I don't know anything about where we should live or what job you would have."

"It can be anywhere you want." Her expression didn't change so he continued. "Is there a place you always dreamed about living?"

"Is there a place you dreamed about living?" she returned without hesitation.

He was surprised she had turned the question back to him. But he put thought to his response. "I don't care where we live, but I like the change of seasons. I like cold and I like hot weather. I like water, but I mostly like your Earth's snow. But more important than any of that is where I would be assigned."

She nodded. "Okay. Once you are done with this assignment, what would you like to do?"

"Fight."

"Is there a place where you can fight?"

"Outer space."

"Can we live in outer space?"

"No."

She rubbed her chin and then squinted at him. "Are you laughing at me?" So, she was beginning to learn his expressions.

"Will you be angry if I say yes?"

She smiled and shook her head. "I'm trying to be helpful, Rafe. Where do you want to live?"

He tilted his head at her easy use of his name. "My plans had been to work with the military. I can do that anywhere. So that brings it back to you. Where would you like to live, Karma?"

"I don't know anyplace but here."

"North America?"

She shook her head. "No. Ohio. Cincinnati."

He absently ate some of the spiced salad. "The North American Exchange is here, so there is a large military presence…"

"And we do have all four seasons."

"Yes."

"We don't have an ocean, but I'm sure we could find a large lake or something."

He was at a loss for words. "Thank you."

She looked down at the table, and he sensed she was suddenly uncomfortable. When he was about to reassure her, she looked up and spoke.

"Yesterday you said something and I came off as dismissive to it. It wasn't because I don't want…a meaningful relationship with you." She swallowed and seemed afraid. He wanted to reassure her but stopped because this was not his time. This was hers. He waited patiently for her to find her words.

"I never thought that…what you're talking about would ever be something I could have. My life is so very…" She shook her head and shut down.

"Karma. It would please me if you would tell me about your life. I understand if you don't want me to—"

"No. I don't mind telling you," she said quickly. "It's just that I'm not exotic or cultured, and I only got education until I was old enough to get a work assignment. By sixteen, I was out on my own. You can't stay at the orphanage once you turn sixteen. They got me a job on a cleaning crew and I had to figure out the rest on my own.

"It was hard. Really hard. If a few kind people hadn't taken me under their wing, I might not have made it. Sometimes, the only thing that kept me going was remembering when I had a real home, a real family.

I think about that and I listen to my music and that's what makes me happy." Her big, brown eyes finally locked onto his and he was mesmerized.

"What you asked for doesn't mean the same thing to me. I've only had that once, and it was with my family and…it means something different for you than it would for me."

Karma's heart was beating a mile a minute. Rafe was so calm as he listened to her, and she didn't know what he was thinking or what she was talking about, only that she needed him to know she could see how there could be confusion with his words and their meaning. But now she felt foolish.

"I'm sure this is common knowledge," he said with barely any inflection or emotion in his words. "But soon, my people will be extinct. When I was a child, I was prized and coddled because a child was a rare occurrence. Everyone I met wanted to be in my company, and they listened to my every thought as if I was a sage. I had to be protected, because someone might take me and raise me as their own. Many want a child but can't have one so when one is born, they are treated in the way royalty is treated among your kind.

"But I was born a male. And that meant I would only ever serve. It is much like your honeybees; there is a queen and there are workers…and I have learned and accepted my place within my society.

"But I cannot forget being treated as if I was Guardian-like. And then one day, I grew into a man and my mother no longer saw me. And my father spent his retirement reliving the glory of his many battles. And my bound-mate has no desire to know me beyond how I can further her goals.

"So, you see, I have a need. It's not for sex. It's not for food. It's not for a servant as a reward for my years of service in the Guard. I didn't even know I had this need until...I saw through your eyes how everything we think of as tradition, is actually pointless.

"I wonder what it would be like to actually enjoy this time and make it into something I want—something we both might want." He inhaled. "Is that different than what you wish for when you want to feel happy?"

Karma's heart felt as if it had lodged in her throat. When she looked at Rafe, she now saw a person—not an alien, not a humanoid, not a Galatian. A person.

"I think we have the same meaning." In that moment their eyes locked onto the other's, recognizing mutual hope, but also deep loss. Karma realized she did want something meaningful, and she wanted it with Rafe Sigur.

"I would like very much to have a meaningful relationship with you."

His lips went up at the sides in a smile, an actual real smile that wasn't just a tint of yellow covering his scales. It was contagious. She couldn't stop the smile from her own face.

"Let's finish eating," he said while using his fingers to put food into his mouth. "This food is delicious, but I want to learn more about you."

"I might have a lot of questions for you, too."

"Ask." He licked his fingers with his long tongue and she paused, having forgotten all thought at the sight of the appendage as it cleaned spices from each of his digits. She could not help but remember that tongue in more personal places.

"Um...it was about the queens but I forget... Oh! Aren't they jealous you're basically marrying a consort?" If she was a queen, she wouldn't stand for giving him to another woman for seven years, or even seven days.

"We have a different word." He made a strange sound with his tongue. "It means that someone is willing to make a personal sacrifice in order to honor another they care for. A queen that has given her bound-mate to a consort has made a sacrifice, and therefore, a grand gesture. And yes," he nodded. "They are jealous. But this type of jealousy gives them status within our community. Does that make sense?"

"I suppose. It's your culture, even if I don't quite get it. But I accept it!" she added quickly so as not to offend him.

His shoulder moved subtly, as if to shrug. "No matter. It's another of those traditions I am forced to adhere to, regardless of whether I agree or not."

Karma suddenly had another question many in her community wondered. She no longer cared—or maybe she already suspected the answer after being involved in the mysterious Exchange.

"Why are only Whites chosen for the lottery?"

He took a moment to consider the question, as if it confused him. "You mean the skin color? Don't your people find white skin more desirable?"

Her back stiffened. "Do you?"

In many cultures, giving an important guest the best they had, like the fatted cow or the prized item, was a sign of their respect. There were places that sacrificed the most desirable of their people to appease whatever God they worshipped.

His eyes moved to take in the areas of Karma's exposed skin. "No. I rather like your brown skin, and so do my Galatian brothers. It feels more...familiar to us." His brothers would have chosen her if they didn't think she had already been chosen for him. He met her eyes again. "But we have no issue with the white-skinned consorts."

His way of phrasing things would have been somewhat humorous except this was a sensitive subject. Her posture relaxed some as she continued. "But people of color never win a chance to enter the Exchange. I'm the first—and I only got in because...well, you know how."

"Everyone has an equal chance—"

She made a dismissive sound. His brow went up at how far she had come from being afraid to voice her opinions. "I don't know, Karma," he had to admit. "The Galatians have nothing to do with the selection process. Any woman within the age range can put in a lottery bid—if they have the funds. But you yourself know there are many people from several regions that object to the practice, and more that just can't afford the price." She didn't appear satisfied by this explanation and in truth, he knew he wasn't being completely candid. But the truth was rather ugly.

"Karma, in truth, we never cared enough to ask the question. When it comes to the Galatian Exchange, I am nothing more than a follower of outdated traditions."

That seemed to change her disposition.

"Now that you're the director of the Exchange, won't this be a question you'll want an answer to?"

Chapter Thirty-two

"You have caused me to consider a great many things, Karma Sigur." He stood and offered his hand to her.

Karma wondered what he was up to, but she couldn't deny that hearing him refer to her in that way sent a pleasant jolt through her body. But she still had several things she wanted to speak to him about. One of which had to do with queens murdering the babies of non-Galatian mothers.

She placed her hand in his, and was reminded of the first time she had felt the rough smoothness of his palm when at the Galatian Exchange. She had been scared to death, but felt protected the moment he had reached out to her.

This felt the same way.

He looked at her while leading her backwards out of the room, never bumping into a thing and carefully side-stepping a chair. She then remembered his tail was his spotter.

Impressed, she followed Rafe as he led her from the kitchen, through the living room, and then into her room.

"I would like to be with you now," he said while unfastening his wrap. He tossed it across the room to land on the chaise.

Karma swore to herself she wouldn't just stare at his prick. Because a relationship was more than sex. It was communication and a mental connection and much,

much more. But when a prick is pale green, more than a foot long, and growing…one doesn't simply ignore it.

She slipped her robe over her shoulders and allowed the delicate silk to pool at her feet.

He made a sound as soft as a whispered moan.

No man had ever made her feel more desired than this one. It allowed her to stand before him boldly without trying to shield herself.

After a moment of scanning her form, he stepped in close and ran his hands lightly down her arms. "They are fools to think it is the color of the skin we care about. It is the skin itself; the delicate softness. That is what we find so beautiful."

Karma stood still, allowing his fingertips to lightly explore her form. When he raised goose pimples along her flesh, causing her nipples to tighten, he groaned again. This time she wanted to mimic him so she reached up and ran her fingertips over his pecs.

The paler scales were smooth, like small pebbles. She wanted to taste him there, to allow her tongue to explore this part of him in the way she had already familiarized herself with the taste and feel of his prick.

Karma leaned forward and placed her lips on one of his nipples. She was at the perfect height to reach it. Her tongue came forward to glide across the small pebble.

Rafe all but froze. Only his prick strained against her, captured between their bodies. She gripped his waist with her hands and pulled him flush against her, enjoying the control he allowed her.

She moved her attention to his other nipple, this time pulling it into her mouth and nipping it lightly.

Rafe's body lurched, and she felt him shift as his prick surged against her.

The power she felt at being able to elicit such a reaction from a warrior as great as he astounded her.

Behind him, she thought of something and held her hand palm up. She didn't have to wait long for the tip of his tail to land lightly along her palm. She stroked the smooth, little scales while nipping and sucking his nipple and Rafe moaned loudly.

The next thing she knew, she was being lifted in his arms and placed on her bed in a move that took less than a blink of an eye.

"Spread for me. I smell you are excited for me to touch you."

Karma's eyes fluttered closed as she spread her legs for him.

His head was instantly buried between her thighs, and the way he had licked his fingers earlier held nothing to the attention he paid her now.

His tongue was like a heat-seeking missile that searched and enjoyed every drop of her juices. Before her essence could glide between the crack of her ass, his tongue was there, collecting and savoring it. The moment it gushed from her vagina, his tongue had already burrowed there, coaxing it into his mouth.

She had become a compilation of nerve endings. She jerked and seized and cried out words that had no meaning as she felt herself being pulled into an explosive finale.

"You're going to cum," he muttered against her pussy. "I feel it." He flicked his tongue against her clit over and over, faster and faster, until her body knotted and released in a huge, orgasmic fit.

Rafe gripped her thighs firmly, holding her flailing body in place as he greedily drank all that pooled from her depths.

"More," he grunted as he pushed his tongue into her pussy, rapidly tongue-fucking her for more.

Karma gripped his head with clawed hands as she pumped against his face, her mouth open in a silent wail.

Rafe was sated when her body finally collapsed back onto the bed. Karma was limp. She couldn't even raise her hands, which had fallen to her sides. How was it possible for him to be this talented?

And then he sat up on his haunches, still between her legs, and he licked his lips with a tongue so long it could have belonged to a snake. Yes, she thought with a pleasant tremor in her tummy. That was why.

Rafe looked down at his lovely consort. He'd always considered her beautiful, but seeing her drunk on the pleasure he'd just given her made her even more irresistible.

It was his turn for release. He knew his mate longed for penetrative sex, which was why he used his tongue inside of her. He hoped that would satisfy her, as the alternative was not an option.

Still between her thighs, Rafe lowered himself over Karma, supporting himself on his hands. His carefully pressed his lower body against her, capturing his prick snuggly between them.

"Would you like me to…?" she asked, her voice now hoarse. She grinned in surprised embarrassment at its sound.

He shook his head slightly. "No. I want you to stay right where you are. You've asked about me entering you. While I can't, I can show you what it would be like."

His consort's eyes seemed to light up in interest. She nodded her consent, and Rafe dipped his head enough to press his face against her neck. Being sure not to crush her, he continued to support himself on elbows while pressing his lower body against her. And then he moved his hips forward, sliding his prick against its tight confines along her belly and torso.

It felt good knowing a large portion of the sensation was feeling himself against her smooth, nude flesh. His precum provided a slick surface and while it wasn't her delicious, tight pussy, gliding his prick between their bodies was an amazing feeling.

Rafe lifted his hips slightly and then rocked forward. He repeated the move, and then repeated it again. Karma did something that delighted and surprised him. She drew her knees up and wrapped her legs around his waist, locking herself to him.

Rafe squeezed his eyes closed as his face remained buried against her neck. Her scent covered him, invading not only his olfactory glands, but also his taste buds. He pumped his hips rapidly against her, barely able to contain himself. But then he felt her hands exploring his back and the ridges there. Her small hands gripped one that was between his shoulder blades and the sensation of pleasure stabbed through him, sending a surge throughout his entire body.

He moaned aloud, knowing he sent the vibration through her body. He came up onto his haunches. His eyes scanned her body, taking in the slick coat of precum that glistened along her dark skin.

He traced the pad of his finger down her thighs as she loosened her grip on his hips. She then reached for his pulsing prick and squeezed the shaft just beneath his prick head, causing the glands there to shoot several electrical currents through him at the same time it sent a stream of precum bubbling from its opening.

He threw his head back and sighed while concentrating on the tight grip she had on him. He pushed his hips forward and then back as her hand glided down his shaft before returning to his prick head.

This time, Rafe helped her. He gripped the base of his shaft, which was also coated with precum. He then pumped his fist down low while she pumped and squeezed her hands up high at his tip.

Together, they jacked his massive prick. He had never done this before, and he had to watch, knowing it wouldn't take long. And he was right. With an uncontrolled shout, an explosion of cum shot toward her. Rafe's hips pistoned forward and his stomach contracted with the force of each shot of cum.

When there was nothing more than several short, weak squirts that glided down Karma's fist, he didn't slump in exhaustion. Rafe could do nothing but blink with renewed arousal at the sight of his seed glistening against her deep-brown skin.

He groaned and reached out to stroke her nipples, which were coated in cum.

"I will not soon forget this beautiful sight..." He gently rubbed her nipple until he heard her soft moan.

"Again, little human?" he asked with a raised brow, delighted she enjoyed the act of mating as much as he did.

"I think I mentioned I like it when you touch me there." Her voice was rough and throaty. Another thrill shot through him.

"I won't soon forget." Rafe leaned forward and licked her nipples until they were hardened pebbles. He allowed it to take several minutes longer than necessary and when her hips began to thrust upward, seeking to rub against the base of his prick and balls, Rafe made a soft fist. He used his knuckle to slowly stroke her clit, not wanting to risk pricking her tender flesh with a talon.

Her responsive shudder reverberated through him and he moaned.

Rafe and Karma made love for hours; touching, stroking, tasting, resting…and then repeating.

"You are insatiable," he said hours later while lying beside her. His tail had gone across his body to collapse over her hip. Its tip didn't even raise.

"You came three times yourself," she reminded him, her voice a tired whisper.

"Would you like to shower again?" he asked.

"No." Her eyes drifted closed. They'd showered the second time he'd cum on her. "But I would like to change this bedding…" Her voice was an even softer whisper.

"I'll help."

But instead of moving to get up, Rafe heard her quiet snores. She was exhausted.

He slowly wrapped his arms around her and when she barely moved, he lifted her gently and moved her into the living room, where he placed her on the oversized couch. He made sure she was covered by the afghan that sat on the nearby chair and then he stood above her and watched her sleep for a few moments.

Rafe returned to the bedroom and stripped away the blankets and quilt. The sheets were still fresh. He found clean bedcoverings in a panel in the hall and quickly made up the bed.

He got a dampened towel and returned to the living room for his mate. He slipped away the afghan and located every drop of his seed and cleaned it from her body before returning her to the bedroom, where he carefully placed her beneath her clean sheets.

He normally didn't find it necessary to sleep beneath blankets and sheets. Besides, his talons did a number on the delicate fabric humans enjoyed. But he did want to lay against her flesh, so he climbed beneath the covers beside her and when he gathered her into his arms, she snuggled against his torso with a sleepy sigh.

He finally closed his eyes in satisfaction and then he too fell asleep, with his consort in his arms.

Chapter Thirty-three

Karma's eyes opened as she was flooded with memories of the night before. She had never spent an entire night having sex. She looked at Rafe, who faced her. His eyes were closed and his breathing was even as he slept. Even his tail, which had draped across her hip, remained motionless.

Had she actually exhausted a Galatian?

She looked at him, feeling free to examine him for the first time, even if it was only with her eyes. Remembering how sharp his hearing was, Karma remained still, only moving her eyes. His even breathing was more rapid than a human's, but his soft breath that brushed her face was no different than any human's.

His tail rose as if it was regarding her. Karma smiled to herself.

"I know you're awake, Rafe," she whispered.

He opened his eyes and looked at her. "I was listening for you to awaken."

"Aren't you tired? I'm still exhausted." She sat up in order to look at the clock on her bedside. It wasn't even 4:00 a.m.!

He stretched, but didn't sit up. "We don't sleep the same as you. But I have no desire to leave this bed. I would like to lay with you."

Karma hesitated. "I may be a bit sore…"

The room was too dark for her to completely know, but she thought he had gained an amused tint.

"We have a cream for that. But I was referring to just lying here until you are fully rested. Would you like more sleep?"

She settled back on the bed, but with his arms no longer around her, Karma felt a slight chill, despite the fact that the room's temperature was at a comfortable level.

Tentatively, she moved closer to Rafe until she was snuggled against his chest. She knew he appreciated the move when his arm immediately held her in place, with her head tucked beneath his chin. She heard his soft hum of contentment.

"I don't know if I can fall back asleep, but this is nice."

"I enjoy spending this time with you." He nudged the top of her head with his chin as his fingertips ran down her side. "How difficult it must be for you to live when you are so delicate. How do humans manage to not damage themselves with such fragile skin?"

She looked up at him. "We're not so fragile."

"Humans are strong, but your skin isn't. You burn under direct sunlight. You cannot withstand cold weather without layers of clothing. I've seen with my own eyes how quickly your skin is affected by water. You bruise with the slightest nudge. I can't imagine bleeding so easily at just the least injury."

She thought everything he said was funny but she didn't dare laugh. She wondered the same things about him, having scales and being able to fly into outer space. But compared to other living things, especially aliens, humans were on the more helpless scale.

"I never thought of it like that. I guess we've adapted. But yes, we would have to be more careful than

335

you would. Your scales are your armor, and your clothes."

"We wear rigging here for modesty purposes," he said. "On Galatia, we rarely bother. Our scales are also weapons."

"They can turn sharp," she said, remembering cutting her fingertips when she tried to scratch him.

He nodded. "We are an apex predator, although I'd rather consider Galatians to be defenders. The only thing more deadly are those that have poison. But they'd have to penetrate us first."

"How do you hurt a Galatian?"

"That, my consort, is a highly guarded secret. It would be best to think of us as invincible."

She lifted her head to look at him and their eyes met. "Do Galatians live hundreds of years, like everyone says?"

He shrugged. "We can live two hundred years or more. But right around that is normal. In human years, I am comparable to an individual in their mid-forties. I am young, but mature."

"Okay. That makes you old enough to be my father."

"I'm old enough to be your grandfather, if we're looking at chronological age. Does that bother you?"

"You are a green man, so I can't say I'm bothered by any of our differences."

"Good. And I am happy you are satisfying your curiosity."

"Well, there is something else that's been on my mind…"

"You have only to ask, my consort."

She inhaled deeply, and then lifted her head again to meet his eyes. "When we mated the first time...before you knew I hadn't had the surgery. Is there a chance I could have gotten pregnant?"

He propped himself up on his elbow and his brow dipped as he looked at her. "You've been wondering about that?"

She nodded. "Yes."

He ran his hand over her naked shoulder. "Karma, it is difficult for Galatians to procreate. For thousands of years, we've tried to find ways to continue our race. Across galaxies we created life-forms in our image that might help us to continue. However, our females could never get pregnant by these male life-forms, and we had limited success with the female ones. The successful matings only occurred with those life-forms that did not have a close match to us. And even then, it took a lot of matings to produce a child only to find that they would never breed and had many disadvantages. As they were sterile, they eventually all died off.

"We have tried with humans and other life-forms that closely match our physical makeup—that way, avoiding the obvious disadvantages, like added limbs, eyes, or even heads. Humans are one of our closest matches. But you're so close that, like with our females, we have a nearly a impossible chance of getting your species with child. It is such a difficult thing and something that hasn't happened in many years.

"But it has happened. And what became of these hybrid human children?"

"There was one child that died right after birth. He was also deemed sterile, even though he was a male."

Karma contemplated her next question. "Did the queens kill the children you created with other species?"

"A *queen* would never kill a child — and especially not one of our own kind." He'd said the word 'queen' very distinctly. "We've worked too hard to create a life-form in our own image to ever allow something so heinous. In fact, queens fought to raise the children from these experiments. But those experiments have long ago been terminated. It was cruel."

Karma studied him and after a moment, she felt better. She wasn't sure if she ever wanted to be a mother, but the chances were slim that she'd want to bring a child into this world.

Karma settled against him again. She had gotten a bad vibe from the queen that was bound to Rafe. She frowned. She would never understand their ability to share. But what if things were beyond their control just as much as it was beyond the males'? It would mean the jealousy was as real as the jealousy she would feel seven years from now.

They talked a while longer before Karma drifted back to sleep. Rafe stayed awake for a while, feeling guilty about the lie he'd told her.

His kind was unaccustomed to lying — and it was pointless, because they easily smelled deception.

Even though he doubted Karma could sense his lie, he didn't like doing it. He knew he wanted a meaningful relationship with her more than ever, and that meant he wanted nothing but honesty between them. It would hurt him if he knew she had been less than truthful with him.

But what other choice did he have? If he thought there was even the slightest chance she was pregnant, then he would have had no choice but to tell her the complete truth about the queens. But there was no need to worry her. She was completely protected as his mate. But if she got pregnant...

He hadn't lied about the queens not harming a hybrid child—if it survived long enough to be born. It was the mother that needed to worry.

Rafe had to leave before they could have a morning meal, but he promised to return before the evening one.

She walked him to the front door and paused awkwardly as he bid his goodbye. Should she kiss him goodbye the way her mother and father always did? She had never kissed him, nor had he kissed her. He didn't actually have lips, but he had a mouth—which contained razor-sharp teeth and a long lizard tongue...

Would he even want to be kissed?

He stared at her as she contemplated these things. "What concerns you, my consort?"

Karma smiled, liking his terms of endearment. She was his little human and his consort. In essence, she was his. It didn't make her feel as if she was a possession. It just made her feel as if she belonged.

Instead of answering him, she stepped up on tiptoes and placed her hands on his cheeks. She pulled him down until he was level with her eyes and then she kissed him.

"Bye, Rafe. Have a good day."

He blinked at her before straightening. "You as well, Karma." He left, shutting the door firmly behind him.

She smiled to herself. Rafe didn't have lips to kiss with, but she had enjoyed the surprised look on his face when she'd done it. And she couldn't deny she had thoroughly enjoyed the intimacy of sharing a kiss with her mate.

She turned and went into the kitchen, where she whipped up a quick breakfast of steak, fried eggs, and skillet potatoes.

Once she'd eaten every scrap of food on her plate, Karma got ready for her day. She'd visit her new friend, make a meal together, come home, and hopefully listen to music with another new friend. And then she'd spend the evening in the company of a man that looked at her as if she was the sun, moon, and stars. And maybe she could normalize kissing for him.

And Karma did exactly that. And she did it the next day, and the day after that as well.

To be continued...

Preview The Galatian Exchange Book Two

Rafe was annoyed by the time he reached the conference hall in his building. He didn't like being late for dinner with his mate, mostly because he knew that she would not have eaten without him.

But also, he had come to look forward to being a family with her. For years, his family had been his brothers in the Guard, and before that he almost remembered family — before he was turned into a man whose voice had been quieted.

His brothers had gathered at his request, and each had spent the evening with their consorts, mating, eating, conversing, while he searched for a man that would be better off dead if he was ever located. And now he had learned something that could jeopardize the Galatian Exchange, as well as the hard-fought human-alien relationship that had taken generations to hone.

Five Galatians came to attention. Only six remaining, counting himself, as Leolo had been returned to his bound-mate.

"Brothers," he said in his native tongue. "Thank you for giving me your time."

"You are our commander, but also our brother," Drago said while releasing his formality. The others followed suit. If Rafe was their commander, then Drago was his second in command. Yet these men were fighting comrades and only held to formalities when it was necessary.

"What's happened?" Kendrick asked. "Drago mentioned that it has something to do with your mate?"

Rafe looked at each of them. They were among the most accomplished warriors within the Galatian Guards.

Kendrick Washington had trained in North America and had a command of North American customs. He was the tallest of them all and willing to interact with humans as a good will gesture.

Titus Grayson had trained in Scotland and spoke English with a thick Scottish accent. He was brutal and his preferred weapon—besides his tail, was a hilted broadsword. He had more kills than any of them.

Paris Frenchman had done his training in the French Union and was the coldest and most detached of the crew. He had a command for languages and was the least patient of them all. An example is the name that he selected for himself. He put absolutely no thought into it.

Haru Bano was the newest and the youngest of their group. From the Japan Union, Haru had mastered and then taught them all several types of fighting styles that helped to keep them unpredictable in battle.

And finally, there was Drago Engström, Rafe's best and oldest friend. He was playful and friendly with an easy personality. It often surprised others when he lopped off heads with a friendly expression still on his face.

"We are a race of warriors," Rafe said. "Others quake in fear and shit themselves when they face us in battle. There are none better than the Galatian Guard— and you are among its top warriors.

"You deserve your reward and you have fought hard for this retirement. But I'm going to ask you to serve once more."

"I am bored of this retirement," Paris stated. "Whatever you want brother, count me in as long as I don't have to watch another military drill."

There was a soft clicking of throats indicating laughter in their language.

"I appreciate that, brother. But this affects your consorts, too. If you assist me with one last task, it will delay your move to your consort's chosen destination."

Everyone exchanged looks that held concern. They were loyal men, but they were also trained to follow rules. The law said that the consorts chose and going against that had never been voiced.

"What is it that you need from us?" Kendrick asked.

"I want us to overthrow the entire North American government."

NOW AVAILABLE

PEPPER PACE BOOKS

The Galatian Exchange Book 2: The Family
The Galatian Exchange Book 3: The Enemies

SHORT STORIES/NOVELLAS
~~***~~
The Way Home
MILF
Blair and the Emoboy
Emoboy the Submissive Dom
1-900-BrownSugar
Someone To Love
My Special Friend
Baby Girl and the Mean Boss
A Wrong Turn Towards Love (An Estill County
Mountain Man Romance)
True's Love (An Estill County Mountain Man
Romance)
The Miseducation of Riley Pranger (An Estill County
Mountain Man Romance)
Christmas Redemption (An Estill County Mountain
Man Romance)
The Delicate Sadness
The Shadow People
The Love Unexpected
The Vinyl Man
Punishment Island
Super G

COLLABORATIONS
~~***~~
Sexy Southern Hometown Heroes
Seduction: An Interracial Romance Anthology Vol. 1
Scandalous Heroes Box set

346

Secrets of the Elite

WRITTEN UNDER BETH JO ANDERSEN
~~***~~
Snatched by Bigfoot!
Bigfoot's Sidepiece
Mated to the Bigfoot!

WRITTEN UNDER KIM CHAMBERS
~~***~~
The Purple World book 1

Sign-up to the Pepper Pace Newsletter!
http://eepurl.com/bGV4tb

About the Author

Pepper Pace creates a unique brand of Interracial/multicultural erotic romance. While her stories span the gamut from humorous to heartfelt, the common theme is crossing racial boundaries. She writes in the genres of science fiction, youth, horror, urban lit and poetry.

www.ingramcontent.com/pod-product-compliance
Lightning Source LLC
Chambersburg PA
CBHW060352260626
47160CB00006B/2282